Fate

by
Amanda Hocking

Second Paperback Edition: September 2010

For information:

http://amandahocking.blogspot.com/

Fate – Book II

ISBN 9781453816868

For my mom and Eric – for enduring my neurosis with only the occasional eye roll.
For Pete, Valerie, Greggor, Bronson, and Fifi – thank you for being a friend.
To Kalli & Kaycee – my number one and two fans

- 1 -

The summer air slid in through the windows, filling the car with the green scent of the park, and the frightening sound of highway traffic. I bit my lip and stared out the window, where children played in the grass. The car was only idling in the parking lot, but I kept imagining Milo losing control and running them over.

My younger brother Milo had just turned sixteen, and he talked constantly about getting his license. His new obsession with cars I blamed entirely on Jack, who drove at excessive speeds in luxury vehicles. Milo changed the instant he laid eyes on his Lamborghini. Things that beautiful captivated people, even gay teenage boys, apparently.

Even though I was a year and a half older than Milo, I still didn't have my license, so Jack was the one giving the driving lessons, and it scared me.

Wearing gigantic sunglasses, Jack sat shotgun, but he didn't really explain things to Milo. He pointed to a pedal and said, "That one makes it go. So push on it and let's go." That's it.

Fortunately, Milo's pretty cautious, so he pressed Jack for more information, but that didn't make his answers any less vague. That might be because Jack's tired. The mid-afternoon August sun shined brightly above us. Ordinarily, that sounds like the best time to drive, but sunlight made Jack groggy. He'd already started to yawn.

Jack is not exactly like everyone else. I really like him, more than I should. He's attractive in his own right, with dancing blue eyes, perpetually disheveled sandy hair, and flawless tanned skin, but he's not what I would call drop-dead gorgeous.

Everything about Jack and his family is complicated, thanks to one major fact: they just happen to be vampires.

They aren't really dangerous to people, or I wouldn't let any of them around my brother. I guess technically they are, since they could easily kill us if they wanted to, but I don't think they want to. They do live off human blood, but they use either blood banks or human donors.

Vampires don't have to drink a person to death, although they can and sometimes do. Jack has never killed anyone, but he's still a relatively young vampire. He was twenty-four when he turned, and that was only sixteen years ago, in comparison with his brother Ezra who has been around for over three-hundred years and Peter's nearly two-hundred.

They're not really brothers, but brothers in the way vampires are. In order to turn, the human's blood fuses with the vampire's blood. Ezra turned Peter, and Peter turned Jack. This makes them close in unusual ways. Peter is attracted to me, or rather his blood is. But because of his attraction, both Jack and Ezra are very fond of me, and Jack much more than he should be.

I know that Jack won't do anything to put me in danger, not intentionally. His ability to monitor danger in relation to human's fragile bodies, like my brother's, is lacking. If we got in a crash, Jack would protect me over Milo, and that makes me nervous.

"Are you sure you really wanna do this today?" I asked, and in the rearview mirror, I saw Milo roll his eyes.

"We can just take you home if you're gonna be this way," Milo glared at me.

Despite his age, Milo had one of those distinct baby faces. His cheeks were chubby, and his brown eyes were innocently large. When he threatened me, he looked more like an angry child then the teenager he was.

"Alice, everything will be fine," Jack promised, suppressing a yawn.

"I'm the sensible one. So if I think something is okay, it probably is," Milo reminded me.

We'd been sitting in the parking lot for twenty minutes while Milo made Jack explain every part of the car to him. Since it was Jack explaining, a disproportionate amount of the time had been spent on the stereo and the seat warmers (which seemed logical for August), but Milo was getting antsy.

When he finally put the car in drive, my heart locked up. Milo drove across the parking lot, jerking on the brake unnecessarily several times.

"Just ease into it," Jack said, and Milo responded.

"Maybe he's not ready." I leaned forward between the seats.

"Alice!" Milo snapped.

Jack lowered his sunglasses enough so he could peer at me over them. "Alice, you've got to lighten up, or we'll really take you home. And I'll let him drive all the way back."

"Fine!" I threw my hands up in the air and fell back in the seat.

Milo drove around the parking lot with more starts and stops than a circle should require. His driving eventually became smoother, and I allowed myself to settle into it.

This was precisely the reason I stuck around. Jack offered me a chance at immortality, but I temporarily declined. I wasn't quite ready to ditch out on my brother yet.

Jack yawned loudly again, and his fatigue washed over me. To wake himself up, he fiddled with the radio, causing the Cure to come blasting out. I opened my mouth to say something about that being too distracting, but Milo slapped his hand away and turned it off.

"I can't concentrate with that," Milo said when Jack looked offended.

"See?" Jack thudded his head tiredly on the headrest of the car. "You've got nothing to worry about with this kid."

"No thanks to you," I muttered. Jack turned towards me, grinning his mischievous, crooked smile. "What?"

"You know, someday you're going to have to learn to drive." Jack's delight only deepened when I grimaced in response. "What? You didn't really expect me to drive you around forever, did you?"

"No. But not today," I said.

"It's all on your time anyway." Jack went back to watching Milo drive.

He'd been trying to hide his ever growing impatience, but he could hide very little from me. For some reason, I felt everything he felt, and sometimes, it made things awkward. He was definitely ready for me to turn. Jack understood what I wanted and tried not to pressure me into turning into a vampire, but it was hard for him.

"Should I take it out on the road?" Milo had paused by the exit of the parking lot and looked at Jack.

"Sorry, kid." Jack shook his head, and Milo looked disappointed. "You did really well today, but I'm pretty beat, and I think your sister's had all that she can take."

Jack got out of the car to switch places with Milo and grumbled something about the sunlight. It didn't help that he wore a tee shirt and shorts, exposing even more of his skin to the sun, but that was his standard uniform, even in winter.

Today he'd gone for a white tee shirt with neon cassette tapes on it and black Dickies with pink Converse. He wasn't exactly the image I'd had in mind when I thought of vampire, but very little about him was stereotypical.

As soon as he hopped in the driver's seat, he fumbled with the stereo until "Mexican Radio" came on. Milo wrinkled his nose, but he hadn't grown up in the eighties the way Jack had.

When we pulled up in front of the brownstone where Milo and I lived, Milo thanked Jack again before getting out. I stayed behind, wanting a minute alone to talk to him. I reached between the seats and turned down the radio.

"Thanks for taking him out like that. I know he really appreciated it."

"Anytime." Jack smiled at me, but there was something droopy about it. Vampires didn't burst into flames, but they were nocturnal. The sun tired them out.

"You should probably get going." I unbuckled my seatbelt and started sliding to get out of the car. "So, I'll see you tomorrow?"

"Nah, I can't. I'm going on that business trip with Ezra," he reminded me. "But I should be back in two days. We aren't doing much more than signing some papers."

In the past few months, Jack had stepped up and started helping Ezra with the family business. They owned a few companies overseas and had lots of stock holdings. Every now and then, Ezra left for a few days to work on something, and Jack finally decided that he should do it. Also, he'd rolled his car, and Ezra demanded that he work for his money to pay for the next one.

"Oh. Right. Well… call me when you get back."

"I always do," Jack grinned, and I got out of the car.

- 2 -

Summer nights were too short. Vampires spent more time indoors in the summer, but heat didn't agree with them anyway.

Jack lived in beautiful house on the lake. It'd be a rather conventional square house if not for the balconies and the turret that connected the house to the garage. As many times as I had been here, it never really stopped being intimidating.

We spent a great deal of the summer in the backyard, either lounging on the stone patio or swimming in the lake or taking out the Jet-Ski's. Milo and I spent so much time on the water that Mae bought us several swimsuits to keep at the house.

I changed into my suit, keeping the towel wrapped around me when I came out of the bathroom, and Milo had already changed into his swim trunks. He sat at island in the kitchen, munching on some grapes, and helping Mae.

Mae had been the eldest when she turned, at twenty-eight. Her skin was flawless white porcelain, and her caramel waves of hair had been pulled into a loose bun. Wearing only her bathing suit and an apron, her warm eyes danced as Milo talked to her.

As a vampire, she didn't eat, and since Milo was an excellent cook, he became her sous chef, helping her prepare all the meals she made for our benefit. I would've protested all the extra work and expense Mae put into it, but it was obvious that she relished this sorta thing.

"Where's Ezra?" I asked, walking over to the island and stealing a grape. Mae was making some kind of fruit dip with cream cheese and yogurt, and slicing up apples, pears, and strawberries.

"He's taking a nap," Mae informed me in her warm, British accent. "He's a little jet lagged from the trip."

Like the other two boys, Ezra was incredibly attractive. His eyes were deep mahogany and infinitely warm. His skin was the same tanned color as Jack and Peter's, and his sandy hair had soft blond streaks through it. The most powerful thing about Ezra was his voice. It was low and resonated through everything. He had a faded accent that came from being born in England, but he hadn't lived in Europe in over two-hundred years.

Through the glass French doors off the dining room, I saw Jack rollicking about with his Great Pyrenees, Matilda. The deck lights revealed the taut muscles of his chest and back as he rolled around with her. The stones of the patio should've left him battered and bruised, but he'd have nothing to show from it.

"Alice, do you wanna try it?" Mae asked, pulling my gaze away from Jack. She held out an apple slice covered in dip, but I shook my head.

"I'm getting pretty chilly. I think I'm gonna head outside."

"I'll be out in a minute," Milo said through the mouthful of the fruit he'd sampled.

"Okay," I nodded and headed out the French doors into the night.

Jack ventured off the patio in his pursuit of Matilda, but I saw easily in the light of the full moon. It was much warmer outside than it had been in the house, but I kept the towel wrapped around me. I walked down the patio onto the small lawn that separated the house from the lake.

Matilda caught sight of me and bounded towards me. She'd knock me over, since she was used to vampires who could handle her lunging at them, but Jack overtook her and playfully tackled her. Then he stood up, brushing the grass from his swim trunks, and grinned at me.

"Are you gonna go swimming with the towel too?" Jack teased.

"Maybe." I pulled the towel more tightly around me, and he laughed.

Matilda sniffed me heartily before concluding that it was only me, and then sauntered off, wagging her tail slowly behind her.

A mischievous glint caught Jack's eye, and after spending a summer getting thrown in the lake, I knew exactly what it meant. Dropping my towel, I turned and ran towards the dock. He trailed a few steps behind me, even though he could easily sprint past me. The sport was in the chase for him.

I almost made it to the edge of the dock when I felt his strong arms looping around my waist. I squealed and let him twirl me around once before he released me, sending me soaring into the air and landing in the lake with a loud splash.

Jack took a running jump and leaped out, flying over me and splashing way out in the lake. He howled excitedly, as if he hadn't made that same jump a million times.

"Jack!" Mae leaned out the French doors and shouted out at him. "You've got to keep it down so the neighbors don't call the police again." It was after midnight on a Wednesday, and the neighbors weren't big fans of the noise.

"Yeah, Alice," Jack said.

"Oh, whatever," I rolled my eyes. "As if I'm even half as loud as you are."

Jack laughed, taking long strokes out farther into the black water. He swam slow circles around me, but I was content to float on my back, staring up at the full moon and the stars shining.

I had never really had the courage to swim too far from the shore when the water was so dark. I always had these horrible visions of being eaten by some unseen monster coming up from the depths of the lake.

Milo joined us in the lake a bit later. Mae stayed inside to continue chopping fruit. She always went overboard trying to feed us. We were just two people, but she cooked like we were an army. It only made it more obvious when they didn't eat anything, but Milo had only made a few comments about it.

Surprisingly, he hadn't really caught on that they weren't human. Jack had been more discreet about his paranormal abilities, but Milo was a smart kid. I thought that he suspected something but let it go, because they didn't seem dangerous and they made me happy.

"It's a really beautiful night out," Milo said. He floated on his back, admiring the night like I was.

"It's been a fantastic summer."

"I can't believe it's almost over," Milo sighed.

14

"Don't remind me!" I cringed.

School was only three short weeks away. Milo tried to convince me that it had little effect on my life, but it changed everything. There'd be no more all-nighters with Jack, and soon everything would get cold and snowy, and Milo would make me do homework.

Something grabbed me and pulled me under. I tried to scream but water buried me. I pictured some evil sea creature coming to eat my soul. Clawing my way to the surface, I grabbed onto something strong and soft and pulled myself up.

As soon as I reached for him, Jack pulled me up out of the water and let me cling on to him. Over my own frightened gasps, I heard him laughing softly, and I realized he'd been the one that grabbed my ankle. After a summer of similar antics, I should've caught on that Jack thought it was funny scaring the crap out of me.

I should've slapped him or told him he was a jerk, but the feel of his arms distracted me. His chest pressed up against mine, and he had to feel the frantic beating of my heart that drove him crazy.

I looked up in his soft blue eyes, and I felt breathless for a whole new reason. His laughter died down, and his smile faltered as his body temperature started to rise, smoldering against my skin.

Ordinarily, he would've pushed me away by now, but he let me linger in his arms. I tilted in towards him, hoping he'd let go just long enough for one innocent kiss.

"Hey! Look! A shooting star!" Milo shouted.

It was just enough for Jack to realize what was happening, so he pushed me back and swam away. Jack did everything he could to keep from letting things get out of hand, and sometimes that meant that he'd physically push me away. It was getting harder to shrug off, though.

Although I hadn't asked about it, his temperature only seemed to rise when things between us got physical. During our one crazy passionate kiss, his skin had felt like it was on fire.

"Did you see it?" Milo asked.

I meant to shoot him an angry glare for disrupting my rare moment with Jack, but then I saw Milo just staring blissfully at the sky. He hadn't been paying attention to anything but the stars, so he hadn't known that he'd interrupted.

"Nah, sorry, I missed it," I said.

"There'll probably be another one," Milo assured me, and I probably sounded very heavy with regret. Sure, I do love a good shooting star, but kisses with Jack were even a rarer commodity.

"I hope so."

I treaded water, and Jack moved on to harassing Matilda. He'd gotten very good at finding ways to ignore me. Poor Matilda stood at the end of the dock, barking her refusal to jump in. Milo tired of his stargazing so he went over to join Jack in cajoling the dog in the water.

Being in the water suddenly didn't feel like much fun. The adrenaline from the near sea monster death, followed by the near kiss, left my body feeling achy and tired. I knew Jack would do his best to steer clear of me for awhile, and even if I understood the routine, it didn't feel good.

"I think I'm gonna head back inside and see if Mae needs a hand," I said to no one in particular, which was just as well. Matilda was far more captivating than I was.

By the time I made it to the shore, I heard the loud splash and their shouts of triumph. Matilda finally jumped in the water. If only my resolution with Jack could be that simple.

Wrapping the towel around me, I stepped in through the French doors. My skin froze instantly, thanks to the arctic draft from the air conditioner. Amy Winehouse blasted out of the stereo, Mae's one new guilty pleasure. Jack was always trying to get her to listen to new music, and so far the only things that took were Winehouse and Norah Jones.

Mae danced around the kitchen, singing into a spatula, and despite my aggravation over the Jack situation, I couldn't help but laugh.

"Oh my gosh!" Mae put her hand over her heart and her golden eyes flashed with embarrassment. "You scared me!"

"Couldn't you hear me come in?" I asked as she turned down the stereo. "Aren't you guys supposed to have super hearing or something?"

"Well, yes, when we're paying attention," Mae smiled sheepishly at me. The fruit snack looked complete and nicely arranged on the island, and she was just cleaning up when I interrupted.

"Do you need a hand?" I offered.

"No, and you need to go put some clothes on first." She nodded at me, and I had begun to shiver. "Unless you're not done for the night."

"Oh, no, I'm definitely done," I replied grimly. The thrill completely wore off the instant Jack pushed me away.

"I should probably go change too." She started untying her apron.

"You don't need to stay in on my account." I held up my hand to stop her. "You can go out there and swim while I clean up."

"Nonsense," Mae laughed, as if she would ever let me clean up after her. She whipped off her apron and set it on the island. "If you and Ezra are in the house, I can't imagine what kind of fun I'd even have with the boys. They'll probably throw frogs at each other."

She wasn't that far off base. When left to their own devices, Jack and Milo turned into very silly little boys. Once, when it was raining, I split up a mudball fight in the backyard. It's very similar to a snowball fight, except with mud. That seemed like a genius idea to them both until Milo started getting bruises, because as it turns out, vampires can throw much harder than weakling sixteen-year-olds.

Mae shook her head and headed off down the hall to change. I followed her to the main bathroom across the hall from her bedroom.

In the bathroom, I changed into my ordinary clothes, and I wondered if I was being too stubborn not letting Mae buy me new clothes. After she'd spent decades buying for only boys, it would thrill her to take me on a shopping trip. The suit I set in the tub to dry had cost over a hundred dollars, and she'd bought me three of them. But then again, they already gave me far too much, and I returned so little.

I tried to dry my hair as best I could and clean myself up. Before I had even finished washing my face, I heard a yell. I turned off the faucet, and Mae was shouting Jack's name, so I rushed out into the kitchen.

Jack was yelling, and he sounded terrified.

Mae stood on the patio when I ran outside. Jack was still several feet away from her, standing closer to the shoreline. When I tried to run past her, Mae grabbed my arm, and her face blanched.

It was too dark for me to really see what was going on, but I could feel pure heartbroken terror. Something terrible had happened, and Jack felt worse about it than he ever had before.

"Ezra!" Jack bellowed, and he stopped walking forward. "Ezra!"

"I'll go get him," Mae whispered nervously. Her hand squeezed my arm so tightly it hurt, but I barely noticed. "Alice, you stay right here. Don't move. I'll be right back."

"Hurry!" Jack pleaded, but she was already gone.

Even though I didn't move any closer, my eyes adjusted to the darkness, and the moonlight splashed on him through the branches of a nearby tree. Something lay limp in his arms, and my breath caught in my throat.

Immediately, I thought that something had happened to Matilda. The boys had gotten too rough, and she'd gotten hurt somehow, and Jack knows how freaked out I get when animals are hurt.

Then Matilda whined by his feet, her white fur soaking wet. I noticed dark patches running through it, dripping off whatever Jack held in his arms. But I still couldn't see it.

It was perfectly visible, but my mind just couldn't process. I felt dizzy and disoriented, like I was looking down at the world from an amazing height. I couldn't make sense of anything.

A wind rustled through the trees, moving the branches, and the moonlight struck him just right. I saw his face, his eyes rolled back into his head, and I saw exactly what Jack held in his arms.

19

"*Milo!*" I screamed, and Mae wrapped her arms around me just in time to keep me from running at Jack.

- 3 -

Ezra ran past us, down the embankment towards Jack and Milo. I kept wailing Milo's name, as if that would help somehow.

I only saw my little brother, bloodied and limp in his arms.

"Get him inside," Ezra told Jack.

Jack cradled Milo like an injured child as they hurried to the house. Ezra placed himself between them and me, shielding me from as much of it as he could. I bucked futilely against Mae's arms as they walked past us, screaming at them, but I don't even know what I said.

"It'll be okay, love," Mae tried to reassure me, but I heard the tremble in her voice. "Ezra will know what to do."

I watched helplessly through the glass doors. With one quick move of his arm, Ezra pushed everything off the island in the kitchen, and Jack laid Milo on the counter. Jack stood off to the side as Ezra inspected my brother.

I couldn't hear them, but neither of them looked good. Finally, Ezra pursed his lips and shook his head.

"No!" I cried, and Mae let me go.

I flew into the house. I reached out for Milo, and Jack grappled me in his arms. Lake water and Milo's blood covered his bare skin, and it felt slimy rubbing against me. I hit him hard in the chest and tried to escape his grip.

"Let me go!" I shouted. "He's my brother! And you killed him!"

"He's not dead," Ezra said, and it startled me enough where I stopped squirming away from Jack.

"Then what's wrong?" I stopped fighting, so Jack loosened his grip on me but didn't let me go. "Can't you fix him? Shouldn't we call 911?"

"I don't think they can do anything for him," Ezra said.

"But you don't know!" I stared down at Milo. Other than the blood, he just looked like he was sleeping. "We just have to call! Where's my cell phone?"

"Alice," Ezra said, and I moved to search for my cell, but Jack wouldn't let me go. "Alice."

"Why aren't you doing anything?" I yelled at him. "We have to do something!"

"We are trying to," Ezra insisted. "Milo broke his neck and cracked his skull. Even if he lives, he'll most likely be brain damaged and paralyzed."

"So you're just going to let him die?" I asked incredulously.

"I don't think that's what anyone's saying," Mae said. I turned to her, trying to understand the conflicted expression on her face.

"We can try the hospitals," Ezra said, watching the slow rise and fall of Milo's chest. "Or… we can turn him."

"Into a vampire?" I swallowed hard.

Jack finally released me and took a step away. When I managed to pull my gaze from Milo, I saw Jack's eyes filled with tears.

"I am so sorry, Alice," Jack apologized, his voice thick with despair.

"His heart is slowing." Ezra looked at me evenly. "You're going to have to make a choice, Alice. Quickly."

"If he turns, he'll live, right?" I asked, surprised I could talk. I found it hard to even breathe.

"If we catch it in time," Ezra said hesitantly. "But it's not a sure thing. If he's already too weakened, the turn might push him over the edge."

"You mean instead of saving him, it might kill him?" The room started spinning, and Jack reached out to steady me, tentatively putting his arm around me.

"I'm sorry," Ezra said simply.

"I can do it," Jack offered, knowing it would make me more comfortable with the decision. He moved closer to Milo. "If this is what you want, I'll do it."

"Do it," I whispered hoarsely.

"Are you sure?" Ezra eyed me seriously.

Ezra wanted to gauge my certainty, but that was impossible to measure. I felt somewhere between total shock and blacked out hysteria. Tears streamed down my cheeks, mixing in with the blood I had rubbed off Jack's chest when he held me to him.

Milo laid on the island, barely breathing and his heart slowing every second. If this was going to happen, it had to happen now, and as far as I could tell, it would be his best chance for survival.

"Everything will be okay, love." Mae was at my side and wrapped an arm around me. I wanted to push her off, but I didn't have the strength.

"We'll see," I said. Jack rummaged through a drawer, wasting precious time we didn't have. "What are you doing?"

"I need a knife." He looked back at Mae for help.

"There's one in the kitchen sink," Mae nodded to it.

Jack sifted through the sink and grabbed the knife Mae used to cut fruit. He walked over to Milo, holding the knife, and his breathing got more ragged. He was afraid of what he was about to do, and that didn't make me feel any better.

"Do you want to see this?" Ezra asked me, sending a new shiver down my spine.

"Yes, of course." I couldn't imagine being anywhere else when this happened, no matter how disturbing it might be. If this was where Milo died or turned, I had to be here, with him.

Jack glanced over at me, his eyes burning with apology. He looked down at Milo and took a deep breath. With one deft move, he sliced open his wrist and blood trickled out. Pressing his wound up against Milo's mouth, he didn't even notice the pain.

"Ezra," Jack shook his head, his voice trembling. "He's not responding."

"Give it time," Ezra said.

"What if he doesn't wake up?" Jack started to panic. His cut already began to close, and he used his other hand to pry it open, allowing his blood to flow into Milo's mouth.

"Give it time," Ezra repeated.

My heart raced wildly, and I knew that wouldn't really help the situation. Whatever was supposed to happen wasn't happening. Jack was terrified, and Mae tightened her grip around me.

Jack gasped sharply. Milo woke up enough to sink his teeth into his arm, but little else seemed to be happening with him. Jack groaned, and I tried to understand what he was feeling, but it was too many things all at once.

Milo coughed, but he still didn't seem to be awake. Jack pulled his arm back before Milo gagged on his blood.

"He's choking!" I yelled, and Mae's arms stopped me from performing CPR.

"No, he's fine," Ezra assured me.

"He's okay?" Jack winced and wrapped a towel around his wrist until the blood stopped.

"It's too soon to tell," Ezra said.

"What do you mean it's too soon?" I struggled against Mae, but she held firm. "If he's breathing, doesn't that mean it worked?"

"It's a process that takes a couple days," Ezra explained, then looked past me at Mae.

"I'll go ready a room for him," Mae said quietly and let me go.

I rushed over to Milo. He coughed and his body shuddered involuntarily. I stroked his hair, damp from the lake and his own blood, and his eyelids trembled but didn't open. Jack's blood covered his lips, and I wanted to wipe it away, but I was afraid to.

"Alice," Ezra said and placed his hand on my arm.

When I finally looked away from Milo, I was surprised to see we were the only two in the kitchen, along with my brother. I'd been so fixated on watching Milo that I hadn't noticed Jack leave the room.

"What?" I tried to focus on Ezra, but my eyes were sore and blurry from crying.

"Why don't you go rest? I'll take Milo and clean him up and make sure he's settled upstairs." Ezra's warm brown eyes tried to soothe me, but I laid an arm over Milo possessively.

"I can clean him up," I insisted, but Ezra shook his head.

"You can't carry him, Alice," Ezra said. "This whole thing has you exhausted and frayed. You need to clear your head a bit, and you can check on Milo later. There's nothing more you can do for him now."

"But-" I tried to think of a convincing argument to stay with him, but there was none. Except that letting Milo out of my sight seemed impossible

Out of nowhere, Mae appeared at my side, and I knew the battle was lost.

"Come on, love," Mae cooed and put her arm around my waist, so she could pry me away from Milo. "He needs to be moved upstairs where he can be more comfortable, and you need a chance to breathe."

Ezra scooped Milo into his arms so he could take him upstairs. If Mae hadn't mentioned that he would be more comfortable elsewhere, I might've fought more to stay with him. But as long as it was better for him, I'd let it happen.

I went to the bathroom to change for the second time that night, and I caught a glimpse of myself in the mirror. Milo's blood covered my pale skin. I took a long hot shower and cried.

After I pulled on Mae's pajamas, I left the bathroom. The panic and fear had died down, leaving an overwhelming sense of guilt and sadness and creeping numbness. It was hard to wrap my mind around everything. One minute, Milo was laughing in the lake. The next he was dying and turning into a vampire.

Jack sat on the steps leading upstairs, morose and freshly showered. As soon as he saw me, his eyes filled with terrified sadness. He felt responsible for Milo, and I didn't even know what happened. In all the worry of trying to figure out how to save him, I'd overlooked how he had gotten that way in the first place.

"Alice, I am so sorry," Jack said, his words rushed and shaky.

"What happened, Jack?" I walked stiffly over to him and sat down on the step below him.

"We were goofing off." He shook his head and tears filled his eyes. "He was running on the dock, but it was wet. He slipped and cracked his head... I am so sorry, Alice. I didn't even think-"

"How is he doing?" I interrupted him.

I don't know if I blamed Jack, but I wasn't ready to ease his guilt. If he and Milo didn't have a habit of letting things get a little too wild, Milo wouldn't have been hurt.

But then again, if I weren't trying to let things get out of hand with me and Jack, I would've still been outside, reining them in. Or if I hadn't invited Milo over tonight. Or if I had never even come over here. Milo never would have been here if it weren't for me.

"Milo's still unconscious. Ezra said that if he's lucky, he should be unconscious through most of this."

"If he's lucky?" I shot him a worried look, and he dropped his eyes. "What does that mean?"

"Turning isn't exactly pleasant." He rubbed his hands together sheepishly.

"So Milo's in pain? Like how much pain?" My eyes widened, and I hoped I hadn't made the wrong choice.

"He's completely out right now. Don't worry. He can't feel anything." Jack tried to brush me off, and that made me more paranoid.

"He's my brother, Jack! I'm going to worry! This whole stupid thing is my fault!"

"None of this is your fault," Jack corrected me sternly, and his eyes were strangely wounded. "Alice, you can't blame yourself for this. You had nothing to do with it."

"Don't tell me what I can or can't feel!"

I tried to stand up, but the weight of the night hit me. I lost my balance, and Jack reached out for me. He pulled me into his arms, and at first, I fought him, just because I felt like fighting something. But his arms felt wonderful and safe around me, and I gave into it. I buried my face in his chest and sobbed.

"It's going to be alright, Alice," Jack whispered. "He's going to be okay. You just need to get some rest."

"There's no way I can rest as long as Milo's…" I trailed off.

I didn't know how to finish the sentence, and I could barely fight off the fatigue anymore. Even though I didn't want to admit it, I didn't know how much longer I could stay awake.

"Mae's sitting with him, and you know she'll make sure he's as comfortable as he can be."

Jack stood up and lifted me in his arms. He carried me upstairs to his room to sleep. I felt too drained and tired to protest. After he laid me down in his bed, he stood next to it, looking hesitant.

"You aren't gonna leave me, are you?" I wanted him with me. I didn't want to be alone.

"Mae wants me to sleep on the couch downstairs," Jack said.

"But I don't want you to."

Still looking unsure, he carefully climbed into bed next to me. I had too much on my mind to get excited about it, but he made me feel safer than I ever thought possible. I rested my head on his chest, listening to his slow heartbeat.

Only one thin wall away from us, my brother laid in a bed, going through his own struggle. I felt guilty for falling asleep when his future remained so uncertain. The exhaustion of the night won out over my guilt, and I passed out in Jack's arms.

- 4 -

Jack was gone when I woke up. I went next door to check on Milo, but he seemed to be mostly the same. He lay in bed, looking pale and frightfully small, but at least his breathing had improved a little. Mae staked out a position next to his bed, and she assured me that he had yet to wake up.

After I got dressed, Ezra addressed the practical aspects of the situation. Milo couldn't go home right now, and I didn't want to be away from him. Our mother was always gone, thanks to work and a gambling addiction, but she would notice if we didn't come home for days. Ezra suggested that I go home, get some clothes, and tell my mom that we were staying at their vacation house for awhile.

Jack returned from his mysterious whereabouts and offered to take me home. Ezra had to repeatedly assure me that Milo would be fine before I got in the car with Jack. I was convinced that Milo would take a turn for the worst as soon as I left.

"He's going to be alright," Jack told me again as we pulled out of the driveway.

"How do you know that? Have you even seen him today?" I glared over at him. It'd hurt me to wake up alone, and he hadn't explained his absence.

"Yeah, I checked on him when I got up. Ezra said everything's going fine. It looks like the change is taking." His earlier guilt seemed to have lessened a bit, since it looked like Milo wouldn't die.

"When did you get up?"

"Awhile ago."

"Where were you?" I asked.

"I had to eat." He shifted uncomfortably.

After all this time, I think he still expected me to go screaming for the hills every time he mentioned that he drank blood. I hadn't gotten used to the idea, but it didn't repulse me. Well, not enough to send me packing, anyway.

"So did you just pick up some girl?" My jealousy flared, but oddly enough, that appeared to relieve him.

"No. We were low on blood at the house, so I went to the bank and picked some up. We're gonna need more blood around with Milo." He said it so matter-of-factly, but in a weird way, it hadn't fully sunk in with me yet.

Milo needed to drink blood.

"When does Milo need to eat?"

"Soon, I think." He looked over at me to see how I was taking things. I must've managed to look pretty okay, because he continued. "At first, he's going to eat a lot. The turning takes a lot out of you, and he won't understand how to gauge his hunger."

"I can't believe this is happening," I groaned. Closing my eyes, I leaned back in the seat and tried not to look as freaked out as I felt.

"It won't be so bad," Jack said. "I mean, I'm not so bad, right?"

"So what's gonna happen?"

"I can't really say for sure."

"What do you mean you can't say? You're a vampire. You know what it's like to be one," I said incredulously.

"Yeah, but it's different for everybody." He wanted to let it go with that, but I kept glaring at him until he continued. "You already know the basics. I don't even know what you're trying to find out."

"This whole turning process," I clarified. "What does that entail exactly?"

"I don't know," Jack said, and I scoffed. "What? I can't really remember, and I've never seen anybody else turn."

I couldn't tell if he was lying or not, but it seemed pretty ridiculous that he couldn't remember the most important event of his life, especially since it hadn't been that long ago. I could understand if Ezra had forgotten, but sixteen years was relatively recent.

"How can you not remember?"

"Do you remember being born?" Jack countered.

"No, but I wasn't twenty-four when it happened."

"Well..." He sighed. We pulled up in front of my brownstone, but we sat in the car as he thought of a way to explain it.

"Mae can remember her turning vividly, and I think Peter can too. But I can't. Mine's all hazy, like a dream I had a very long time ago. I just can't remember pain very well, I guess."

"So it is really painful?" I asked, even though I wasn't sure I'd want to know.

"Your body dies," Jack said softly. "Not all of it, but enough where you really feel it. But it only lasts a few days, and then everything feels really wonderful."

"Is there anything they can do for the pain?"

"You're really so much better off talking to Ezra about all of this," he said.

"Do you think I made the right choice?"

"I think you made the only choice," Jack told me solemnly. Then he smiled crookedly, trying to brighten my mood. "Come on. Let's go pack your stuff so we can hurry up and have a sleepover."

"You make it sound so much more fun than it really is," I muttered and got out of the car.

"Hey, any time you spend with me is fun!" Jack said, following me out.

"Oh, yeah, last night was a total hoot." I meant it at as some kind of joke, but the hurt look on Jack's face meant I cut a lot deeper than I meant to. "I didn't mean it like that."

"Nah, you're right," he brushed me off and went into the apartment building in front of me.

The apartment looked the same as it always had, but it felt smaller somehow. Thankfully, my mother was at work, because I wasn't ready for a conversation with her. It'd be too hard telling her Milo wasn't coming home, even if I was just feeding her a lie about staying in a vacation house.

Milo's room was immaculate, making it easy to find the things that I needed to pack. He mostly needed clothes, and I picked out what I thought were his favorites.

Jack tagged along for moral support, and he ended up being a huge motivator. I tended to stand and stare until he prompted me to do something, like pick up a shirt.

Going through all Milo's stuff was hard. It felt like an invasion of privacy and the kind of the thing I would do when he was dead.

After we got Milo's stuff, I went in my room to grab my clothes. As long as Milo was turning, I didn't plan to leave him, so I'd need things for myself.

Before we left, I wrote a note for my mother and kept it as simple as I could. I told her we were at a vacation house for the next few days, and I'd have my cell if she needed me.

The note didn't sound very convincing, mostly because it was from me. Milo usually did that kind of thing.

"How long is this gonna take?" I asked on the car ride back.

"The car ride?" Jack was willfully playing dumb, and I didn't appreciate it. "Like five more minutes."

"How long will it take for Milo to turn?" I carefully enunciated all the words.

"I don't know, Alice."

"What do you know?" I snapped.

"I told you that you need to talk to Ezra about all of this," Jack said. "I don't know why you think I was kidding. We're almost home now. You can run inside and interrogate him until your heart's content."

"I will." I crossed my arms over my chest, as if I had won something.

"Yeah. I know you will."

Jack carried the bags inside when we got to his house. Matilda waited by the door for his return, but even she seemed oddly subdued.

The entire mood of the house had changed. Everybody waited on edge for Milo to be okay.

Jack went upstairs and I started following him. I wanted to check on Milo again, but Ezra appeared at the top of the steps. Something about the way he looked made me freeze, but Jack kept going, brushing past him with my luggage.

"Did something happen?" I asked Ezra.

"He's fine," Ezra reassured me and descended the stairs. "But I don't think you should see him right now."

"Why not?" I straightened up for a fight. Nobody could keep me from my brother, not even an all-powerful vampire. He placed his hand on my arm, and some of my anger relented.

"Let's talk." Moving his hand to the small of my back, he ushered me to the living room.

"Are you sure nothing happened?" I repeated.

"He woke up," Ezra allowed carefully, and my heart sped up.

"He did? Is he okay? What did he say?" My excitement was overwhelming, but he gestured to couch.

"Please, sit. We need to talk."

"What?" I collapsed back on the couch, feeling nauseous.

"He is turning, and rather rapidly at that." Ezra sat next to me. "He's young and strong, and the change should be completely over within a few days. He's going to be alright."

"Oh, that's wonderful," I breathed deeply. A weight lifted off my shoulders, and a surge of relief went through me. Then I noticed the grim expression on Ezra's face. "So why do you still look like you have bad news?"

"I don't. Not really," he qualified, forcing a smile. "You just can't see him for awhile."

"What do you mean?" I narrowed my eyes at him.

"At least until the change is complete, and he can get a grip on his hunger," he elaborated, and I remembered what Jack said in the car. "You can't go near him until things are under control."

"He's going to try and bite me?" I shook my head, disbelieving. "He hasn't fully turned yet. He just woke up."

"He's already eating, Alice."

My chest tightened, and my head swam. I thought I still had time. I don't know what I planned on doing with that time, but I thought he'd be human for just a little longer.

But he was drinking blood less than twenty-four hours after biting Jack. He was Milo the vampire, and he would kill me if I got too close to him.

"It will get better. I promise." Ezra placed his hand on mine, trying to comfort me. "You can be around all of us without any problems, and it will be the same with Milo. It takes time to get a handle on things. At the rate he's going, it shouldn't be that long."

"So…" My mouth felt dry, and I swallowed hard. "Do I need to go home?"

"No, of course not. We wouldn't expect you to go home while all this is going on, and Milo is still fairly incapacitated. He shouldn't leave the room for a day or two. By the time he does, he should be in control enough." He smiled, as if that was reassuring in some way.

"Awesome," I said wryly.

"I know the situation isn't ideal, but he's going to live, Alice. And he's going to be better than he was before. You're not going to have to worry about him anymore."

"I know, I know." I closed my eyes, letting it all sink in.

I knew I should be grateful to them. They saved Milo's life and gave him an amazing gift, but it didn't really feel like it then.

When it came to my little brother drinking blood and turning into something that would rip my head off, it felt a lot more like a curse.

"Did he say anything?" I asked.

"Nothing that's coherent," Ezra shook his head. "He's not exactly conscious."

"But you just said that he woke up and he's eating." I felt bewildered.

"Yes, but he's more…" He paused, trying to think of how he wanted to phrase it. "Delirious? He's not completely there yet. It's more instinct and confusion than anything else."

"Has he asked for me?"

"He hasn't asked for anything. He only mumbles complaints of pain and hunger," Ezra reiterated. "Mae is doing her best to see that he feels as little pain and hunger as possible."

"So… what happens next?" I asked. "He turns, and then what?"

"Let's just get through this, and take things from there," Ezra hedged the question.

"Why? What does that mean?"

"There's no blanket answer for this. We'll have to see exactly how Milo reacts to everything before we can say with any certainty what's going to happen. So far, he's turning differently than anybody else I've encountered," Ezra explained carefully.

"You're supposed to know everything," I said, growing frustrated.

"I understand your impatience, but there's really nothing more I can tell you." Ezra smiled sadly at me.

Jack lumbered down the stairs, and I wondered if he was responding to the quickened beat of my heart. He was so sensitive to it, and it alerted him whenever I was upset about anything. He read my emotions almost better than me since he had a direct link to my heart.

"How is everything going down here?" Jack was full of forced cheer, and his overly broad smile masked the anxiety underneath it.

"How do you think they're going?" I cast a look at him.

"Well, I just checked in on your brother." He ignored my glare and tried to give me information he hoped would comfort me. "He's asleep again, but he's looking really good. I think you're gonna be really happy when you see him."

"He's not a house that you're remodeling," I grimaced at his poor choice of words.

He made Milo sound like some kind of fixer upper that they were working on, and while that wasn't very far from the truth, I didn't want to think of it that way.

"Sorry." Jack shifted uncomfortably. "Mae sent me down here to feed you."

"I'm not hungry." Stress destroyed my appetite, but I hadn't eaten in a long time, and my stomach already reminded me of it.

"Why don't you let Jack make you some food and I'll go make sure everything is going well with Milo?" Ezra posed it like a question, but there was no mistaking it for anything but an order.

"I'm perfectly capable of making food for myself," I said as I stood up. For some reason, I had resorted to refuting their generosity with pouting.

"Fine, I'll watch you make food then," Jack rolled his eyes.

In the kitchen, I made a show of slamming things down and banging drawers. Jack sighed and watched me make the angriest peanut butter sandwich in the world.

But for all the stomping around and tantrum throwing I did, I wasn't angry with Jack or Ezra or anyone. I was just scared.

- 5 -

Even standing in the hallway, I could smell Peter and hated what it did to me. The ache I tried to ignore burned unbearably inside me, and my heart sped up so quickly, it made me weak.

Thankfully, Jack was downstairs, doing his penance by washing my laundry. Under normal circumstances, Mae would be happy to do it, but she'd been preoccupied with Milo, who required 24-hour care.

I'd been here for almost three days, and I had seen almost nothing of her. I hadn't seen Milo since Ezra warned me not to.

That left me with a lot of time to wander around the house feeling lost and confused. Jack tried to console me while simultaneously keeping his distance, and it did little to make me feel better.

He'd been sleeping on the couch downstairs, leaving me with his room. I snooped through his drawers in hopes of finding something incriminating, but everything was innocent. He had a trunk of graphic novels in his closet that I leafed through, but it was hard to focus on anything.

I should have found comfort in this, because it meant that I would never have to give Milo up. Maybe if I had already turned I would feel that way, if I could completely understand what was in store for him. Instead, I had Jack's vague assurance that being a vampire was awesome, and that was about it.

What if it did something horrible to Milo? And he got sick or died or turned into something completely vile? What if he stopped being Milo, the timid over protective geek I loved, and turned into some overzealous blood sucker?

Or what if he turned out fine, but he hated me for letting him turn? And for lying to him about vampires? What if I had to spend the rest of eternity with him hating me?

When I tired of searching through Jack's room and driving myself mad with worry, I finally gave into Peter. I stood in the hallway for a long while, just breathing in the intoxicating, tangy scent that Peter left behind.

Since Peter took off last spring after the incident where he nearly killed me, Mae simply shut the door to his room. No one talked about whether or not he would be back, although he hadn't packed any of his things.

The unspoken consensus was that Ezra would find a cure for us, and life would go back to normal. Not that I even knew what it would mean to be "back to normal" anymore.

I opened Peter's bedroom door, checking the hall both ways just to make sure that Jack wasn't around. Nobody had forbid me from · entering his room. I doubted that Mae and Ezra would care at all, but Jack was liable to take offense.

Even mentioning Peter's name made him tense up, and I hoped that someday, he'd be able to move past that. I began to doubt that Jack would ever want anything to do with Peter again, regardless of how our relationships resolved themselves.

His room was just as he had left it, but I barely noticed. I closed my eyes, breathing in more deeply, and a wonderful heat surged through me. There was a physical pull inside me, and I was drawn into his room.

Peter had been gone for months, and my body still clamored to get in every last drop of him.

On the floor in front of Peter's massive bookcases, a white rug had been stained with a few drops of my blood. I remembered the terrible ecstasy when Peter bit me, and the way the life drained from me in this beautiful, peaceful feeling. Nothing, not even my magical kiss with Jack, had ever felt as good as that.

Even now, knowing what I know and having all that I have, I knew that if Peter offered to bite me in exchange for my death, I would gladly make the trade. My feelings for him were positively suicidal.

I walked around Peter's room, admiring his odd collection of things. His furniture seemed to be primarily antiques, and everything was natural wood or white. His bed smelled too sweetly of him, so I deliberately steered clear of his white linens.

His shelves were lined with books from every day and age, and I let my fingers travel over their worn bindings. Then I noticed something that made my already shortened breath catch.

Peter had an entire section of books on vampires, and I don't mean things like Bram Stroker or Anne Rice. They were books with titles like *A Vampire Dictionary* and *A Brief History of Vampyres*.

I pulled the latter from the shelf, carefully opening the cover to the yellowed pages. The moldy smell overwhelmed me, and I sneezed.

I sat back down on the chair by the bookcase, and I looked through it. It had no table of contents, but a page appeared to be missing. It started with a foreword:

"I am not the oldest of my kind, nor do I claim to be an expert on them. However, in my many years of existence, I have found little written on the subject of vampyres, other than questionable folklore.

"In an effort to dispel the mythology and to create a guide for the newly turned, I have decided to write this book. In no means is it to be taken as a 'Bible' for my kind, but rather, as the title suggests, a brief history of vampyres as far as I can tell."

My fingers began to tremble, and I was afraid I'd rip the fragile pages out. Knowing vampires had a history was disconcerting.

I knew they existed, but the only ones I knew were Jack and his family, and they weren't particularly frightening or disturbing. But thinking of vampires as a whole, an entire species of creatures out there, feeding on the living for the past millennia… it sent chills down my spine.

The first chapter was simply titled *"In the Beginning."*

"Perhaps what is most unusual about vampyres is that while we carry many of the same traits of humans, we lack any real creation story of our own. Some vampyres still cling onto the religion of the people, while others banish it, saying that we are proof that God does not exist.

"What I have found to be true is much less sensational than one would hope. We have neither a direct line with God nor the devil. We are no closer to the meaning of life than any other human.

"Vampyres have not existed as long as humans have, by our best record, and I was unable to find anything on the first vampyre. More precisely, I have never

encountered a vampyre who admitted to being the first one, or any other vampyre who met him.

"Our first documented appearance happened to coincide with a plague, which leads me to believe that we are some kind of plague ourselves."

"I see you found some light reading," Ezra interrupted, startling me so badly that I jumped up from the chair and dropped the book onto the floor.

"I-I just- I was just curious," I stumbled and felt my cheeks burn with shame.

"There's no harm in being curious." Ezra waved off my apology and walked over to me.

He picked the book up off the floor and held it for me to take. I hesitated for a moment, afraid that it might be some kind of trick, although he didn't seem much like the tricking kind.

"I just don't know very much about you." I took the book from him, and I lowered my eyes and held it close to me.

"We haven't been as forthcoming as you'd like?" Ezra raised an eyebrow, and I wasn't sure if he was being skeptical or sincere.

"No, it's not that," I corrected myself quickly. "It's just…"

What was it exactly? They had been incredibly open with me. When I had questions, Jack answered them to the best of his ability, but somehow, that wasn't enough. As much as I knew, it seemed liked there was twice as much that I didn't know.

"It's because it's personal now," Ezra nodded knowingly. "Before, we were merely a curiosity to you, or an opportunity."

"No, no!" I interrupted him forcefully. "You're not some sideshow to me."

45

"No, I know that. It was a poor choice of words on my part," Ezra said, calming me. "I know how much you care for us.

"But... you'd always known us as this, and whether you understood us completely was irrelevant," he continued. "You saw that we were happy and well. But now that it's struck Milo, it's not enough to know that we're content. You need to understand everything about us."

"Yeah," I nodded. "So?"

"So... you want me to tell you everything," he smiled sadly.

"Yeah, kinda."

"I have bad news," he exhaled. "There's not much more to tell."

"How can there not be much to tell?" My voice quavered with incredulity. "You're telling me that the little bit you've confessed to me in the past few months covers the entire history of your species?"

"No, of course not," he laughed at my fervor. "We have an extensive history, and that book you're holding right now is a very good source of a lot of it. But it's much like any other history book you've read. You'd be more interested in a biology book."

"Is there one?" I asked hopefully.

"There are a few," Ezra shrugged as if none of them were that good. "Peter has some, I'm sure.

"But there are many problems with a biology book about vampires. Autopsies are impossible," he went on. "Whatever kills a vampire tends to destroy everything inside him, making it impossible to dissect it all and see how it differs from a human. But that's only half the problem."

"What's the other half of the problem?"

"Have you heard about the bumblebee?" Ezra leaned back against the end of the Peter's four-post bed, crossing his feet over his ankles.

"What are you talking about?" I shook my head, confused by the abrupt subject change.

"According to an aerodynamic study done in the early 20th century, the bumblebee can't possibly fly," Ezra explained. "Its wings are much too small and can't beat fast enough to carry the weight of its body."

"What?" I furrowed my brow and decided it must be a riddle. "So… What? How do they get around then?"

"They fly, of course," he smiled at me.

"But you just said…" I sighed and shook my head. "What does this have to do with vampire biology?"

"Nothing." Ezra shrugged. "The bumblebee existed despite scientific evidence to the contrary, much like myself. Eventually, scientists figured out they were looking at the wings wrong and discovered the magic in the flight of the bumblebee.

"Unfortunately, science has yet to figure out the magic of us," Ezra finished, looking apologetic.

"So you're saying that nobody knows the answers to my questions?" I asked.

"Yes and no." He stood up. "You'll find some things, but it won't be enough. You look through Peter's books and see if you can come across anything that might help you feel better."

"Thanks," I said.

With that, Ezra nodded at me and strode out of the room. I sighed and listened for his departing footsteps, but there were none.

The only thing I could hear was music wafting from Milo's room that sounded like Mozart.

I settled back in the chair and opened the book where I had left off. As I read on, I found that the faded italics offered little in what I wanted, just as Ezra predicted.

It was interesting though, telling the story of the unnamed author and his transformation into a vampire. He described it as excruciating, but in the end, very brief and hard to define. There was just pain, and then an unquenchable thirst.

The only new information was that some vampires turned more than others. While most retained a sense of their humanity, some of them lost it entirely. They were crazed bloodthirsty monsters, and they didn't live very long because humans and vampires couldn't stomach a creature like that.

I had just finished reading that passage when I heard a disgusted scoff at the door, frightening me so much I yelped. I half-expected to find Milo standing there, with shiny new fangs and that animal look in his eyes the book described.

Instead, it was just Jack, standing in the doorway and frowning darkly at me.

"You scared me!" I pointed out in an attempt to alleviate his glare.

"What are you doing in Peter's room?" He fought to keep the edge off his voice, but he did a poor job. The last time I'd been in this room, I'd almost died, and he strained to keep his eyes from my dried blood on the rug.

"Reading." I held up the book for him to see, but his expression never changed. "It's a book about vampires. I figured that I better bone up since everybody around me seems to be one."

"Why don't you take the book and go somewhere else to read?" Jack meant to ask it, but it came off as a demand.

I could've argued with him, and I would've been perfectly justified in doing so. But it felt like too much work, and the scent of Peter distracted me anyway. Thoughts of him kept lurking in my head, keeping my mind in a fog.

Jack stood just outside the doorway, refusing to step inside. When I slid past him out the door, he finally started to relax a bit.

"What do you have?" Jack touched the book, moving it so he could read the title. Immediately, he let go of the book and rolled his eyes.

"What?" I looked down at the cover, trying to figure out what displeased him. Nondescript leather with the words *A Brief History of Vampyres* emblazed in the cover. "It's just a book."

"It's Peter's book," Jack grumbled.

"Yeah, but you knew that when I was in his room." I gestured back to the bookcases in his room and gave him a peculiar look. "Just because Peter owns something doesn't-"

"No, he doesn't just own it," Jack corrected me. "He wrote it. That's his biography."

"What are you talking about?" I flipped open the book, looking for some mention of the author, but I found something that contradicted Jack. "No, it says right here the author is very old when he wrote this, and the book itself is incredibly old, and Peter isn't even two-hundred yet."

"Yeah, he wrote it when he'd been turned for like twenty years, but he didn't think anyone would think anything of it if they knew how young he was. That's why it doesn't mention who he is or how old he is exactly."

"But..." I tried to think of something to counter it with, but I didn't even know why it was so important to me that I counter his argument at all.

"Was that the first book you picked up?" Jack narrowed his eyes, and his tone took an entirely different turn.

He was vaguely jealous, but mostly, the whole vampire bonding thing sickened him. My blood, Peter's blood, they only seemed to exist to drive Jack insane.

I felt the same way he did. I hated that my pulse quickened just at the memory of Peter, or that I was automatically drawn to his book. Any connection to Peter felt like a betrayal, and I couldn't stand it anymore.

"It's just a book!"

"Whatever." Jack shook his head and shut Peter's bedroom door. When he looked back at me, he wrinkled his nose. "You smell like him."

"Sorry."

"Have you eaten today?" He abruptly changed the subject, and he softened. "I can order you a pizza or something."

"I'm okay," I shook my head. "I had a bagel earlier."

"Right." Jack stood awkwardly in front of me for a moment, and then stepped away from me. "I'm gonna go check on your brother."

"Good idea. Tell him I say hi."

He nodded and walked to the end of the hall, into the room I couldn't go. I was alone in the hall, holding Peter's book, and I couldn't decide whether I wanted to read it or not.

Part of me wanted to read it even more now that I knew it was the story of Peter. Anything to get a better understanding of him would be amazing.

The rest of me knew it was a path I didn't want to go down anymore. After he tried to kill me, a choice had been made, and Peter was no longer an option for me.

While Jack hadn't requested it, I knew that a shower would fare better with him. I went into his room and discarded the book on his bed before picking out a change of clothes. Getting clean and worrying about Milo's condition were enough. I would decide what to do about the book later.

The curtains layered the windows so thick the sun never stood a chance. No matter the time of day, darkness shrouded the house. My vision wasn't as advanced as theirs, so Jack put a night light in the bathroom that adjoined his room.

I heard a rustling, and that must've been what awoke me from my sleep. The clock on the nightstand said it was only two in the afternoon, so I couldn't imagine that anyone would be awake. I hadn't gone to bed until seven in the morning, and Jack had still been awake playing Xbox.

I rolled back over, burying myself in the thick blankets of Jack's bed.

When I heard the rustling again, I barely stirred, and decided that it must be the dog. I had overtaken Jack's room, and it led to some confusion with Matilda. She usually slept at the end of his bed, but he was sleeping on the couch. She couldn't decide if her loyalties lied more with him or the bed.

"Go to sleep, Matilda," I muttered.

I was awake enough where I felt the movement. It wasn't actually a rustling that had woken me, because the motion was nearly soundless. But there was something – almost like an electric breeze – moving about the room.

Someone was in the room with me. There was silence and a shadowy presence that I couldn't explain.

"Matilda?" I whispered.

By now, I knew it wasn't her, but I wanted to play along. My heart raced, but I wasn't sure if Jack would notice that if he were asleep.

I sat up, my eyes searching the darkness. I hoped to see her massive white shape lurking somewhere, but the night light from the bathroom cast little light. Then I saw a glimpse of a shadow rush in front of it.

Before I could yell, the bed moved, and whoever it was had gotten on the bed with me. I could scream, but by the time anyone heard, it would be too late for them to do anything. So I sat in the darkness and waited for whatever came next.

- 6 -

"Jeez, Alice, settle down," a voice chuckled in the dark, only a few inches from my face. "You're gonna give yourself a heart attack."

"What? Who's there?" I asked, my words shaking. The voice sounded familiar, but I couldn't place it.

"Shame on you," he said with a mock disapproval. "You don't even recognize your own brother?"

"Milo?" I scrambled to turn on the bedside lamp.

I gasped as soon as I saw him. He looked like my brother but not. The baby fat had been chiseled away to cheek bones and a strong jaw. His skin had never been scarred by acne, but it appeared even smoother and more flawless.

The change aged him, but in a good way. He no longer looked like a boy teetering on puberty but rather a young man in his late teens. His brown eyes had gotten more amazing, but his crooked, unsure grin remained the same.

"Milo?" I repeated, struggling to grasp that my little brother had become this rather stunning creature before me.

"The one and only." His voice still sounded much like his own, but it was deeper and more velvet. It lacked the squeaky insecure quality that had once been so distinctly him.

Without thinking, I reached out and touched his face. His skin felt soft and temperate, but before I could register anything more, something flicked across his face. He jumped back from my touch.

"What? Did I do something?" I asked, pulling my hand back.

"I'm just not strong enough yet." Milo backed closer to the wall but stayed in my room, bathed in the soft lamp glow.

"For what?" I asked.

"You're the first... human I've been around." His face contorted, looking confused and torn. "I could smell you when I was in my room, and I thought I had a handle on it. But I wasn't prepared for how your pulse would feel on my skin..." Guilt flashed across his face at finding me appetizing.

"I'm sorry. I should've known better. I'm always doing the same things to Jack, and you think I would've learned by now." I forced a smile at him, but his expression only got more sour. "What?"

"So... you know?" Milo asked quietly.

"You mean... that they're vampires?"

"I knew that you had to." He stared past me into the darkness. "As soon as I could understand what was happening, and Mae explained it to me... She told me that you knew, and I knew you had to. But, I guess I didn't really believe it until I heard you say it."

"Why wouldn't you believe it?" I furrowed my brow. If he could believe that he was becoming a vampire, how would it be a stretch to believe that I had known about them?

"How could you not tell me about this?" Milo sounded so angry and hurt, and I flinched.

I remembered what Jack had said. When vampires first turn, all their emotions are right at the surface. Everything is so much more intense, making it harder to control. Self-control had always been Milo's strong suit, but that's how he could be in the same room with me so soon.

"I-I didn't know how to tell you," I stuttered. "I even tried to once. But you would've just thought I was crazy."

"You should've tried harder!" Milo snapped.

I stared at my brother, at the new exquisite contours of his face. I felt an immense sense of relief and love, but I had this feeling that I didn't really recognize the boy glowering at me from the shadows of the room.

I imagined this was how the dad felt when that creepy little boy came back from the *Pet Sematary*. That thought was followed by the thick Maine drawl saying, "Sometimes, dead is better." I stifled the chill running over me.

"I'm sorry, Milo. You're right. And it was so hard keeping this from you. I just..." I sighed and shook my head. "It was a hard decision. Just like this one."

"What one?" His eyes flashed with confusion, and I wondered how much Mae had told him.

"The one... to turn you" I swallowed hard and studied his face for his reaction. His eyes dropped from mine, and he softened. "Did they tell you what happened?"

"Jack did," Milo nodded. "He said it was his fault, and I was dying. So you asked him to turn me. To save me."

"I didn't know what else to do."

"I'm not angry with you," Milo absolved me. "I'm sure I would've done the same thing in your situation."

He shifted against the wall, and I noticed for the first time the way his clothes fit against his body. In that simple movement, I saw the way the muscles moved subtly underneath his shirt. Soft would be a good way to describe him before, but now he looked like a jungle cat recoiled before an attack.

To know something is entirely different from seeing it so blatantly in front of me. Everything about him had changed, and only time would tell how much of him was still my brother.

"You're a vampire," I said breathlessly.

"I am," Milo agreed with a wry smile.

"How do you feel?"

"Pretty amazing actually." His smile widened and his stance broadened. "At first, it hurt like hell and I was sure I was going to die. Or at least I hoped I would. But now I feel better than I've ever felt."

"Really?" I asked hopefully.

"Yeah." Milo nodded, but his smile faltered. "Well, except for the hunger. It's hard to get used to, but eating… Wow. There aren't even words for it."

"So you're eating?" I asked, even though I knew the answer.

"If I wasn't, I couldn't be here with you," Milo said with a strange threatening sound to his voice, and I involuntarily shrunk back in the bed. "I'm not even supposed to be out of my room now. But I woke up hungry, so I had some blood bags in the room. Mae was completely passed out in the chair, and I was sick of being locked up."

"They think you're going to eat me?" I tucked a tangle of my hair behind my ear and hoped my voice stayed even. He looked pained but said nothing. "Do... do you want to?"

"I'm not going to!" Milo insisted, but he dropped his eyes to the floor. "I want to. It's impossible not to."

"Don't kid yourself, Alice. They're all thinking about it." He looked back up at me, his russet eyes full of warning. "It's really not safe for you here."

"I think I'm pretty safe here," I reassured him.

"You have no idea," he said ominously, and then narrowed his eyes at me. "Do you let them bite you?"

"No." I floundered under his judgmental gaze. "Well, it's complicated."

"Not Jack." Milo's voice had gotten small and plaintive and... jealous.

Definitely jealous. Everything he felt got more intense when he turned, including his crush on Jack. But more than his emotions were powerful. Physically, Milo was stronger, but just standing there talking to me, there was something menacing about him.

"Not Jack," I answered quickly. "Once with Peter, but it was a very difficult situation."

"What's going on?" He stood up straighter and sniffed the air. "Something just happened."

"What are you talking about?" I looked around the room.

"You. Something happened to you. You're..." His eyes changed, and I recognized that burning hunger behind them. "Everything about you... It's like... You want me to bite you?"

"No!" I shouted, alarmed.

"I don't understand." His face betrayed the struggle going on within him, and when he took a step closer to me, it finally dawned on me that I could actually be in danger. "What did you do?"

"I didn't do-" I started to argue, but then I realized exactly what I'd done.

I'd thought of Peter, and my body turned itself into the most delectable thing a vampire could imagine when I thought of him. It affected Jack the hardest, but since Milo was so new, he had no defense for it.

"Milo!" Jack shouted, appearing in the doorway.

With a great effort, Milo pulled his eyes away from me, and he exchanged a look with Jack that I couldn't read. Milo swallowed hard and his breathing had grown more labored, but he managed to keep his focus on Jack.

"Go back to your room," Jack told him.

Milo shivered and walked past him. Jack stayed frozen in the doorway until I heard the bedroom door shut as Milo went back into his room.

"What the hell were you doing?" Jack turned back me, his voice full of venom.

"I didn't do anything," I said. "He came into my room while I was sleeping!"

"You should've yelled for me or Mae!" Jack crossed his arms over his chest. "And you've got to stop thinking about Peter! Do you want to get yourself killed?"

"It's so impossible!" I groaned and flopped back onto the bed. "You know, in the real world, its okay to just think about people! There's not little mind police checking to make sure that your pulse hasn't quickened!"

"I know," Jack sighed apologetically. "We're just a little more sensitive than everyone else."

"What was that, by the way?" I looked back over at him.

"What?"

"That look you had with Milo. You were like... I don't know. Connected." A weird pang of envy stabbed at me that I tried to ignore. "You guys aren't like... lovers or something?"

"No, no, of course not!" Jack laughed, and the clear sound of it made everything about me lighten and relax. "But we are more 'connected,' I guess. Because I turned him, it makes us closer."

I wasn't sure how I felt about that, but I'd better hurry and get used to it because there'd be nothing I could do about. The one thing I knew for sure about vampirism is that it was permanent.

"Are you okay?" Jack walked closer to the bed and looked me over.

"If I said no, would you stay here with me longer?"

Knowing Milo was alright had taken a giant weight off my shoulders, and it made me aware of how little time I'd really spent with Jack lately. I missed him terribly.

"I shouldn't..." Jack trailed off, but I'd won.

Lifting up the covers, he crawled into bed with me. I snuggled up next to him and relished the feel of his strong arms around me.

Despite Milo's earlier proclamation, I knew there was nowhere in the world I was safer than in Jack's arms.

"Everything's gonna be okay." He stroked my hair gently, and I rested my head on his chest, letting his heart thud slowly in my ear. "Milo's going to be just fine. He just has to adjust to everything."

"I don't want to talk about adjusting or how everything is going be fine or okay or great in the future," I said tiredly. "I just want to lay here with you."

Jack settled into bed and I felt him relax with me. We rarely got to fall asleep together, let alone curled up in bed. The moments were few and far between, and I wanted to hang onto this one as long as I could.

We were woken up much too soon. I had been in the middle of a dream, and then I heard someone clearing their throat loudly in the hallway.

As I started coming to, I felt Jack's arms pull away from me, and I clung onto them. He laughed quietly into my hair, but that only annoyed the interloper in the hall.

"Ahem!" Mae coughed loudly.

"What?" Jack groaned.

"It's time to get up," Mae said.

"But I'm still sleeping," he yawned.

"Too bad." To enunciate her point, she clapped her hands loudly. "Get up!"

"I'm up!" Jack insisted and freed himself from me so he could sit up.

When Jack sat up, he cleared my view so I could see Mae standing in the hallway. Wearing an elegant housecoat, she had her hands on her hips. Just the way she looked at Jack made me feel guilty.

"What do you think you're doing?" Mae asked wearily.

"Getting up, like you asked." Jack leaned back and stretched, and I watched the wonderful muscles of his back ripple underneath his tee shirt.

"I meant, what do you do you think you're doing in that bed, with her?" She nodded at me, but she never took her eyes of him. "Did you think that since you left the bedside lamp on it would make it okay?"

"Kinda." He smiled at her, but she was in no mood for it.

"Get up. We all need to talk downstairs." Mae took a step away, but Jack stopped her.

"Hey, hey. Did Milo tell you about his little excursion last night?" Jack asked, and his voice took a more accusing tone. "When he was on your watch?"

"We'll talk about all that when you get downstairs." She turned sharply, her housecoat billowing behind her, and disappeared down the hall.

"Its way too early for a lecture," I muttered into the pillow.

"You're telling me."

He looked back at me, and his smile deepened, growing more genuine. He reached over and brushed a hair back from my eyes. His hand rested on my cheek for a moment, and it grew warmer, but he let it linger.

"You're really beautiful when you sleep," he murmured.

"I am not." My cheeks reddened and I buried my face deeper in the pillow. He laughed, and reluctantly dropped his hand.

"Dibs on the shower." The bed moved as he got up, and I turned my head so I could get a better view of him as he went over to the closet.

"There's like twenty-seven showers in the house. Are you calling dibs on all of them?"

"Maybe," Jack laughed and went into his closet.

I didn't really mind him showering first. It gave me more time to lie in bed, burying myself deep in the covers.

I knew that many a love story had been written full of longing glances from across the room that could sustain a smoldering romance, but I couldn't see how. I had spent the night curled up in Jack's arms, and that wasn't enough anymore.

It was worse than a lecture.

Ezra sat on the couch, and Mae sat on the floor next to him, resting her head on his knee. Her long honey waves of hair cascaded around her, and he absently ran his fingers through it.

Jack stretched out on the chaise lounge with Matilda sprawled out by his feet.

Milo stood off to the side, fiddling with the floor length curtains next to him. Under the bright lights of the living room, he was even more brilliant. He was still clearly my brother, but what he would've looked like in a few years if he worked out more and had a stylist.

It was hard not to stare at him when I walked in the room, but something distracted me.

They were all poised around me like it was an intervention. Jack sat up straighter when I came in. I sat in a chair and waited for whatever they were going to dump on me.

"So," I said when it appeared nobody else would speak. "What's going on?"

"I heard you had a visitor last night," Ezra said, his accent lilting with a hint of dissatisfaction.

Milo's cheeks colored with shame. Absently, he fiddled with the curtain and almost yanked it down. He reddened deeper and spouted apologizes that Mae just brushed away.

His movements were clumsily graceful. The way his slender fingers picked at everything was oddly elegant, but he didn't understand how to control it or have any mastery of his strength.

He took a step away from the curtains and almost stumbled into the chair but caught himself with amazing ease. Milo gave up on movement and collapsed into the chair.

"The good news is that this is all perfectly normal." Ezra watched Milo with a bemused smile.

"You're just getting your bearings, love," Mae said reassuringly. "We've all been through it."

"Not all of us," I whispered under my breath, and Jack shot a disappointed look my way.

"This is just so weird!" Milo lamented.

He meant to lean back in the chair, and he nearly tipped it over. He scoffed at himself, and underneath his perfect new features, I saw the frustrated little boy he had always been.

Whenever he uncovered a problem he couldn't solve, he furrowed his brow and his eyes got faraway. Seeing him look that way again was reassuring.

"As you can see, Milo turned quite smoothly," Ezra said to me. "He's had very little problems, and he seems to have a rather large amount of self-control."

"This is the least amount of control I've ever had in my life!" Milo scoffed.

"You'll get it all back, plus so much more," Mae told him. "You should've seen Jack after he first turned. He was a horrible mess."

"Everyone is a little out of control in the beginning," Ezra said. "Which is exactly why you never should've gone into Alice's room last night."

"I'm sorry!" The way Milo said it, I knew he'd already apologized a hundred times.

"Everything turned out fine." I waved off Ezra's concern. "It really wasn't that big of a deal."

"Yeah, it kinda was," Jack said seriously, looking over at me. "If I hadn't woken up…"

"If he hadn't eaten before he saw you, there wouldn't have been enough time for anyone to intercede," Ezra agreed.

I hated the idea that Milo could kill me. They could all kill me, and according to Milo, they all wanted to. It didn't seem fair that he was the only one guilt ridden and required a chaperone.

"Well, it'll never happen again, and I'm still alive," I said.

"You have no sense of self preservation." Jack gave me a skeptical look.

"Obviously not," I met his gaze evenly. If I cared anything for my life, I wouldn't spend all my free time with a pack of vampires.

"That leads us to now," Ezra said, but I didn't follow. "Milo can't go home, for many reasons. He's got to stay on with us."

"Sure," I nodded.

Milo couldn't go back to his normal life at school, and with everything going well for him, I would just turn, and nothing tied us back to our old lives.

"You, on the other hand, will not." Ezra spoke slowly, letting the weight of his words sink in.

"What?" I shook my head. "What are you talking about? Why wouldn't I stay? Milo was the only reason I even wanted to go back to my life, and he's here now!"

"Alice." Ezra held a hand up to calm me, and I could feel Jack struggle to reign in his own emotions to soothe me.

"You'll be out here all the time anyway," Jack offered.

"I don't understand. If... if I can be here all the time, then why do I need to go?" A lump wedged itself in my throat.

"It's not safe for you," Ezra tried to reason with me. "Milo's very dangerous to humans right now, and he wouldn't be able to live with himself if something happened to you."

"Why..." I trailed off, unable to form the words I desperately wanted to ask. Why couldn't I just turn? Was this their way of saying they no longer wanted me?

"And there's your mother," Ezra continued, ignoring my open ended question. "You left a letter indicating that you and Milo were going away with us for awhile. If both of you were to disappear, she would find that suspicious and send the police."

"But if Milo just vanishes, you think she'd be fine with that?" I asked dubiously.

"No, we'll have an explanation for that," Ezra shook his head. "We'll have that all figured out by tomorrow."

"Tomorrow?" I asked breathlessly.

"Yes. You'll go home tomorrow," Ezra said.

"Milo will have enough time to ready himself to visit your mother, one last time, and we'll have enough time to get things in order," Mae elaborated, smiling at me.

They were kicking me out, pushing me away from everything that I cared about, and they were doing it with a smile.

Before Milo got hurt, I hadn't planned to turn so soon. It shouldn't matter if I left, because nothing had really changed from a few days ago.

But somehow, everything had changed. I was being left behind.

"I know this is hard for you, but it's for the best," Ezra said, and the finality in his voice let me know this wasn't open for discussion.

"No, it's no problem," I shrugged and blinked hard to fight back tears. I stood up before I decided where I wanted to go, so I mumbled a lame excuse.

Mae called after me, and Milo watched me. I just walked past them, through the kitchen, and out the French doors onto the patio bathed in moonlight.

After spending the past three days inside frigid air conditioning, the warm humidity of the night hit me like a sauna. Fireflies danced through the branches of the weeping willow by the lake, and I walked out on the dock, wiping at my eyes.

I looked at the planks of wood stretching about before me, at the source of all my problems. If Milo had never slipped, if he'd never hit his head, then everything could just go back to normal.

My grasp on normal was getting very tenuous.

I didn't like this hurt and confusion welling up inside me. It had the definite sting of loneliness, and that was one thing that I had become unprepared for. With everyone I loved immortal, it never occurred to me that I would be left alone.

Heavy footfalls echoed on the boards behind me, and I wiped at my eyes. I didn't want to cry, let alone have an audience. I kept my arms wrapped around me, and I refused to turn back to see Jack as he came up behind me.

"Alice. It's really not so bad."

"No, I know," I nodded in agreement. My tears stopped enough · where I could look at him. "I just wasn't thinking. If I had been thinking, I would've realized that I'd have to go soon."

"Alice," he groaned, seeing through me. "It's for your safety, and ours."

"No, I know," I insisted. "I get it. Completely. You don't have to worry about me."

"Nobody blames you for being hurt."

"I'm not hurt!" I snapped, and he rolled his eyes.

"Why do you always have to be so damn obstinate?" Jack asked, growing frustrated with me.

"I'm not. I have no idea what you're talking about." I shook my head.

He exhaled and tried a different approach. He reached out for me, but I pulled back, and he let his arm fall to his side.

"I don't know why you're mad at me. I had nothing to do with this."

"It's your fault Milo's a vampire," I pointed out, and then instantly regretted it. He looked so wounded, and I wanted to say something to take it back.

"You're right," Jack replied thickly. "You're absolutely right. This is my fault." He lowered his eyes. "You take as much time as you need. I'll be in the house."

"Jack," I said, but he just shook his head.

"Take all the time you need, Alice." He turned and walked back to the house, his footsteps heavier and slower this time.

I stared out at the black water surrounding me. Jack almost never did anything wrong, but he and Milo got the brunt of my anger or frustration because they took it so willingly.

It wasn't fair to them and led me to believe that I was most likely a terrible person. No wonder they didn't want me around anymore.

It would all just be so much simpler if I had been the one that had slipped on the dock and hit my head instead of Milo. I was jealous of the fact that he had almost died.

- 8 -

Since Milo managed honor roll grades, it wasn't a stretch to think he'd been offered a scholarship to a fancy boarding school. It wouldn't even seem that strange that he hadn't mentioned it to our mother. With her work schedule, they barely saw each other.

Ezra printed off documents to certify Milo would be attending Chester Arthur Preparatory School outside of Albany, New York. The semester was slated to start one week from today, and it was recommended that students get out there a week early to acclimate themselves with the school.

Or at least that's what the letter claimed.

They had an extensive story to go with it. Milo went over it with Ezra and Mae all evening.

Jack had done his best to try to cheer me up, but there was little he could do. As time dragged on, I only got more nervous and upset as I thought about the life I'd return to.

Milo called our mother and arranged a time for them to talk. Mae helped me pack up my things, talking the entire time about how things were going to be so much more fun this way. Her reasons almost entirely depended on the phrase "absence makes the heart grow fonder," but I nodded as if I believed everything she said.

Once Mae's Jetta was loaded with my things, I stood in the entryway, waiting by the garage door. Jack was next to me, twirling the car keys around his fingers. We waited for Milo, but he didn't have to pack, so I didn't understand what could be taking him so long.

"What is he doing?" I asked, pulling at the hem of my shirt. If we were going to leave then I wanted to hurry and get it over with.

"He'll be down in a minute." Jack scratched the back of his neck and looked away from me, a clear sign that he didn't want to tell me something.

"What?" I asked. "What's he doing?"

"He's eating." He looked at me and shrugged. "He's going to be out in the world with people for the first time. It's better if he's not hungry."

"Do you need to eat?"

"No. I'm good. Thanks for asking, though." His eyes inspected me, looking for revulsion or fear, but when he didn't find any, he eventually looked away.

"Is he gonna eat my mom?" I had a serious risk of vomiting every time I thought about Milo drinking blood, but apparently, I did a good job masking it.

"That's why he's eating," Jack said. "We're hoping to avoid that entire situation."

"Excellent," I sighed.

"I'll be there to bodyguard." He flexed his muscles to prove that he was up for the job and grinned at me. "It's gonna be fine."

"I know," I said grimly. "Everything's always going to be fine. Great. Good. Okay."

"He's just about ready!" Mae declared, interrupting the worried look Jack gave me. When she saw me, her face fell. "Oh, Alice, love, you just look so pitiful."

"Sorry." I tried to force a smile as she placed her hands on my arms.

"You will be back, you know?" Her eyes glistened with wet tears, and it made me feel a little better she was sad to see me go. At least someone would miss me. "We're not banishing you."

"I know," I nodded, smiling a bit more genuinely.

"You're part of the family now." She tucked a stray strand of hair behind my ear. "This is just how things have to be. For now."

"I know," I repeated. And I did know. It didn't change the fact that this still hurt.

Mae threw her arms around me and pulled me close to her, hugging me so tight I could hardly breathe. She whispered in my hair, "Oh, love, you have no idea how marvelous everything will be when it's all said and done."

"Mae, honey, I think you're smothering her." Jack tapped her on the shoulder.

"Oh, sorry!" Mae let go of me and took a step back, and I tried not to gasp for breath. "I keep forgetting how fragile you still are."

Down the hall, I heard Milo's clumsy footsteps, and Ezra reassured Milo that everything would be alright. When they walked into the entryway, Ezra had his arm on Milo's back, and Milo looked pale.

"We can follow behind you if you want," Ezra said. Jack was going with us, but Ezra and Mae had planned to stay at the house.

"No, I'll be fine." Milo sounded better than he looked, and I wondered if I should take them up on the offer.

"Are you sure?" Mae reached out and stroked his face, a gesture that I couldn't do anymore. If I did, he'd be too tempted to rip open an artery.

"Come on. Everybody's great. Let's get this show on the road." Jack sensed my discomfort, and he wanted to get this over with.

Reluctantly, Mae let us leave. I didn't like how nervous she was about this, but there wasn't very much about any of it that I did like.

When we went into the garage, I walked ahead of Milo and reached the Jetta first. I grabbed for the passenger side door, planning to sit shotgun as I always did, and Milo growled at me.

"Did you just growl at me?" I asked dubiously.

"I might have," Milo admitted with anger in his eyes.

"Why would you growl at me?"

"Alice," Jack said sharply. He stood on the other side of the car beside the driver's side door, and he looked at me from over the top of it. "Get in the backseat."

"Why?"

"Just do it," Jack said firmly

"But that's stupid!" I protested. "Just because Milo's a vampire, he gets shotgun? That's not fair. It doesn't even make sense."

"Just get in the back!" Milo snapped. I looked at him, and violence brewed in his eyes.

"This is bogus," I grumbled but got in the backseat.

"This would be so much easier if you didn't fight everything," Jack said as he started the car.

"You really didn't realize what you were getting into with her, did you?" Milo said.

I bit my tongue, but it wasn't an easy feat. Who the hell did Milo think he was? I wanted to shout at him, but I couldn't, because he would literally bite my head off if I did.

That was so unfair, too. He got away with being a random dick because he could kill me. Milo never would've talked to me like that before.

On the positive side, I didn't feel so bad that I wouldn't get to be around them as much anymore. In fact, I was pretty sure that I wouldn't even miss Milo at all. He'd probably growl at me if I touched the television remote or something.

I sulked through the car ride home. Jack had Dinosaur Jr. in the CD player, and that filled up the silence. Milo said a couple things that I couldn't hear from the backseat, making me hate them all the more.

When we pulled up in front of the apartment building, I leapt out of the car. Jack grabbed my bags from the trunk, and he and Milo followed me inside.

We rode up the elevator in silence, and Milo tensed up. His jaw set, and he kept clenching and unclenching his fists. I looked over at Jack to see if he noticed, but he kept his expression blank.

"Are you okay?" I asked Milo quietly outside our apartment door.

"Yeah," he nodded, but he definitely looked pale.

"Maybe we should do this another time," I suggested. I really wanted to get this over with, but not that the expense of my mother or my brother, even if he really pissed me off.

"No. Let's do this." Milo pulled the keys out of his pocket and unlocked the door.

A light was on over the kitchen sink, but the rest of the apartment was dark. Milo still looked like Milo, but his drastic changes would be less noticeable in dim lighting.

A scratched Led Zeppelin record played softly in the living room, with Robert Plant crooning about when the levees break.

"Mom?" I said cautiously, following Milo inside.

"Oh, good, you're finally here." Mom burst out from her bedroom, a cigarette glowing in her hand, and her hair looked less frizzy than it usually did. Too-red lipstick stained her lips. "I don't have much longer to wait."

"You're going somewhere?" I asked.

Milo deliberately moved into the shadows of the apartment, but I lingered in the light of the kitchen. Jack set my bag on the floor and hovered next to me, hoping to catch my mother's attention.

She flitted about the living room, searching for something, so she hadn't noticed him. The last time they met, Mom had swooned over him.

"Yes, yes, in a bit," Mom waved me away and found what she'd been looking for – a tumbler of brandy. Taking a long drink, she turned back to look at us. She finally saw Jack and inhaled deeply. "Oh, I didn't realize you had guests."

"It's good to see you, Miss Bonham," Jack gave her a little half wave, and she placed her hand over her chest.

"You were at a vacation house, weren't you?" Mom asked and sat down in a chair in the living room. Apparently, he made her too weak in the knees to stand anymore.

"Um, yeah," Jack nodded, going along with the lie I had told her earlier.

"Did you do a lot of swimming?" Mom was undoubtedly picturing him in swim trunks, and I wanted to gag.

Milo made a strange sound, and Jack suddenly stepped forward, closer to him.

"We did tons of swimming. It was fantastic," I blurted out. "But Mom, Milo really needs to talk to you. He, uh, has something major to tell you."

"Oh?" Mom struggled to pull her gaze from Jack to Milo, but her eyes didn't have to travel far. Jack moved even closer to Milo, and things were not going as well as everyone had promised they would.

"Yeah, it's really great news," Jack added in an attempt to sway her.

"Here." Milo thrust his hand forward, holding out a crumpled letter. His voice had taken on an icy tone, and if Jack hadn't been here to distract Mom, she wouldn't have bought any of this.

"What are you shoving at me?" Mom made no attempt to get up and retrieve the letter from him.

"It's a letter," Jack said and pried the paper from Milo's fingers. When he handed it to her, their fingers briefly touched, and Milo made that sound again.

"A letter?" Mom peered down at the paper once she had recovered from touching Jack. She tried to smooth it out, but the dim light and her poor eyesight made it almost impossible for her to read. "Well, what's this about?" She looked back up at Milo. "Just spit it out."

"I've been accepted to a boarding school in New York," Milo answered stiffly. "Thanks to my grades, I've received a full scholarship. The semester starts in a week, and they want me to get there early. So I'm going to leave tomorrow."

"What?" Mom looked confused. Milo was the good one, and she wasn't used to him not making any sense. "Why didn't you tell me about this sooner?"

"I was waiting for the right time to tell you," Milo said.

"That's why we want to the vacation house," Jack smiled too broadly. "As one last hoorah before he goes."

"What?" Mom repeated. "I don't understand why you wouldn't tell me about this."

"I was afraid you'd be angry about me leaving." Milo didn't sound afraid or apologetic, though. He sounded like a robot.

"Why would I be angry? All I've ever done is stress how important a good education is for you kids, so you don't end up like me." Mom softened and looked down at the letter, trying to read it in the darkness. "So you're leaving tomorrow?"

"Yeah."

"How are you getting there?" Mom asked.

"Plane. Jack bought the ticket for me." Milo gestured towards him, and Jack smiled at her.

"Oh." Mom swallowed and looked at me for the first time. "You knew about this?"

"Um, yeah," I shrugged.

"And you didn't tell me?" Mom snapped.

"No. I didn't. Neither did Milo. But thanks for getting angry with me," I said.

"Oh, never mind." She glanced at the clock and downed the rest of her brandy. "I don't really have time for this." She stood up, brushing hair back from her forehead. "But you're leaving tomorrow, right? So I'll have a chance to say a proper goodbye to you then?"

"Yeah," Milo lied. He was leaving tonight, and she wouldn't realize it until it was too late. He'd leave a note explaining that the plane left before she woke up.

"Alright then." Mom nodded once and put out her cigarette in the ashtray. She grabbed her oversized purse from the table and headed over to the shadows where Milo hid by the door.

"Have a good time tonight," Jack interjected, putting himself between her and Milo. It was still too soon for Milo to handle her going in for a hug.

"Oh, I will." Mom touched her hair, taken back by Jack's interruption, and unable to figure out how to rectify it. She smiled at him, and then turned to me with her usual scowl. "You. We'll talk later."

After she walked out of the apartment, I tried not to think about how tremendously sad that was. That was the last time Milo was ever going to see his mother, and he couldn't even hug her goodbye.

She hadn't always been the greatest mom and spent most of her time anywhere but home, but she was still our mother. She deserved a better goodbye than that.

"Oh, hell," Jack exhaled shakily once she had left, and I saw his whole body relax. "You've gotta get that under control."

"I'm trying!" Milo insisted. "But it wasn't my fault! You saw the way she was fawning all over you-" His voice turned into a low snarl, and Jack held up a hand to stop him.

"Yeah, I was there, but seriously." Jack shook his head. "You can't be like that!"

"Be like what?" I asked, confused. Milo was having issues with bloodlust, but I didn't understand why it was solely directed at our mother.

"Nothing," Milo said sheepishly.

"Go pack up the rest of your stuff." Jack gestured to his room. "Let's get out of here before you do something really stupid."

"Sorry." Milo slunk off to his room.

Once he was gone, I whirled on Jack, and whispered fiercely, "What was that about? What's going on?"

"Remember how things were complicated before?" Jack asked, shooting a glance over his shoulder to make sure that Milo was out of earshot. "Well, they just got a whole lot worse."

"What are you talking about?" I narrowed my eyes at him.

"Milo is jealous."

"Of what?"

"Well..." He scratched the back of his head and sighed. "Everyone who interacts with me."

"What?"

"Okay see... the thing is, vampires bond with whoever turns them," Jack elaborated. "I told you about how close I was to Peter and

80

Ezra because we shared the same blood. Well… since Milo drank my blood, we're really bonded. And it's different than it was with Peter because apparently, Milo had a crush on me before he turned. And with the bonding, that's intensified."

"You've got to be kidding me." My arms had been crossed over my chest, but they fell to my side. "Holy hell. First your brother, now my brother. It's like this whole thing is completely impossible."

"No, it's not like with Peter," Jack shook his head. "Milo's like a brother to me, and that's all. And this is just new. My blood is still fresh, and he doesn't have a handle on any of his emotions. This'll fade. With time."

"How much time?" I demanded.

"The thing is… there's so much uncharted territory with you," he tried to explain, but I laughed hollowly and shook my head.

"You don't know. You don't even know if it will fade. This is all assumptions!"

"Shh!" Jack looked nervously back at Milo's room, but when he didn't come out, he turned back to me. "No, the bond does fade. Okay? When I first turned, it was like hero worship with me and Peter."

"That was sixteen years ago," I said incredulously. "Do you really plan on waiting sixteen years for this?"

"It'll stop sooner. I just can't say the time frame, but I really don't think it was that long with Peter and me."

"Whatever." I rolled my eyes. "Milo will stop. Peter will stop. Everything will stop. And one day, it'll be happily ever after. But instead of things getting better, more stuff just keeps piling up on top of it."

"You know what the problem is? You're looking at this all with mortal eyes," Jack decided. "You see time finitely, and that's not the case. This will take time, but we have time."

"No. You have time. Because the last time I checked-" I stopped and held my fingers to my throat. "Yep. That's a pulse. That's mortal blood in these veins, Jack. I'm not a damn vampire."

"Yeah, now. But this is just temporary."

"Maybe," I said. "But right now, you're whispering and standing like three feet away from me. Because if you weren't, my brother might kill me, or your brother might kill you. And until that stops, you can't really get any closer than you are now."

Jack sighed and looked sadly at me. Milo came out of his room, and Jack dropped his eyes and took a step away from me.

Yeah, this was all going to work out perfectly. Jack was now afraid of my little brother. Everything was right on track.

"I'm all packed." Milo had two duffle bags and a garbage bag of stuff in his hands.

"We should probably get going," Jack said, taking a step towards the door. "You've had enough excitement for today."

"Alice, I'm sorry about all of this," Milo said sincerely, and softness returned to his face. I hated him for it, because just then, I really wanted to be mad, and I couldn't. "I know how much trouble this is for you, and I never meant for that."

"Don't be silly," I shook my head. "None of this is your fault. You are a victim of circumstance."

"I'll see you soon, okay?" Milo promised.

"Yeah, I know," I lied. He looked at me expectantly for a moment. "I would hug you if, y'know, I could. But you'll get it under control soon. Okay?"

"Yeah," Milo smiled wanly.

Jack held the door open for him, and gave me one last apologetic look as Milo escaped out into the hall. "I'll talk to you soon. Have fun."

Once the door shut, it hit me. I was alone in the apartment. Thanks to Milo's complete lack of a social life, I could count the times I'd been home alone on two hands. The only time was when I skipped school, and Milo still went. Otherwise, he was always here.

And he was never going to be here again.

A few minutes ago, I mustered some pretty wicked anger at him, but it was all gone. The reality of everything sunk in.

No one would be here to lecture me about bedtimes or homework, or scoff at me when I watched reality TV, or make me supper.

For the first time in over sixteen years, I was alone. My little brother was really gone.

- 9 -

After becoming accustomed to the subzero temperatures at Jack's, I was dying in my own apartment. To beat the heat, I drenched my tank top and underwear in cold water and put them on. It was the closest thing I had to a lake in my backyard.

To pass the time, I buried myself in Peter's biography, although I wasn't convinced that he had actually written it. Jack seemed sure of it, and he had been offended by me reading *A Brief History of Vampyres*.

Still, it was hard to think of Peter wanting to write anything down. Whenever I was around him, he wanted nothing to do with expressing himself, but Ezra had said he had been a different man before the love of his life died.

I felt strangely betrayed at the thought of Elise, Peter's girlfriend that'd been murdered a long time ago. She was his one true love, or something ridiculous like that.

Every part of my being claimed that I was meant for him, and because of her, because of a vampire that had died before I was even born, he refused me. I will never be with him, and the way things are going now, I'll never be anything except a lone corpse in the ground.

So far in the book, Peter has yet to mention Elise, and I hope he doesn't. Jack said he was very young when he wrote it, so he probably hadn't even met her yet.

He explained how he turned, what he could remember of it. Apparently, the transformation was something hard to articulate.

"My mind was an excited fog. It felt like I was waking up and falling asleep at the same time. My body was shifting and dying. There were times where I could literally feel my organs sliding about, as if my gut had been cut open and filled with eels.

"I couldn't decipher dreams from reality, and I recall singing 'Ava Maria' repeatedly so I could hear my own voice. The sound of it meant that I was still there, that there was still some part of me on this earth."

Imagine, Peter writhing in a bed as his body died. His beautiful face contorting and twisting with pain, and through it all, he's singing. I'm sure that he had an amazing voice, but it seemed strange to think he would sing.

I often tried to figure out why Peter had turned Jack. They were opposites in nearly every way, and Peter was always running off on his own. He didn't seem to have the inclination for companionship, not like Jack did. It didn't make sense that he would turn someone knowing the attachment that would create with him.

In the book, Peter says almost nothing of his mortal life. Only going as far as to say that he was riding a horse that bucked him. The horse took off, and he was left dying on the side of the road. A stranger came upon him, and seeing the shape Peter was in, decided that turning him was the only way to save his life.

After that, Peter describes an intense feeling of loyalty and affection for the vampire.

"It wasn't like anything I had ever felt before. In my previous life, I had a father, a brother, friends. But no other bond had ever felt this strong. I could sense

everything that he felt, as if I was feeling it for myself. When he went too far away from me, there would be an awful panic inside, as if I wouldn't be able to survive without him.

"There was nothing carnal about it, however. It was as if I was an extension of him. Being away from him would be as painful as being severed from my own limbs.

"Fortunately, he treated me with respect and dignity, like an equal or a brother. Many other fledgling vampyres did not acquire such a happy fate."

That explained a bit more about what was going on with Milo and Jack, but it didn't make me feel any better about it. I knew eventually that it would fade, as it had with Peter and Ezra, but even in the book, Peter did nothing to illuminate a time frame.

He moved onto the first time he saw a young man turn into a vampire. He described a disturbing scene that I wasn't excited to repeat for myself.

I lay in bed, reading the book and listening to Elliott Smith. As the sun set on the third day, I still hadn't heard from either Milo or Jack. I made it halfway through Peter's book, and I was trying to read slowly.

Night settled on my room, making it too dark for me to read, and I stared at my phone, willing it to ring.

Milo needed time to get the hang of being a vampire, and his new jealous streak made it more dangerous for me to hang around Jack, but this was ridiculous. They both promised to talk to me soon, and it had been three days.

One entire day was spent consoling my mother when she learned that Milo left without really saying goodbye. After crying a lot, she started drinking even more, and ended up yelling profanities at me and throwing things.

On top of everything, school was less than two weeks away. Once summer vacation drew to a close, I'd have to deal with curfews and school that'd keep me away from Jack and Milo even more.

I was going to spend the rest of my life cooped up inside this apartment by myself, and they didn't even have the decency to call and give me one last blowout before deserting me for the rest of time.

In some form of misplaced pride, I'd been waiting for one of them to call or text me. But I was tired of waiting. I couldn't stand the thought of spending another night suffocating in my tiny room.

Hi. What are you doing? I text messaged Jack.

Not much. What about you? Jack responded. It took him three minutes to answer, which was an unusually long time for him, especially since it was after ten o'clock at night. Even he never slept in this late.

Even less. I haven't done anything in three days. I tried to lay on the guilt.

You haven't talked to Jane? Jack was suggesting that I hang out with Jane.

Wow. Things were worse than I thought. After Peter, Jane was Jack's least favorite person in the whole world. And he was encouraging me to hang out with her? Wow.

Not so much. But I guess I could. Great idea. I replied.

Right now, Jane was probably getting drunk or giving oral sex or something. If it were earlier, we might be able to do something more reasonable, like shop. But with only two weeks until school, I knew that for her, every night would be a blur of alcohol and debauchery.

I'm just pretty busy lately. Sorry. Jack texted.

No. I totally get it. It's great. I'll just do something else. That's what I said, but I knew that I was going to spend the night in bed crying myself to sleep.

No. Wait. Are you ready? Jack text messaged back, but it was too little too late.

Never mind. I'm good. I responded.

Just be ready and outside in like fifteen minutes, okay?

I didn't reply to that. I couldn't even decide if I wanted to get ready and go outside to meet him. I honestly didn't want a pity hang out, even if I really did miss him. It was stupid how much I missed him. But I was bored and lonely and couldn't stand it.

Almost grudgingly, I got up and pulled on a pair of jeans. I wore a white tank top and pulled my hair back in a ponytail. I quickly applied some eyeliner and mascara, and then ducked out the door, unsure if I was making the right decision or not.

When the black Jetta pulled up, I got my answer. It was absolutely the wrong decision.

Mae had come to pick me up.

I considered turning around and going back inside. What would I achieve by hanging out with her? I'd feel stupid and pathetic all night, and I was just prolonging the inevitable. When a guy sends his sister to hang out with you instead of him, I think that's the beginning of the end.

"Hello, love," Mae said when she had rolled down the car window. She leaned across the passenger seat towards me, looking sheepish. "Sorry, Alice. I know it's not quite what you hoped for, but Jack thought you needed to get out of the house."

"You know what? I'm actually fine." I chewed my lip. "He's um... he's mistaken. I'm sure you have better things to do then baby-sit me, so I'll just go back in."

"Nonsense! You know how much I love spending time with you. So come on. Get in the car."

"You really don't have to do this," I said.

"I know." She nodded towards the empty seat, so I sighed and I got in the car. "It'll be fun. You'll see."

"I bet," I leaned my head back on the seat as she pulled away. "The last time somebody came in place of Jack was when Peter picked me up. And we all know how well that turned out."

"This isn't like that." Mae shook her head. "Jack really wanted to see you. He just can't right now."

"What is he doing? Teaching Milo how to turn into a bat?" I mocked, and Mae scowled.

"A lot goes into being a vampire, you know," she told me gravely. "Plus, he's been helping Ezra with the business. He was supposed to fly out to Tokyo yesterday, but..." She shook her head, pursing her lips.

"But what?" I sat up straighter.

"Something must be different in your blood," Mae exhaled, talking more to herself than me. "I don't understand it. But something makes you all so eager to bond. Who was your father?"

"My father?" I wrinkled my nose. "What does he have to do with anything?"

"I'm trying to understand your ancestry, because you and Milo are both so unique. I'm wondering if we've been looking at this all wrong. Maybe you weren't meant for Peter. Maybe you were just meant to be a vampire." Mae chewed her lip, looking sad and faraway. "We're just a means to an end for you."

"What are you talking about?" I asked. "An end to what?"

"You both bond so easily. It's unlike anything we've ever encountered," Mae said wearily.

"Milo's super possessive of Jack, right?" I better just hurry up and resign myself to a life of mortal celibacy. "Jack kind of told me the other day."

"These things just take time."

"Why is that the answer to everything?" I scoffed. "All I ever get from you guys is that everything takes time and everything's complicated."

"What else am I supposed to say?" Mae asked pointedly. "That this will never get better, no matter how much time we have? If that's what you want to hear, I'll be happy to tell you that."

"If that's the truth, then yeah, that's what you should say," I said.

"Of course that's not the truth!" Mae rolled her eyes. "Alice, the only constant in life is that everything is always changing. And that's a little scary, but it means that things can't be bad or hard forever."

"And they can't be good or easy forever either," I countered.

"You've just got to trust me on this one." Mae turned to me, smiling warmly at me. "I don't know how yet, but things will end up the way they're supposed to be."

"Thanks for the blanket answer."

"Let's just forget about all of this," Mae suggested. "Let's just go have a girls' night. Just the two of us."

"It's after ten on a Tuesday. How much do you really think is open?" I asked.

"We'll find something," Mae insisted. "We'll make do."

We made do with a Wal-Mart that was open 24-hours, a Denny's where she watched me eat, and a Blockbuster. We went back to my apartment, even though the whole point of the evening was supposed to be to get me out of the house.

Mae had never been inside before, but she ooed and awed over all our second-hand junk like it was astounding. She painted my nails and played with my hair while we watched *Silence of the Lambs*. It was one of my favorite movies because it was so terrible, and I felt better knowing that I was forcing her to watch something so terrible.

And despite my best attempts to hate everything about the night, she did manage to cheer me up a little bit. Of course, that went away completely when she left, when I was alone again.

- 10 -

I couldn't get out to his car fast enough.

When Jack texted me the next day and asked to hang out, I hated myself for getting so excited about it. Even though I felt ridiculous, I spent an hour preening.

I rushed outside, and Jack sat in the Jetta, grinning broadly. Pat Benetar blasted out when I opened the door. He turned it down when I hopped in, but I barely even cared.

We were alone for the first time in what felt like forever. Nobody growled at me or chastised us for being too close. I could just be with him.

"Hey," Jack smiled.

"I don't wanna go to your house."

"Why not?" He cocked an eyebrow.

"Because." I pulled my knee up to my chest and looked at him, refusing to elaborate on my answer. I expected him to drive away or press me further, but he just nodded.

"Okay," he smirked. "Where do you wanna go?"

"I don't care where. Just drive."

"You got it." His eyes glinted, and he sped away from my apartment.

The buildings were a blur of lights beside us, and he had this weird ability to weave through openings in traffic that weren't even there.

"So... how's life with Milo?" I asked cautiously.

I wasn't sure if I really wanted to know, but I needed to know. I had to make sure Milo was okay, and I wanted to hear how Jack felt about it.

"Good," Jack shrugged noncommittally. "I like your brother. I like having him around."

"I see," I murmured.

"He's already much better. Pretty soon you'll be able to be around all the time. And I'm sure it will be all the time. He really misses you too." Jack looked over to see if I believed him, and I wasn't sure that I did. "He talks about you a lot. He just isn't always thrilled when I talk about you."

"Really?" I raised an eyebrow. "You guys talk about me? What do you say?"

"I don't know," he laughed. My heart flipped happily, and I settled deeper into the seat. "Nothing bad, if that's what you're getting at."

"I just wonder what you say about me when I'm not around."

"What do you say about me when I'm not around?" Jack countered.

"Hasn't Milo told you?" I figured that by now, Milo had spilled everything.

"Yeah, he has, because apparently, all you ever tell him is that you're not interested in me." He tried to play it off with a smile, but I saw the hurt behind his eyes. "So yeah. I got all the juicy details."

"That's not all I say."

"So then what do you say?" Jack asked, watching me from the corner of his eyes.

"That you're the most dashing, handsome stranger I've ever met," I said with a dramatic Southern drawl and batted my eyes at him, making him laugh. "No, I don't know. I try not to say anything about you."

"Why not?"

"Cause." I shrugged. "I don't know. It's hard to talk about you."

"How is it hard?"

"Well… what am I supposed to say about you?" I squirmed.

"You're supposed to say whatever you want."

"Things are a little too complicated for me to say what I want," I said finally.

I didn't know what I felt for Jack because I wouldn't let myself think about it. To quantify it as something would put expectations and shatter things. I liked being around him and I missed him when he wasn't there, and that was as far as I was willing to admit.

"Fair enough." He ran a hand through his sandy hair.

He turned to me, looking like he might say more, but his phone rang in his pocket. Cursing under his breath, he pulled it from his pocket.

"Hello?" Jack answered his phone. "Yeah. Yeah…. I'm with her now…. Yeah… Yes… Okay… Yes…. I get it… I got it…. No. I'm fine….Yep… Okay…. Okay… Bye." He sighed and then shoved his phone in his pocket.

"What was that about?" I asked.

"We're going to my house."

"What? Why? Who was that?" I tensed up at the thought of his house. It suddenly felt like so much drama.

"Milo." He pursed his lips. "He wants to see you."

"Does he really? Or is he just against the idea of us being alone together?"

"Both, probably."

"I'm a little offended actually." I watched out the window at the changing scenery as Jack switched directions towards his house. "Peter never got this jealous over the time we spent together."

"Yeah, well, Peter's a total idiot," Jack grumbled.

"Have you heard from him lately?" I asked offhandedly.

"Why are you asking about him?" Jack had very little tolerance for the sound of Peter's name, but I wanted to know anyway.

"I was just wondering if anybody had heard from him," I shrugged. "That's all. I can be curious, can't I?"

"I'd prefer it if you weren't," he admitted wearily. When I didn't say anything for a little bit, he continued, "You took the book."

"Ezra said I could."

"Is everything to your satisfaction?" he asked icily.

"It's a book, Jack!" I didn't even want to dignify it with a response. "What do you think is going to happen? I'm going to run off with it and leave you in the love triangle with my brother? It wouldn't even be a triangle anymore. It would just be an angle."

"An oblique angle," Jack said, and his bout of jealousy was quickly replaced with glee. "Ha! I told you I would work that in!"

"What are you talking about?" I didn't understand what he was getting at, but he grinned foolishly, so I was swept up in it.

"Remember? That time I took you to the concert after we first met?" His eyes danced. "And you asked what my angle was, and I said isosceles, but really I should've said oblique. And I said that I'd remember it for next time, and I did!"

"Wow," I laughed.

At least we arrived at his house on a happy note. As soon as we walked inside, Matilda ran to greet us, and Milo followed her.

Seeing him was still an adjustment, and I wondered how long it would take me to get used to him. He walked like he was about to trip over his own feet but would elegantly catch himself. He was like Bambi learning to walk –all stumbles and a graceful bound.

"Hey," Milo sounded out of breath and his smile was too bright.

He brushed his hair from his forehead, and he was even wearing it different now. It had always been just a standard guy cut, but he went for a more popular style.

"How are you?" Milo fidgeted with his sleeve. He did a weird head bob, and he reminded me of Mike Meyers from *Wayne's World*. Was this Milo's interpretation of cool?

"Good," I answered unsurely. "You're looking really... good. I like your hair."

"Thanks." He touched it self-consciously and blushed. It was a glimpse of cute Milo that made me miss him again. "Mae did it."

"She loves hair," I said.

"Yeah," Milo agreed absently.

He looked over to Jack and rubbed the back of his head, and that's when it finally dawned on me. He wanted to impress Jack. He lacked the ability to mask his crush, and he had no clue what to do with himself.

Newly gay, newly vampire, and barely old enough to drive.

I felt like the biggest bitch in the world for being irritated with him. Sure, he messed up my non-relationship with Jack, but he was just a scared, confused kid. He was going through a whole huge thing that I couldn't help him with at all, and I should be happy he had someone like Jack to show him around.

"You guys have a nice drive?" Milo looked at Jack, and his eyes were hoping that we didn't have too nice of a drive.

"It was good," Jack nodded.

He chewed the inside of his cheek, growing uncomfortable with the way Milo looked at him, but I think that was for my benefit. Ordinarily, I'm sure he would brush off Milo's adoring gaze, but with me there, it felt... well, everything just felt really, really awkward.

"So, while you were gone I totally found that thing and I got to the next level," Milo announced randomly, and it took me a second to realize he was talking about some kind of video game.

"Oh, yeah, really?" Jack looked impressed, which was a bit too much for Milo.

"Yeah!" Milo beamed. "Here, I'll show you!"

With that, he reached out and took Jack's hand to drag him off to the living room. The gesture was probably meant to be flirtatious in some way, but it only succeeded in making him look more like a little boy.

"I'm going to go check out the game," Jack shot me an apologetic smile as Milo pulled him away.

Once they were gone, I took a deep breath. Things are weird, but Milo's still Milo, Jack's still Jack, and pretty soon we'll have this all sorted out. Soon. That's what I've gotta believe.

"Why are you hiding in here?" Mae walked into the entryway to claim me. "I saw the boys go in the living room with those stupid games, and I couldn't believe they left you stranded."

"I wasn't really stranded," I said, but she looped her arm through mine, leading me on through the house.

"It's just so strange not having you around all the time."

"At least you don't have to make so much food," I said, and she laughed.

"I know I'm a horrible cook, but I still love baking!"

I thought she'd take me into the living room, where she'd harass the boys until they quit playing video games. Instead, she took me past the living room and down the hallway, to Ezra's den at the far end of the house.

It was what I'd expected of a rich vampire's den. The walls were lined with bookcases covered in books and antiquities. A massive mahogany desk sat in the center of the room with high end computer equipment on it. A reproduction of Rembrandt's The Mill hung above the distressed leather sofa. Behind his desk, a massive window revealed the blackened lake behind the house.

Ezra sat at the desk, staring at the computer monitor. If Mae hadn't been dragging me in, I never would've entered his den. I didn't want to break his concentration, but Mae thought nothing of it.

"Hello, love!" Mae chirped, and Ezra looked up from the screen to smile at us. "And what, pray tell, has your attention?"

"Nothing of real importance." He leaned back in his chair, giving the screen one last look, before turning his attention fully to us. "Just a stock tip someone told me to check into. I don't think it's going to be fruitful but…" He shook his head.

"Ezra doesn't care what he's looking up on the computer as long he's looking it up," Mae said with a bemused smile. "The other day I caught him watching a video of an elephant painting with his trunk."

"It was an elephant painting," Ezra said, but that only succeeded in making Mae giggle. "And I suppose you've seen an elephant paint?"

"No, but it's just a weird thing for you to be interested in," Mae said, and I concurred with her entirely.

"Technology fascinates me," Ezra allowed, then rested his eyes on me. "I can watch an elephant paint live on the internet. That sounds like nothing to you, but when I was a younger man, the poor animal would've been dead by the time I heard about it. This right here – this is magic."

"You'll never cease to amaze me, darling." Mae looked at him with complete adoration. It made me uncomfortable witnessing it, as if I were spying on some private moment.

"I should hope not," Ezra smiled back at her. She left my side and walked over to him, giving him a small but passionate kiss on the lips.

"I never will," she promised and headed out of the room. "Well, I'm sure you two have a lot to talk about." Before shutting the door behind her, she smiled sadly at me.

"Mae's never been one for subtlety," Ezra sighed, staring at the closed door. "Go ahead. Have a seat."

"Okay?" I carefully sat down on the sofa behind me. "You have something to tell me"

"It's not something I need to tell you so much as a conversation we need to have." Ezra moved his chair over so he wasn't hiding behind the computer. He tried to look relaxed, but he was hesitant to meet my eyes. "Your brother's turning was quite unexpected."

"For both of us," I agreed.

"In the end, I don't think it's a bad decision." He looked at a spot on the Oriental rug on the floor, thinking. "Once everything is sorted out, he'll be a very good fit. It'll be a wonderful opportunity for you both. I know how important he is to you."

"Yes, he is," I swallowed hard.

"As you're finding out, new vampires require a lot of time and energy," Ezra went on. "All of us have spent hours with him, helping him transition.

"We had a plan for you to turn when you felt that Milo was ready." He licked his lips, and my heart thudded painfully. "But his turning has changed your plan."

"What do you mean?" I asked.

"Milo needs too much right now, and you'd need just as much if you were to turn," Ezra explained. "It would be impractical and unfair to both of you to have two very young, very new vampires in the house. Jack isn't that old and wouldn't be up for the responsibility of siring you both into this."

"Oh." I couldn't think enough to argue against it. I just stared vacantly in front of me.

"It's only temporary," Ezra added quickly. "We're only postponing things. Actually, we're sticking to the original time frame."

"Wait. The original timeline? You mean... you mean like one or two more years?"

"You can finish out high school this way," Ezra said, like that was something that really mattered to me.

"I don't care about high school!" I snapped.

"I know," Ezra sighed. "But an education is important."

"Why does this just keep getting harder and harder?" Tears brimmed in my eyes, but I didn't even fight them off. He knew this would upset me, which is why he'd told me alone.

"I don't know." He came over and sat next to me on the couch. To comfort me, he put his hand on my back. "I am sorry this is so hard for you, Alice. I truly am. In the meantime, you can still stay here as much as you want."

"Yeah, right. Like Milo could handle that right now. Or like Peter could, if he ever decides to come back."

"Milo will settle down soon, enough where you can be around as much as you'd like," Ezra assured me, but I noticed that he made no mention of Peter.

"Can I ask you something?" I looked at him directly. "Do you think... I'm ever going to turn? I mean, is it ever really going to make sense for me? Or would I be better off getting on with my life and pretending that I never met any of you?"

"I can't answer that for you, Alice." His deep voice sounded saddened by my question. "I've always told you that regardless of how we feel, you need to do what's best for you. And if you don't think that's this life, then it isn't."

"Like I have any idea what's best for me." Folding my arms on my knees, I buried my face in them. Ezra seeing me cry like that embarrassed me.

"I think you do." His hand felt strong and gentle as he rubbed my back.

After a solid minute of crying, I decided that was enough and lifted my head. I wiped at my damp cheeks, pushing strands of hair off my face. I took a deep breath and reminded myself this wasn't the end of the world. It was only a postponement.

"Do they know?" I asked, thinking of how cheery Mae and Jack had been.

"Jack got on about you turning last night, but I was evasive," Ezra said. "No, I haven't told him or Milo that you're going to hold off."

"Are you going to tell them?"

"You can tell them if you want, or I can, or we can. We can do it now, or next week. Whatever you're comfortable with." He brushed his hair off his forehead and looked out the window. "I know neither of them will take it well."

"Not tonight," I decided. It seemed like far too much watching Jack get sad and angry over this. Feeling it myself was enough without having to feel it for him too.

"That's understandable."

"So I probably need to get myself in order before I go back out there, or they'll know something's up." I smoothed out my hair.

"You know what would cheer you up?" Ezra asked, getting to his feet. "Watching an elephant paint. It's really much more entertaining than it sounds."

"Okay," I laughed a little and got up.

After Ezra showed me the video, he gave me a brief tour of his den, explaining some of his favorite books and the painting on the wall. He'd actually lived in Amsterdam shortly after Rembrandt died, so that had always held some significance to him.

When I finally looked like my normal self, we headed out in the living room to see what everyone else was up to.

For most of the night, Jack and Milo played video games, but nobody complained. I felt rather sad and lonely, and while I did my best to mask it, Mae noticed and let me curl up with her on the couch.

The time passed much quicker then I wanted it to, and before I knew it, the sun was rising and Jack was giving me a ride home. If I had been awake enough to talk, he probably would've noticed something was up, and I didn't want to talk about it. I didn't even want to think about it.

- 11 -

Nine days left of freedom, and Jack couldn't return a stupid text message. I couldn't spend another night locked up inside the stifling heat of the apartment. In anticipation of escape, I had gotten all dolled up, and I looked ridiculously foxy, at least for me. I could not stay inside looking that good.

Three text messages and one hour later, when I still hadn't heard from Jack, I resorted to calling him.

"Alice," Jack answered the phone, and he didn't sound happy. So that was a good start.

"Jack."

"What can I do for you?" he asked, and someone talked behind him. "Hold on." Before I could say anything, the sound muffled as he moved the phone away from his mouth. "No! Can you just wait? I'm on the phone." He scoffed. "I don't care! Just hold on!"

"Jack, what's going on?" I thought I heard Milo shouting in the background. "Is something wrong?"

"No, everything's fine." Jack was talking into the phone again, sounding irritated. "Look, now's not really a good time to talk. Can I call you back later?"

"Like when later?"

"I don't know." He growled and yelled at something happening around him. "No! Knock it off! You can wait one second for-" He exhaled angrily, and then spoke to me again. "Alice, I'm sorry. I gotta go. I'll call you later, though."

"Alright, fine." I'd barely gotten the word "fine" out of my mouth before he hung up. He didn't even say goodbye.

I collapsed back on the bed, knowing it'd mess up my hair. My nails were freshly painted a dark violet, and I had pulled out a fancy new top that did amazing things for my cleavage.

Not to mention that I had put on my one pair of black heels that looked fantastic, even though they killed to walk in. My eyes were in dramatic smoky makeup that would wash off when I started bawling in approximately five seconds.

After a whirlwind romance with a pair of vampires, somehow my life had amounted to waiting by the phone in hopes someone would call. Getting all dressed up with no place to go.

My phone buzzed in my hand, and out of the blue, my supposed best friend Jane texted me. Immediately after being blown off by Jack for the hundredth time this week, Jane sent me good news.

There's a big party at Andrew Sullivan's house. I'll drive. You in?

My first instinct was to decline, but I decided that it was a sign. I had asked Ezra if it would ever make sense for me to turn, or if I was better off moving on with my life.

Jack practically hung up on me, and Jane invited me out into the real world. My path looked clearer.

Yeah. I'm actually already to go out. When can you get here? I responded.

Twenty minutes? Jane texted back.

Great. See you then.

I rolled out of bed and hurried to the bathroom to make sure I looked okay. With one last quick look over, I realized that something was missing. That something that screamed, "Let's go crazy."

I dashed back into my room and changed into the final touch: a bright purple thong that Jane had insisted getting for me from Victoria's Secret, "just in case" Jack ever decided... well, he was never going to decide that, so it seemed like a moot point.

Jane pulled up in her father's car with Moby playing so loud, I'm surprised it didn't blow the speakers. The whole car smelled of the strawberry lip gloss she layered on. With an overly happy "Hey girl," she offered me some, and I took it.

She looked amazing. She'd always reminded me of some tragic socialite, like Edie Sedgwick, the way everything about her was perfect and completely poised to end up exploited.

While she drove, she laughed too much at things that weren't funny and danced to the music so that the car weaved all over the highway.

"Jane!" I grabbed the wheel to keep the car from slamming into a divider. She giggled and put both her hands on the wheel, but it took an effort to keep her eyes focused on something as mundane as the road. "Jane, what's going?"

"I'm rolling." Jane leaned towards me, as if confessing a secret, and held her fingers out to me about an inch apart. "Just a little."

"Of course you are," I sighed, and she took this as my displeasure in not being high myself. She squealed and let go of the wheel so she could search through her glittery purse. "Jane!"

"Just hold on! I know have some more X in here!" Lip gloss, condoms, and cash flew out of her purse as she dug through it, and I groaned.

"I don't want any! Just take the wheel back!" I'd never done ecstasy, and I didn't want to try right now, while steering the car from the passenger seat.

"Oh whatever." She turned her attention back to the road. Then her eyes widened. "Oh! Quick! That's Andy's exit!" She snatched the wheel from me and skidded across three lanes of traffic without looking before flying up the freeway exit and lurching to a stop.

"This is still better than sitting at home," I muttered to myself.

Magically, we got to Andrew Sullivan's house without dying. We got out of the car, and Jane stumbled in her heels as we walked up to the house. It was pretty amazing that she even remembered where Andy lived, let alone how to get there.

From outside, I could hear the music, and the entryway was clogged with teenagers. Jane separated from me as soon as we went in, but I'm not sure if it was by choice, or if she was just sucked up by male hormones.

I'd been there for all of five minutes before someone spilled beer on me, and I knew that I was in dire need of a drink myself.

In the kitchen, an attractive guy poured shots for all the girls in the room, and he insisted I take one. He made some swarthy comment I could barely understand over the blaring bass, but I let myself take it as a compliment. Bright blue vodka burned when it went down, but it burned good.

"Your eyes are the same color as the drink," he told me after I had downed the shot, and I laughed as if I actually thought it was funny. My eyes were more gray than blue, and nothing in nature was the same shade as that vodka. "You want another drink?"

"Yeah!" I shouted.

It felt warm in my belly and left a fake blue taste in my mouth. I think it was supposed to be blue raspberry, but artificially flavoring never, ever tasted like raspberries. It all just tasted like blue, the same way that grape Kool-Aid tasted like purple.

"My name's Jordan," he said.

He leaned in closer as he poured me another shot, and he smelled really good. He probably did a lot of drugs. Boys that smoked a lot of pot always put on too much cologne to mask the smell. But so what? At least they smelled good when they leaned in close.

He poured himself a shot, then clinked his glass with mine.

"Cheers!" Jordan laughed. I laughed too, because he did and the alcohol was starting to spread warm through me.

When the hair fell in his eyes, I realized that he was probably very attractive, but it was hard for me to gauge anymore. Peter had been so incredibly gorgeous that everything else paled in comparison, and Jack looked pretty foxy himself.

But I didn't want to think of Peter or Jack so I took another shot, and I tried to focus on Jordan and his eyes and his wonderful cologne.

"You should probably slow down," Jordan suggested as I downed my fourth shot, but he never stopped pouring them for me.

I felt myself moving closer to him, touching his chest and leaning in on him like I wanted him, and some stupid desperate part of me did want him. He'd been pouring shots for several girls, but now we were alone in the corner. He singled me out, and he was foxy, so I was flattered.

"You look like a light weight." This is what Jordan said after he poured me yet another shot.

He'd known me for less than a half-hour, and the only thing he'd done in that time was talk about Lil Wayne and ply me with alcohol.

I'd drank before, several times. At least twice, I'd gotten really tipsy on fruity schnapps with Jane, but I'd never been really and truly drunk. Not like Jane.

Not surprisingly, five straight shots of vodka hit me pretty hard.

One minute, I was standing there talking to Jordan. I felt a little warm and a little light, but still entirely in control of myself.

Then, suddenly, everything changed. I'd go to move my arm an inch and it'd move a foot. I tried to take a step, and I ran into the island. I knew I was repeating myself, but I just couldn't remember anything that had happened a minute before.

Here's what I can remember: In the kitchen talking to Jordan, and he finally cut me off when it was obvious that I was entirely gone. I yelled things at him, but he just laughed. A girl in a tube top offered to make out with me. Someone threw a football, and it hit me. I walked into a wall. There were so many stairs, and I couldn't figure out how to climb them. Jane told me I looked pretty, but she was making out with an ugly guy with curly hair. There was a lot of stumbling and leaning on Jordan, who didn't seem to mind.

The next thing that I remember clearly I was in a darkened room. I know that I had been conscious the entire time, but I felt like I was just waking up.

All I knew is that I was on a bed, making out with someone that smelled insanely good, presumably Jordan. We were kissing pretty intensely, and his fingers had just started pulling down the string on my bright purple thong, alerting me to the moment I was in.

Vampire or no vampire in my life, I hadn't planned to give up my virginity to some guy who thought it was a good idea to pour too many shots for a girl. I know that a moment ago, kissing him had felt good, but it suddenly just felt wrong.

Before I could even push him off me, my pocket started to vibrate.

"You're vibrating." Jordan stopped kissing me, so I took the opportunity and pushed him off me.

"It's my phone," I mumbled.

"Ignore it." He put his hand on me, trying to keep me in bed with him, but I shook him off and got up. The ground felt precarious under me, but at least I had taken off my shoes at some point so I could actually walk.

"I've gotta take this," I said, but I just wanted an excuse to be away from him. Without even checking the ID, I answered. "Hello?"

"Alice?" Jack sounded confused. Just hearing his voice made my heart soar, and combining that with too much to drink, I started crying in relief.

"Jack!" I squealed. "Jack! I'm so glad you called! Oh, Jack!" I searched around the darkened room for a door, but I stumbled into furniture. "Dammit! Why is it so dark in here?"

"Why don't you just come back in bed?" That was Jordan's helpful advice.

"Because I just want to leave! Where is the stupid door?" I cried, and tears streamed down my cheeks now.

"What's going on?" Jack asked, his voice tight with anxiety. Which made sense since I was sobbing and complaining that I was trapped in the dark, but really, I was just too drunk to find a door. "Alice? Are you okay?"

"No!" I stomped my foot. "I want out!"

"I'm getting the door!" Jordan said. Out of nowhere, a rectangle of light flooded the room, revealing the door.

"Thank you!" I smiled at him as I walked past, but he just nodded. As soon as he realized that I wasn't going any farther, he lost interest.

"Alice!" Jack shouted, trying to get my attention. "What's going on? Are you alright?"

"I don't know!" I had to yell so he could hear me over the music and the chatter of the party. I plugged my open ear so I could hear him better, but he was still hard to make out.

"Where are you?" Jack asked.

"I don't know!"

"Look, I'm coming to get you!" Jack decided.

"How do you know where I'm at? I don't know where I'm at!" I tried to walk down the stairs and talk on the phone, and I stumbled into the railing and dropped the phone. When I picked it up, Jack was yelling panicked hellos. "Jack?"

"Alice! Go outside!"

I fought my way through throngs of people. I could hear Jack saying things on the phone, but I couldn't understand them. It wasn't until I'd finally made it out the front door and the sound dampened that I could hear him again.

"-need you to look around," he was saying.

"You need me to do what?" I asked. I half-expected it to be some kind of magic trick, and Jack would already be waiting out front for me, but he wasn't.

"You're outside?"

"Yep, I'm outside, and I'm not wearing any shoes."

"Do you see any street signs? Any landmarks? Anything to tell me where you are?" Jack asked.

"Um…" I scoured the area around me. I could hear the traffic from the highway and I saw a billboard a block away. "I think I'm right off of 494 by a billboard for 93X. Is that good?"

"Yeah, I can work with that," Jack sounded relieved. "Just stay where you are. I'll be there in a minute."

"Okay," I nodded, even though he couldn't see me.

"Call me if you need to. But I'll be there really quick," he assured me.

"Okay," I repeated, and he hung up the phone.

I should've let him know that I actually wasn't in any danger. Well, not in any immediate danger. After all, I was drunk, shoeless, and sitting on the curb outside of a house party.

Jack pulled up a few minutes later in the Lamborghini, which was how he traveled when speed was a necessity. He stopped right in front of me and dove out of the car, leaving it on and the door open.

"Are you okay?" Jack crouched down in front of me to inspect me for injuries, pushing my damp hair out of my eyes.

My eyes were puffy from crying, beer stained my fancy top, and my feet were very dirty from walking around the party, but overall, I was okay.

"I think so," I nodded.

"You're drunk," Jack smirked.

"I think so."

"Okay. Let's get you home." He stood up and took my hands so he could help me to my feet. Before we got in the car, he gave me a once over to make sure. His eyes got hard and the hand that was holding mine got very cold. "Your pants are undone."

"What?" I looked down at my jeans, and I couldn't remember undoing them. Then I remembered being upstairs making out with Jordan. "Oh. Yeah. That. I didn't do anything."

"You didn't do anything?" Jack let go of my hand and eyed me up severely.

"No, I didn't. I mean, like kissing, but you know, just that. It was nothing at all." I started zipping up my pants when something occurred to me. "I'm wearing a purple a thong."

"You're wearing a purple thong?" Jack raised an eyebrow, but since I was drunk, I couldn't get a read on his emotions. I didn't know if it was an intrigued I'd-like-to-see-more eyebrow, or a disapproving you're-a-huge-slut eyebrow.

"Yeah. Wanna see?" I offered.

"Just get in the car," Jack said, not unkindly, and walked around to the driver's seat.

"Sorry," I mumbled. When I got in the car, a tear slid down my cheek, but I tried to wipe it away before he noticed.

"That's what you were doing when I called?" He kept his voice even, but the car squealed away from the house. His hands gripped the steering wheel too tightly, and I sunk deeper into the seat.

"He kept pouring me shots, and I don't remember most of the night. I don't even remember how I got in the room. But when I realized what was going on, I pushed him off of me, and then you just happened to call like a second later." I played with my hair and shook my head.

"I don't know why I have to explain myself to you, anyway," I said. "You were too busy to even talk to me tonight. It's not my fault that you decided to grace me with your presence the one time I'm actually out doing something."

"Oh, yeah. Because I'm just busy partying it up all the time. That's why I can't talk to you," Jack scoffed.

"I was just sick of sitting in that stupid apartment waiting for you!" I snapped. "So when Jane texted me-"

"I should've known she'd be the source of all this," he laughed darkly.

"You're the one that suggested I hang out with her while you're so 'busy.'" When I made the little air quotes for busy, he rolled his eyes.

"I didn't mean it. I just felt guilty for leaving you alone all the time, but I took it back right away. That's why I had Mae come get you."

"Oh, yeah, thank you for that, by the way. Great idea."

"What? You love Mae!" Jack looked at me dubiously. "How was that not a great idea?"

"Because! I wanted to see you!" I shouted, then instantly regretted saying it.

"Do you think that this is what I wanted?" Jack countered. "That I wanted you to hang out with Jane, getting drunk, and messing around with random date rapists? Yeah, this is exactly what I wanted, Alice."

"It's not my fault that that's what it feels like." I crossed my arms over my chest.

"Well, good thing you got smashed tonight so you could figure it all out!"

"You couldn't even return a text message today!" I yelled. "And when I called, you couldn't wait to get off the phone! I've barely talked to you lately! And you just..." Biting my lip, I didn't even finish the thought.

"I couldn't stay on the phone with you! I shouldn't even have answered the phone in the first place. Things almost got really out of control because I didn't want to hurt your feelings, and now you're mad at me because that wasn't good enough for you?" He shook his head.

"It was a five second phone call! What could've gotten so out of control?" I asked skeptically.

"Milo!"

"Milo?" I looked at him, waiting for him elaborate, but he didn't. "What? Did he... I don't know. I can't even think of anything he could've been doing that would be out of control."

"I was teaching him to eat."

"What?" The air went out of my lungs, and a nauseous feeling crept up inside of me. "I thought... I thought he was eating."

"Out of bags," he said quietly. "But... he needs to learn how to do it with live... people."

"Why?" I asked. "Why does he have to know?"

"Because there isn't always bags, and because it happens, and because when he does it I want to make sure he doesn't kill somebody." Saying it made him uncomfortable, but he sounded more angry than he did embarrassed. "As it was, he could've killed her tonight. He was going crazy while I was on the phone with you, and I had to stop and show him how so he didn't break her neck."

"You had to show him how?" My mouth went dry and I gripped onto the car to keep my hands from shaking. "You bit a girl tonight?"

"I am a vampire, Alice," Jack sounded weary, but he wouldn't look me in the eye.

I remembered how amazing and intense it felt when Peter drank my blood, and how crazed and delirious Jack got just over the taste of it. For vampires, drinking blood from a person was far more intimate than sex. Tonight, Jack had been that intimate with someone else, and it made me sick to my stomach.

"Pull over!" I screamed. The combination of Jack's confession and the vodka were not mixing well, and I felt like I was going to throw up at any second.

"Alice?"

"Pull over now!"

He pulled sharply onto the grass next to the highway. I opened the car door and swung my legs out. As soon as my bare feet hit the grass, I started to feel better, and the cool night blew against me.

I kept swallowing until I felt like I was okay, then sat back up. I left the door open and my feet in the grass, though, just to be on the safe side.

"Are you okay?" Jack had completely softened from earlier, and he reached out to touch me, but I pulled away.

"I'll be fine. I just need a minute."

Closing my eyes, I did my best not to think about Jack biting another girl. To feel that close with somebody, it was impossible to describe. When Peter drank my blood, his heartbeat was my heartbeat. Knowing that Jack was capable of feeling that with anyone else, when he hadn't even felt that with me...

"I know why you're upset and I don't blame you." His voice was low and apologetic. "But Milo has to learn. He's still so volatile. In all honesty, I should've waited, and if I had, I probably wouldn't have had to physically demonstrate."

"But I didn't want to wait," he said. "I want to get through all of · this as quickly as possible, so he can be independent, and you can turn. I did this so you could hurry up and come live with us."

"I'm not going to turn," I said, and my words came out harsher than I meant.

"What?"

"I talked to Ezra the other day." I finally opened my eyes and glanced over at him, and his blue eyes swam with confusion and pain. "He said that I still have to hold off for a couple years. It's not safe or healthy for Milo. I don't think you can rush through this, no matter how hard you try."

"But…" He stared off at nothing, digesting it all.

"Maybe this is all a sign," I said thickly when he didn't speak. "I don't mean just tonight. Everything with Milo and Peter. It's like everything in the universe is saying that this won't work for me."

"Two years really isn't that long," Jack said quickly.

"Jack! You know that's not the only thing!" I leaned my head back on the seat.

"Alice…" He breathed deeply. When he spoke, his voice was barely a whisper. "When I called, it was because something felt off. I knew something was going on with you. And by the time I got to the exit, I knew exactly where you were at. I could feel you, scared and alone. I can't just turn that off. You can't just throw this away."

"What am I supposed to do?" I asked.

He looked at me desperately, and a longing radiated from him. The alcohol was either wearing off or he was overpowering it. A panicked need overtook him because he thought he was losing me.

I leaned over and pressed my lips against his, and he gave into it. He wrapped his arms around me, pulling me as close to him as he could without hurting me, and his mouth worked ferociously against mine. He tasted amazing, and his skin burned hot.

We'd only been kissing for a few seconds when abruptly, he stopped, and pushed me back from him. Gently but firmly, he held me at arm's length and struggled to catch his breath.

"Alice, that's way too dangerous," he panted.

"You're really not helping the case, you know?" I pulled away from his arms and slunk down in the seat.

"The only reason I have any restraint is because I just ate," Jack said, leaning back. "Otherwise, that could've been very bad."

"Thanks for reminding me about that," I grimaced.

"You can't really talk. At least what I did, I did because it's how I survive and it was to help your little brother. You just did that... for fun. And you can't use being drunk as an excuse because you wore a purple thong. That was premeditated."

"It was not! I wore the panties cause I wanted to feel fun and dangerous!"

"You're dangerous alright," Jack muttered.

"Whatever." I slammed the car door shut. "Just take me home."

"Can do."

Neither of us spoke the rest of the way home, because that seemed like the safest bet. I was hurt, angry, and disappointed in both of us, and he felt pretty much the same. When he finally pulled up in front of my apartment, he sighed and turned to me.

"Look, Alice, I don't want you to go home mad."

"Neither do I," I said. "So. Fix it."

"Okay," Jack laughed. "Since you can't turn right away anyway, I can stop rushing Milo. That means that I can put less time into getting him ready, and I can make more time for you. You won't feel so shut out."

"Thank you." I bit my lip and looked at him gratefully.

"I don't know if this helps any, but I really, really wanna kiss you right now," Jack said with a sad smile. "And yeah, I did wanna see your purple thong."

"I don't know how that helps," I smiled. It stung a little, because I knew it couldn't happen, but it made me feel better knowing that he still wanted it to.

"Yeah, I guess it doesn't really." He pushed a hair off my forehead, and he looked at me intently. When he breathed in deeply, his eyes went wistful. "Go. Before I give in."

"Okay," I nodded and opened the car door.

"I'll call you. Tomorrow. I promise."

Jack waited outside until I was safely in the apartment. When I went into my bedroom, I looked out the window, and he was still waiting outside. I watched him for a few minutes, but then he finally pulled away.

After sleeping fitfully, "Time Warp," Jack's ringtone, woke me up first thing in the afternoon. When I rolled over and picked up my phone, I found a text message that sent a nervous shiver through me.

Text me as soon as you get this. That was all it said.

- 12 -

I assumed the worst. Like Milo had gone on a rampage or Mae had developed vampire cancer or something.

What's wrong? Is everything okay? I texted Jack.

Nothing. Everything's great. I just wanted to get you here as soon as possible. Jack replied almost instantly.

Why? Did something happen? I texted back and sat up in bed.

The sun hadn't fully set yet, and reddish light streamed in through a gap in my curtains. He was up early, at least for him. Something had to have woken him, and he wanted me over there. My mind raced, trying to figure out what it could be.

Peter. That had to be it. Peter had come back.

Jack still hadn't replied, so I got out of bed and searched through my room for something to wear. I wanted to look good if Peter came back. Technically, he was my intended. Kinda. I think.

I really, really don't understand vampire biology, and I didn't really understand Peter either.

I had discarded three shirts on my floor when my phone started to ring. Not like text message but actual incoming call ringing, and my heart skipped a beat.

"Jack? What's going on?" I demanded breathlessly when I picked up the phone.

"You're totally freaking out right now," he laughed. I was mid-heart attack by then, and he laughed.

"Why is that funny?" I asked, but hearing him laugh made my nerves settle down.

"You're so paranoid!" Jack continued laughing. "Milo told me you would freak out if I just told you to text me without an explanation." I heard Milo say something in the background, and Jack laughed harder. "Yeah, she is. I think she's getting pissed now, though."

"Good call," I said.

"Sorry." He suppressed his laughter. "We just had a big night of fun planned, and I wanted you to get over here so you can get ready."

"A big night?"

"Yeah. We're going out," he said mischievously.

"Out?" I echoed.

The last time Jack and I had actually gone out anywhere, it was like a month ago. We went to Valley Fair, this amusement park in Shakopee. Even though we didn't get there until almost ten, the park was pretty packed.

We hardly waited in line for anything. Everyone offered to let Jack go in front of them, and by association, me too.

That sounds awesome, but after this chick wearing only a bikini top and Daisy Dukes shorts tried to steal my seat next to him on the Wild Thing, I kind of freaked out and said I was never going in public with him again.

"Don't sound so nervous. It's not gonna be like Valley Fair. I promise," he said.

"Okay?" I said, because that was the only thing I could really do.

"Awesome. So I'll pick you up in like ten minutes."

"No, wait! I'm still in my pajamas and everything!" I was just wearing girl boxers and a wife beater. I couldn't imagine anywhere this would be a good look.

"Mae has some clothes for you. You're getting ready here. Trust me," Jack insisted wickedly. "It's better this way."

"What is going on?" I asked, baffled.

"Just be outside in ten minutes."

"Jack!" I shouted, but he'd hung up. And if I wasn't downstairs in eleven minutes, he'd probably come up and get me.

I ran a brush through my hair but it was still a ridiculous mess, so I pulled it back in a messy bun. I slipped on my flip-flops and ran downstairs, just in time to see Jack pulling up out front.

"You know, I don't think you'll even need Mae's clothes," Jack grinned and turned down the Beastie Boys when I got in the car. "You look smoking hot in that. I mean, are those even shorts? Or just slightly long underwear?"

"They're pajamas!" I blushed and struggled to pull down the boxers so they covered my legs better.

"You slept over at my house lots of times, and you never wore those shorts." He started driving and pretended like he was watching the road, but I could see him appraising me out of the corner of his eye.

"Your house is cold. I have to wear warm pajamas. My house is like ten million degrees. And I wanted to put on real clothes, but you didn't give me enough time, so this is all your fault."

"Hey, I am not complaining," he laughed. "And I'm definitely turning the thermostat up the next time you stay over."

"Oh will you stop looking at me like that!" I rolled my eyes at him. "You've seen me in a bikini before. Get over it! Its pajamas!"

"Sorry!" Jack smirked. "You're right. You look nice is all."

"Where are we going anyway?" I tried to change the subject.

"My house."

"After that."

"Oh, you'll see." His smile was definitely wicked, and I wondered what exactly I had in store for me.

When we got to his house, he had still refused to give away any clues. Matilda ran to greet us, and Jack shouted that we were home, so Mae followed the dog.

"Oh, Jack, you didn't even give her time to get dressed?" Mae scolded him and wrapped her arms around me to shield me from the instant cold of their house.

"She's just gonna change anyway," he shrugged.

"She doesn't need to freeze until she does!"

She led me through the house, back towards her room, where I'd presumably get ready. Milo, who'd been in the living room, ran out to greet us. If I wasn't mistaken, he looked even better than he did the last time that I saw him, and he was taller too. The change was still taking its full effect on him.

"Has he told you where we're going yet?" Milo asked.

"No." I looked to Mae for help.

"You're going to a club," she smiled thinly at me, and Jack scoffed behind us.

"It's supposed to be a surprise!" Jack complained.

"Oh, quit, it still is," Mae shook her head.

"Like a dance club?" I asked.

As far as I knew, Jack wasn't that into dance clubs, and while I didn't hate them, it wouldn't really be that exciting for me to go to one.

"I don't know if I really approve of the idea, but Ezra's not here to talk him out of it, so here we are," Mae said tiredly and steered me away from the boys to her room. "Why don't you go ahead and hop in the shower, and when you get out, we'll pick out some clothes."

I was confused, but I did as I was told. I went to the master bathroom and took a shower. They had a million shampoos and body washes, and they always made my hair and skin feel amazing afterwards.

Wrapping myself in a fluffy robe, I opened the bedroom door to find Mae waiting. Clothes covered her bed. On closer inspection, many of them still had the tags on, and they all looked to be about my size (which had to be at least two sizes bigger than Mae).

"Is there anything you really like?" Mae had a puzzled, serious look on her face, as if she was having trouble making an important decision.

"Well… they all look really nice," I said, but that was an understatement. "What exactly am I getting dressed up for? It might help me pick something out."

"Well-" Mae said when the bedroom door opened, cutting her off.

"Oh good! You're out of the shower!" Milo burst into the room.

Whenever I went out to something special, he helped me get ready. This wouldn't be any different, and it would actually be kinda nice to do something normal with him. Relatively speaking.

"Sure am." I eyed them both up. "Where am I going tonight?"

"A club," Milo replied and exchanged a look with Mae. "A vampire club!" He squealed with delight and looked far gayer than he ever had in his mortal life.

"What?" I didn't think I understood him right, so I looked at Mae. "What's he talking about?"

"A vampire club." Mae smiled in way that I knew that she wasn't as keen about the idea as Milo. "We told you a little bit about them before. They're similar to a regular bar or club, but with obvious differences. Jack frequents one off Hennepin Avenue, and I've been there a few times."

"Obvious differences?" I asked. "Like what? Do they have a keg of blood?"

"No, no." Mae laughed nervously and looked away. "Well, not exactly. They do have some kind of blood on... tap." If that was meant to ease my nerves, it failed. "Humans go all the time, though, and they have bouncers. People aren't..." She sighed as she floundered for words. "They don't harm people there."

"That's where Jack goes to eat, isn't it?" I gulped.

"Yes. They have donors there. And most of them know that's what they are." Mae tilted her head, thinking. "They call them bloodwhores. But mostly it's people and vampires doing what anybody does at a club."

"Getting drunk and looking for sex?" I raised an eyebrow.

"Some of them, yes," Mae laughed. "But it's all in fun."

"It's gonna be a blast," Milo said. "I'm so excited to get out of this house and actually do something. Especially with other vampires! Aren't you excited?"

"Yeah," I nodded, but I didn't really know how to feel about it.

I'd never met any other vampires, not that I knew of, anyway. I'd love to see what they'd be like. And dancing and being out is exactly how I wanted to spend my last few days before school.

On the other hand, I was going to be in a room full of vampires, which still had some frightening implications. Thinking about Jack eating made me physically ill, and the prospect of seeing where he got his "food" didn't thrill me either. There could be someone there he had bitten, someone who knew him more intimately than I did, and that thought made me sick.

"Are you okay, love?" Mae asked me.

"Yeah, I'm fine," I lied.

"You look really pale," Milo agreed. His eyes softened with worry. "Are you sure you're okay? Do you not want to go? We don't have to go. We just thought it might be fun." He desperately wanted to do this, and he would give it up for me, so I just shook my head.

"I want to. Really. I do," I said, and sighing, I decided to explain my ambivalence. "I don't want to see anyone that Jack's... bitten."

"Oh," Mae nodded.

"What?" Milo gave her an odd look.

"You don't understand because you've never been bitten," Mae told him, then turned to me. "Jack doesn't feel it like you feel it. Being bitten is not the same as biting, and it's not the same when you do it for food, versus pleasure."

"I don't follow," I shook my head. Milo sat on the bed, on top of the clothes, and listened. Apparently, this was new information to him, too.

"It feels amazing," she said. "Few things in life are better than drinking someone's blood. But in order for the prey-predator relationship to work, humans willingly give themselves to us, and that happens because they develop an emotional attachment that we don't feel. For us, it's purely physical."

"That sounds like something a guy says after he cheats on you," I pointed out dryly.

"I suppose it does," she smiled. "But it's the truth. Your feelings on this are slightly misleading. Your only experience is with Peter, and you're bonded. When you love each other, it's intimate and intense. But just eating, that's nothing really."

"Uh huh," I said skeptically.

"Let me put it this way: Ezra bites other people," Mae said. "And on occasion, so do I. This doesn't bother me, and it doesn't bother him when I do it. If he let someone bite him, that would bother me. That would be tantamount to cheating."

"I think I understand."

What I had felt with Peter had been because we were already bonded and I was victim. If anyone bit me, I'd feel similarly, but if I bit someone else, I'd feel good, but without all the emotional connection.

"When you're a vampire, you'll understand," she assured me, but that only touched on another raw nerve. Realizing this, she smiled and brushed past it. "Anyway, let's get you dressed."

"I know you love jeans, but I'm thinking a skirt, definitely." Milo hopped off the bed so he could inspect the clothes.

I just agreed with everything they said as Mae and Milo sifted through the clothes. Milo spoke animatedly about everything. Being a vampire sat very well with him. I had never seen him so comfortable in his own skin before. Jack's tutelage must've been helping, because it was an improvement from even a few days ago.

Mae did my makeup, since that was one area that Milo had never been any help with. He left to finish getting ready while she styled my hair and assured me that I would have fun. I asked why she wasn't going, and she just shrugged and said she was too old for it.

When she finished, she paraded me out into the kitchen to show the boys. Jack leaned on the island, looking rather handsome. He traded in his shorts uniform for dark washed denim and a fitted shirt.

As soon as he saw me, he grinned happily and let out a long whistle, making Matilda bark.

"Look at you." Jack stood up straight and looked me over. His eyes lingered at the hem of my skirt, and I squirmed. "I might like that skirt even more than I like those little short things you were wearing this morning."

"Jack," Mae said disapprovingly.

"You're the one that dressed her up," Jack pointed out.

"Just be good," Mae warned him.

"I'm always good," he muttered.

"You do look really good," Milo said.

"So do you," I told him. He'd changed his shirt, and he did something infinitesimal to his hair, but he did look good.

"I want you kids to have fun, but you need to be careful," Mae said gravely. "And I'm talking to you, Jack. You need to keep your eyes on both of them. Milo's really young, and Alice is... well, you need to watch them both."

"I know," Jack rolled eyes. "I got it when we had this conversation twenty times this morning." He started edging towards the door, and I followed.

"Stay close to Jack, and don't go anywhere with anyone, okay?" Mae said, looking at me directly. "And just remember. Vampires are like men. They only think about one thing."

"So vampire men really only think about one thing?" Milo asked with a deviant glint in his eye.

"You only think about one thing?" I teased, looking up at Jack.

"I'm thinking about one thing right now." His tone was joking, but he looked at me seriously. He felt dangerously close to me, and my pulse quickened.

"Jack!" Mae snapped.

"Being good!" Jack turned away from me.

"You better be," she said. "I'm trusting you. They're both in your care, and I expect them to come back in the exact same condition they are now. Is that clear?"

"It's been clear all day." Jack walked backwards to the door, so he could mount his escape while still looking at her, and Milo and I trailed right after him. "You know, I'm middle aged, Mae. You think you'd start trusting me by now."

"I would if you acted your age for a change!" Mae called after him, but he was already slipping into the garage.

I waved at her before I left, and she pursed her lips and hugged herself. She already regretted her decision to let us go.

I didn't feel that nervous. After all, I was with two vampires that would kill anyone that tried to mess with me. What was the worst that could happen?

- 13 -

We parked by First Avenue, but it wasn't until we got out of the car that I realized that it was the same parking garage where'd I first met Jack. He said he'd just gotten done eating when he ran into me, and then saved my life from some ridiculous hooligans.

It was so weird to think that if I hadn't stumbled into the garage that night, my entire life would've turned out different.

"You coming?" Jack asked, looking at me curiously. He and Milo had taken a couple steps ahead of me, but I stood just outside the car.

"Yeah," I nodded, and slowly followed them.

People littered the sidewalk, doing similar things as us. Summer was ending, and girls were getting the short skirts and halter tops out of their system. The Minneapolis skyline towered over us, and the music from clubs and voices of people echoed off the buildings.

I looked down the street at the brightly lit marquees announcing clubs and restaurants and plays, and I wondered what there would be outside marking the vampire club.

"What's this place called anyway?" I asked.

"It doesn't really have a name," Jack said. "It's like an underground thing."

"Well, what do people call it? Like, the ones that don't know it's a vampire club? Or even the ones that do?" I asked.

People were probably within hearing distance, but I didn't lower my voice or hide the term "vampire." They were drunk or on cellphones or too embroiled in their own drama to notice me. Most of them only gave a fleeting glance at Jack and Milo.

"I don't know," Jack shrugged. "I think they call it V or something."

"That's not very creative," I scowled.

"Yeah, I thought it'd be something sexier," Milo agreed.

"It's an underground vampire club," Jack scoffed. "It doesn't need a 'creative' name to entice people."

"He has a point," Milo said.

"I still expected more from them," I said.

Jack directed us to turn off Hennepin, leading us away from the glittery lights of the gay club flashing down the street. People were still around, but much less than there were before. Without all the bright lights announcing venues, the yellow streetlamps made it seem much darker. The traffic had even dissipated.

"We're almost there," Jack slowed. He held out his hand to me, and I didn't understand so I looked at him. "Give me your hand. You're with me and I want everyone to know it."

"Okay?" I let Jack take my hand, and looked over to Milo to make sure he wasn't going to growl and attack me for touching Jack.

"He's got it under control," Jack said, slowing so we were barely walking, and Milo stayed a few paces ahead of us. When Jack spoke, he lowered his voice to just above a whisper. "Stay by me. And try not to get excited or think about Peter. But if you do, you find me. If somebody's gonna bite you, it's gonna be me."

"Is that a threat or a promise?" I smiled up at him.

"Both," Jack laughed. "No. Sorry. Neither. I'm being good. But just stay by me."

"You're making this sound dangerous." My stomach filled with butterflies, and I thought of the worried look on Mae's face. "Why are we going here if it's hazardous?"

"It's slightly riskier than hanging out with us in the first place," Jack said. "But you needed to get out and have fun. And I won't let anything happen to you. So..." He shrugged. "Milo. Hold up."

Jack stopped next to a nondescript doorway in the middle of the block. The nearest streetlight had completely gone out, making it eerily dark for downtown. He squeezed my hand briefly, and I felt his temperature warm up just slightly, but it wasn't out of control.

Milo came back to where we were standing, and Jack nodded at a large black door. Milo raised his eyebrows, and then opened it.

The door opened into a narrow entryway that glowed red from the bulb above. Two giant bouncers stood there, nearly blocking our path inside. They nodded at Jack and Milo, but something about the way they looked at me when I walked past assured me that they were vampires, and I hurried past them.

At the end of the narrow hall, a steep set of cement stairs led down into black nothingness. The only light in the stairway came from the red one by the front door.

We walked into complete darkness, but that wasn't a problem for most attendees. For my puny human eyes, it was disorienting. I clung onto Jack, and he never let me go.

I could hear the music pulsing, some kind of heavy electronica. Jack whispered that we had reached the main level, but I still couldn't see anything. We walked a little farther, and Jack opened the door, bathing us in cool, blue light and making the walls echo with the music.

Considering we were in the basement, the ceilings of the room were amazingly high above the dance floor. Five hundred or more people smashed onto the floor, dancing wildly. Slender arms waved in the air, and bodies moved delicately and perfectly in time with the music. Never had I seen movements so graceful.

A long, metallic bar lined the far side of the room, and based on the bottles lining the back wall, I assumed it was an actual bar, full of alcoholic drinks for the humans. Several very attractive men and women stood behind it, manning it for drinks. The stools in front of it were full, and a line of sweaty humans waited to be served.

I turned to look for Milo, but he'd already disappeared onto the dance floor. Jack smiled at me and pulled me into the crowd.

The people moving around us were stunningly beautiful. A girl with pixie white-blonde hair smiled at me, and I noticed the fading bite marks on her neck.

Jack moved gracefully, and I tried to keep up with him. He kept his hands on me the entire time, keeping me close to him, and I loved it. The blue from the light made his eyes glow, and his happiness was infectious. The speed of my dancing and Jack's proximity made my heart pound.

Other bodies pushed up against me as people danced around us. It almost felt like they were grabbing at me, but I had to be imagining things. Then I felt a sharp prick as someone scratched the back of my neck, and Jack stopped dancing.

They hadn't scratched hard enough to draw blood, thankfully. Jack kept his arm around me, and when I looked around, I saw the crowd had closed in on us.

Jack started to lead me off the floor, towards a doorway into another room. Someone touched me, letting their fingertips glide lightly down my arm, almost caressing me. I looked back, expecting whoever touched me to slink away into the crowd, but he just stood there. Not dancing, not moving, just staring at me.

He was gorgeous, with thick hair slicked back. His eyes were a mesmerizing black and burned straight through me. He smiled at me in a seductively evil way.

I'd been frozen in a trance, and Jack dragged me away. When I noticed it, I managed to look away, and the way my lungs burned reminded to breathe.

The crowd broke, and the light shifted from blue to dull red. We slipped through a doorway into the next room. The walls dampened sound of music.

This room was smaller than the last and dressed more like a bar or a coffee shop than a club. Lots of doors and darkened hallways led out of it. Soft couches filled the room.

A small bar sat in a dark corner with a bartender behind it. There weren't any bottles lining the wall, and I figured it had to be an entirely different kind of bar.

On the couch nearest to us, a stunningly beautiful woman laid with her head lulled back. Her clothing was black leather and so tight I couldn't believe she could move. A pretty young girl was curled up on her lap. Her eyes were closed, and a thin line of blood trailed down her neck. The vampire holding her looked at me and smiled as she licked the blood from her lips.

"Stop it," Jack murmured in my ear.

"What?" I asked, pulling my attention from the vampire to look about the room.

Scenes similar to the one on the couch played out all over. Some people (or vampires) were simply sitting and talking, and some were just making out. But others were openly feeding on humans.

As soon as we entered the room, everyone seemed to turn and look at us. Vampires with their stunning, entrancing eyes, kept fixing their gaze on me, and I would forget to breathe.

"Stop," Jack repeated and jerked my hand so I would focus on him.

"What?" I looked up at him, away from everyone in the room.

"Don't look at anyone," he said.

"Why not?"

"You keep letting them… captivate you." He looked over the top of my head, and he was starting to think that maybe this was a bad idea. "Don't do that."

"Sorry," I said, but I wasn't exactly sure how to fix that.

"Don't be sorry. Just…" He shook his head. "Come on." He pulled me off to the side of the room, to a mostly empty couch.

When he sat down, I sat close to him. On the other side of him was a girl with hair that shown purple under the light, and her lipstick was black. She'd been sipping something out of a tall wine glass, and she turned her attention to us.

She smiled, mostly at me, and her fangs were more pronounced than Jack's were. Almost comically so, and I wondered if that was a natural occurrence or if she did something to make them like that.

"You're new here," she purred, directly to me, and her voice sounded like honey and helium.

"Yeah," I said, and Jack dropped his arm around me.

"You, I've seen around before." She narrowed her eyes at him. Her makeup was so thick and heavy around her eyes, as if she wore a kind of mask. She bit her lip, carefully so the fangs wouldn't tear her skin, and tried to place him. "Did we fuck?"

"No, I can't say that we have," Jack replied quickly. I tensed up, which I knew was a bad idea since I was supposed to keep my heart rate down.

It never occurred to me that Jack had sex. I realized that vampires probably had sex, that Mae and Ezra did, and I definitely considered the prospect of me having sex with Jack, but I had never thought about it actually happening. Not only had Jack most likely bitten girls here, he had probably slept with some of them.

"Pity," the girl said, and her eyes dropped back to me. Her smile tilted, and she noticed the change in my heart rate. "So you're that kind of girl."

"What kind of girl is that?" I asked tightly.

"Where are my manners?" She laughed, a tinkley, fragile sound, like breaking glass. "I haven't even introduced myself. My name is Violet."

She held out her hand to me and only me. It was covered in one of those lace fingerless gloves that Madonna used to wear, and I took her hand and shook it.

"I'm Alice." I let go of her lacy, tepid hand and looked up at Jack. "This is Jack."

"Jack." She clicked her tongue and looked at him. "We never-"

"Nope," he repeated with an edge to his voice.

"Are you sure?" Violet looked dubious. "Cause I have a really excellent memory, and I could swear that we knocked boots?" She winked at me and elbowed Jack playfully in the ribs.

"I'm quite certain," he said icily.

"Yeah! You did this thing-"

"Stop," Jack told her, his voice low and even. "I know what you're doing, and I want you to stop." She batted her eyes innocently, and he turned to me. "When she mentioned it the first time, your heart sped up, and now she's just saying things to make it race. She's trying to set you off."

"It's beating like a moth caught in jar," Violet smiled wistfully at me. "I can't help myself. It sounds so beautiful."

"I'm sorry."

"You have nothing to be sorry for," Jack reassured me quietly.

Blushing, I curled up closer to him. Even in the dimly lit room, I could see the way Violet looked at me with pure thirst in her eyes. Jack would never let anything happen to me, and I don't think she wanted to kill me. But she wanted to taste me, and that was a weird thing to know.

"Are you gonna go back to one of the rooms?" She nodded toward the dark doorways that led out of the room, and I wondered what kind of rooms they were. "I would kill just to watch."

"We're good, thanks," Jack said.

Violet kept her eyes locked on me and slid closer to Jack, pressing her body against him. He tried to recoil, but I was at the end of the couch and he didn't want to smash me.

"You're just a little treat, aren't you?" Violet winked at me.

"Alright, that's fun." Jack stood up, pulling me to my feet with him.

"We must not have messed around, otherwise you wouldn't be turning me down," she laughed at him. "I can do things, for the both of you that you've only ever dreamed about."

"Yep. I'm really missing out." Jack steered me towards the bar in the corner, and Violet cackled behind us. "I'm sorry. This was a terrible idea. I've never brought a human here before, and I didn't really know what to expect."

"It's not so bad," I said.

At the bar, Jack moved me in front of him, so my stomach was pressed against the wood. He stood behind me with his arms on either side of me. The vampires had freaked him out, and he wanted to surround me.

Oddly, I didn't feel the slightest bit anxious, and my emotions tended to mirror his. Something about being in this room, it made me strangely sedate.

The bartender came over to take our order and gave Jack a bewildered look.

"I'd like a drink. Just whatever you have handy," Jack told him, and that only deepened the bartender's confusion. "Do you have any vodka back here?"

"All the light drinks are out there." The bartender gestured to the dance floor. He looked at me, then up at Jack. "Are you sure you really want a drink?"

"Yep," Jack said, and when the bartender continued eyeing me up, Jack added, "She's just for looks."

"Whatever floats your boat, buddy," the bartender shook his head and walked away to get a drink.

"You know what? Cancel the drink." He slid his arm around me and stepped back from the bar.

"What's going on?" I asked.

"This was a stupid idea, and we're getting out of here." He looked around uneasily as he led me away. "Everyone is looking at you like... I don't know."

"What about Milo?" I asked. We were just about out of the room, back to the dance floor where my words would be drowned out, so I stopped.

"I'll text him when we get outside," Jack said.

"He won't hear it. It's too loud. And even if he does, he wouldn't answer. He's having fun."

"Then we'll leave him here, and he can call when he's ready," Jack said.

"We can't just leave him here!" I insisted. Milo might be a vampire, but he's still my little brother, and I wasn't prepared to leave him alone on his first night out.

Jack tried to reason with me, so I jerked my hand away from him and crossed my arms over my chest. Behind us, the vampire in black leather with the girl on her lap whistled loudly at my display, so both Jack and I turned to look at her.

"She's a firecracker!" the vampire laughed, but it was that lazy, blissed-out laugh people have when they're really high. "You've got your hands full with that one, don't you?"

"I make do," Jack told her, but looked severely at me. "Alice…"

"I'm not leaving Milo here," I persisted.

"Well, I'm not dragging you out there to look for him." He pursed his lips when he glanced out at the crowded dance floor. Going across the room wouldn't be so bad, let alone wading through there for any length of time, with all those people grabbing at me.

"I can keep an eye on her for you, if you need to me to," the vampire offered. She patted the girl on her lap. "And I know how hard it is to keep the flies away from the food."

"Just keep an eye on her, nothing else," Jack warned her.

"Cross my heart and hope to die." She crossed her heart with her long black fingernail.

"I'll be right back." He hesitated before leaving, and then placed his hands on my cheeks and quickly, he kissed me. Keeping his face close to mine, he whispered, "Don't let anybody touch you."

"I won't."

"Good." Reluctantly, he turned and disappeared in the writhing bodies on the dance floor.

"What's your name?" my vampire baby-sitter asked me.

"Alice." I hugged myself and tried to keep my eyes fixated on her and the girl on her lap, and not on the room full of leering vampires around me.

"Olivia," she gestured to herself, and then to the girl on her lap. "This is Hannah. She's mine."

"Congratulations," I said lamely, unsure of what else to say.

"Thanks," Olivia laughed. "It's tricky what you have with him." She nodded at the door after Jack. "Why hasn't he turned you?"

"It's a complicated situation." I rubbed my arms. The girl on Olivia's lap stirred, and she stroked her hair to quiet her. "Why haven't you turned Hannah?"

"I wouldn't have any reason to keep her if I did," Olivia said, but she looked at her with some affection. "You've heard the saying 'why buy the cow if you get the milk for free?' Well, if I bought the cow, I wouldn't get any milk at all."

She wanted Hannah for her blood, and nothing else.

"So why do you think he should turn me?" I asked.

"He loves you," Olivia sounded surprised when she looked up at me. "You must know that." I shifted uneasily but didn't answer her. "And I'm betting that he's not getting any milk either." She narrowed her bleary eyes at me, genuinely appraising me for the first time. "I bet you're a virgin in every sense of the word."

"Not entirely," I raised my chin defiantly, as if I had showed her in some way.

"He's never bitten you?"

"He's tasted me." When I told her that, her eyes widened.

"And he hasn't bitten you?" She was stunned and unbelieving. "That boy has some restraint. But it's only a matter of time before he slips, and with that much pent up, he'd go way too far."

"We have things under control," I said unconvincingly.

"Well, hello there," a deep voice said from behind me.

I whirled around to see the vampire that had touched me on the dance floor. His black eyes glowed at me. A strand of black hair came loose, so he pushed it back with unpleasantly long nails, at least for a man.

"That's Alice!" Violet announced with her shrill, sparkling laugh. She leapt off the couch and skipped over to us, stopping so close to him that they were almost touching. "Isn't she a treat?"

"Sweet as pie," he purred with an exaggerated southern drawl, reminding me of when Hannibal Lector mocked Clarisse Starling in *Silence of the Lambs*. He breathed in deeply, leaning in closer to me, but I couldn't think enough to step back. "Breathe, honey."

With that, I gasped and filled my lungs with precious oxygen. Whatever he did to me, it was far worse than even what Peter could do. My mind was less of a fog, but my body lost the ability to do anything, like breathe or blink or move.

"You are precious!" he smiled hungrily, and Violet giggled next to him.

"Oh, leave her alone," Olivia said. Her voice gained some strength and lost its bleary edge as she came to my aide. "She's just a kid, and her boyfriend's out there in the other room."

"What's it to you?" He looked past me at her, and I caught a glimpse of primal rage flashing in his eyes.

"He left her in charge," Violet smirked, leaning in close to him. "He left her alone."

"What do you want?" I asked when I finally found my voice.

"You're so scared!" This fact amused him too much, and he sounded a tad aroused. "I'd just like us to be friends. Me, you, and Violet." He spread his arms openly, as if he expected me to run into them. "To put you at ease, I'll introduce myself. My name is Lucian."

"His name's not really Lucian," Violet confessed. "It's actually Hector, but that doesn't sound nearly as decedent." He glared at her, and she recoiled but forced a smile at me. "But trust me, sweetie, he's all vampire."

"So am I," Olivia interjected. "Why don't you two go prey on someone you stand a chance with? This girl isn't going anywhere with you."

"You must be getting senile in your old age, Olivia," Lucian snarled at her. "Because I didn't say anything about going anywhere. We're just having a friendly little chat. Isn't that right, Alice?"

"I'm not much for talking," I said.

My heart beat erratically and much too fast. Both Violet and Lucian had that eye-fluttering pleasurable look, and I knew they were tuned into it.

"My god, that's beautiful," Lucian murmured, almost inaudible. "It's so delicate and frantic. Like a fly caught in a spider web, desperately beating its tiny wings… but it's not going anywhere."

"You guys are big into the insect metaphors," I whispered.

"Here's another: 'Welcome to my parlor,'" Lucian smiled, this time purposely showing me his fangs. Like Violet's, they were sharper and larger than Jack's, and all the more frightening.

"My boyfriend is right out there, and he'll kill you," I warned them breathlessly. "He left Olivia in charge, and she takes her responsibility seriously."

"That drugged out old hag?" Lucian laughed and leaned in closer to me. "She's not going to do anything. If your boyfriend really cared, he wouldn't have brought you here in the first place. I think he wanted this to happen."

"That's not true," I said, and his eyes dropped to my throat as he leaned closer to me.

"Oh, Alice, I'm afraid you've really fallen into a rabbit hole this time," he whispered, and I closed my eyes.

"Lucian!" Olivia shouted. "Oh, Hannah, will you move!" A moment later, she appeared next to me. "I told you to back off!"

"Olivia, Olivia," Violet said, stepping away from us to take care of Olivia. Lucian leaned back up straighter but didn't move away from me. "Aren't you sick of that tired old blood bag you're always taking around with you?"

"Violet, not right now." Olivia sounded disgusted. "I'm trying to keep this girl out your hands. She's not yours. There are plenty of other girls here that you can go crazy with."

"I'm here too, Olivia," Violet batted her eyes at her and rubbed her arm seductively on Olivia's. "I know you're always traipsing around with those little dolls of yours. When was the last time you were with a real woman?"

Olivia was momentarily distracted by Violet, and that was all the time that Lucian needed. His arms were around me, so strong and tight, that I couldn't breathe or move or even scream.

He carried me away, quick and nauseating. The wind whipped through my hair, and he had my face pressed into the unyielding muscles of his chest. If he didn't let me go soon, I would suffocate.

He let go of me, and as soon as I could gasp for air, I started to scream.

In a dim narrow hallway, Lucien dropped me heavily onto the cement. He sprawled out on the floor a few feet from me, and Jack stood between us. On the other side of Lucian, Milo blocked the door back to the club where we'd come from, and behind him, Olivia growled.

"Get up," Jack said, his voice trembling with restraint, and Lucian scrambled to his feet. "Get out of here before I rip out your throat."

"You shouldn't have brought her if you didn't want to share her!" Lucian shouted, almost plaintively.

Milo made a move towards him, but Olivia grabbed his arms and held him back. Lucian snuck past them and hurried away.

Jack glared after him for a second, but before Olivia released Milo, Jack turned and dropped to his knees next to me. He touched my forehead and let out an uneasy breath. With great effort, he pulled his eyes away to look me completely over. His breath came out in shallow rasps, and I felt a hungry panic from him that I didn't understand.

"Are you okay?" Jack asked.

"Yeah," I nodded. "Are you? What's the matter?"

"I'm okay." His hand trembled when he pulled it from my forehead, and I noticed something dark staining his fingers. "You're bleeding."

"Oh no," I whispered.

"Alice... do you trust me?" Jack kept his eyes fixed on me. I nodded. "Good." He leaned over and gently, he kissed my forehead.

Milo yelled in protest, but Olivia restrained him. Softly, I felt Jack's mouth on my wound, and that simple touch sent shivers of pleasure through me. He wanted me so badly I could hardly stand it. I moaned, and Jack sprang back from me, panting hoarsely.

"What did you do?" Milo shouted.

"I needed the bleeding to stop!" Jack licked his lips and looked at me hungrily. "My saliva will make it heal quicker."

"Take her out the back way," Olivia said, sounding far more worried than I felt. "It'll be easier than going through the club."

I couldn't feel worried or frightened. Jack overwhelmed me with his thirst, and that left me wantonly reciprocating.

I sat on the floor with my back against the wall, only vaguely aware of my throbbing headache. Jack crouched across from me, pressing himself tightly against the other wall. His blue eyes stayed locked on mine. He willed himself to stay there, and I wanted his will to break.

"Jack!" Milo said, and he gripped my arm painfully as he yanked me to my feet. He hadn't gotten the magnitude of his new strength, and I was lucky he hadn't snapped my arm in half.

"Sorry," Jack mumbled, standing up. Milo managed to break us out of the trance, but we were both pretty dazed.

"We gotta get out of here," Milo said, looking back over his shoulder.

"Yeah, right, okay." Jack nodded but made no effort to move. He just stared dumbly at me, and he shook his head to clear it. "I, uh, I don't know where the back exit is."

"Oh, hell." Olivia rolled her eyes. She slid in between us, her long hair brushing like silk across my skin. "Grab the girl. We have to hurry." She was already jetting ahead, gliding lightly in her knee-high boots.

I could never keep up with her, and I was about to say that when Milo tried to put his arms around me. At the same time, Jack made the same play, and they bumped into each other.

"I got her." Jack scooped me up in his arms before Milo could stop him.

"Just be careful," Milo warned.

As soon as Jack had me in his arms, he flew after Olivia. We raced down winding passageways that appeared to be an intricate labyrinth in the basement. At least that's what I could tell from what I could see, but most of it was completely black.

Abruptly, we burst through a set of heavy doors. We were outside, with a set of cement stairs leading up to the sidewalk.

At the top, Jack set me down, and I looked around. I could see the marquee for Barfly glittering brightly, but we were hidden in an alley, next to a stairwell I had never noticed before.

Olivia waited for us, crossing her arms over her chest in a way that pushed out her ample bosom. A full moon splashed in between the buildings, lighting her face, and she was even more exquisite than I had first believed.

"Thanks," Jack told her. He moved a couple feet away from me, because he didn't trust himself right now.

"You have to be careful," Olivia cautioned him. "What were you thinking bringing her here?"

"I don't know." He scratched his head and looked at the ground. "I'd never brought anyone here, and the girls I'd met here never seemed like they in were any danger."

"That's because they're whores." Olivia looked at Jack like he was an idiot. In response, he kicked an empty bottle with his foot. "They let people bite them! If you had wanted to share her, you probably wouldn't have had a problem."

"What the hell happened in there?" Milo asked.

"I don't know really." I shook my head. "There were these vampires, Violet and Lucian. And they were into me, and Jack went to look for you, so they pounced."

"What were you doing?" Jack lifted his head to look at Milo. "You disappeared in there."

"I was dancing," Milo said. "I didn't know we'd have to run out ten minutes later because you didn't realize it wouldn't be a good idea to bring a human to a vampire bar!"

"You guys can sort it out later," Olivia interrupted. "You should get out of here."

"Yeah, you're right," Jack said. "Thank you. You'll never know how much I appreciate what you did tonight."

"Yeah, well, I've been there," Olivia shrugged, but her expression got more severe. "You need to hurry up and turn her, unless you're ready to bury her."

"It's complicated," Jack sounded exasperated, and I knew it touched the same raw nerve it did me.

"Maybe, but death is simple." She pointed to the end of the alley. "Now get out of here."

"Thank you," Jack repeated.

"Thanks," I echoed.

"Take care of yourself, kid," Olivia smiled at me before going back down the stairs, into the darkness that led to the hidden vampire club.

Jack took my hand as we walked towards the car. All the clubs downtown were letting out, so the streets were more crowded than before. Milo and Jack had put me in between them, and Milo scoured the crowd, as if a vampire would attack us on a crowded street.

Neither of them said anything until we reached the car.

"Well, that was fun," Milo sighed as he leaned back in the seat.

"I am so sorry." Jack started the car and wouldn't look at me. "I should've known better."

"It's okay," I reassured him. "Everybody's okay. And it was a really interesting night. I learned a couple things, and that's something."

"There's easier ways to learn," Jack said.

"I had a blast!" Milo interjected. "I mean, until the whole Alice-almost-getting-slaughtered thing. That wasn't fun. But the running away kind of was. I felt like Matt Damon."

155

"What does Matt Damon run away from?" I looked in the backseat at him, but he gave me cockeyed grin.

"I don't know. I just felt like him," Milo shrugged.

It was such a 180 from how he used to be. Everything I did used to make him nervous and scared, but I had almost been murdered, and he made jokes on the ride home. He was still sweet and geeky, but he'd lost his insecurities and paranoia.

"At least you wore your pajamas here," Jack said as we got closer to his house.

"Why?" I asked.

"Because you're spending the night at my house tonight." He swallowed hard and looked at me out the corner of his eyes. "I just want you there tonight. Okay?"

"Okay," I nodded.

"Oh, slumber party," Milo said, but Jack didn't even crack a smile.

The night had really gotten to him. On top of what had already happened, he wasn't thrilled about explaining it to Mae. Even I was dreading it, and I hadn't really done anything wrong. Neither had Jack per se, but neither of them saw it that way.

After Mae lectured Jack about his careless behavior, she'd wept over what could've befallen me and held me close to her while listening to Etta James. Jack hid and Milo tried to lighten the mood.

Eventually, everyone just showered and went to bed. I don't know how they all faired at sleeping, but I did terrible. Maybe it was the adrenaline of the night, or all the new questions I had swirling in my head.

After seeing all the gorgeous vampires at the club, I knew that Jack had to have hooked up with at least one or two of them for sex or blood.

As Mae had pointed out before we left, vampires and men only think about thing one thing, and while she'd implied that vampires only want blood, Jack couldn't completely turn off the man part of himself.

It shouldn't matter to me, since we're not together, and even if we were, that was a long time ago. Or if it wasn't, it was still before he met me, and I can't really blame him for not being psychic.

But I was a virgin in almost every way (except for once when Peter had bitten me, and Jordan had made it to second base the other night). It intimidated me to be with someone so much more experienced than me.

Plus, Jack had tasted my blood at the club, and that left this lingering maddening desire. Finally, I gave up and went downstairs.

Milo slept in his room next door so I was careful to tiptoe out. Milo's hearing had greatly improved, and he found it distracting to sleep, so he had a white noise machine in his room anyway.

Even though it was after seven in the morning, every shade in the house was drawn so no natural light could sneak in. Everything was submerged in pitch black, except for Jack's room, which they had outfitted with a night light for me.

I maneuvered the stairs without making a sound, but I stubbed my toe three times. I couldn't make it farther without help, so I flicked on the kitchen light at the bottom of the steps, and I went into the living room.

The dim light didn't faze Jack, who lay curled up on the couch underneath a dark comforter. Matilda slept on the floor next to him, and she lifted her head when I came into the room and thumped her tail.

"Jack?" I whispered. "Jack?"

"What?" Jack mumbled, moving his head against the pillow. He became aware that he talked to someone, and he opened his eyes and looked at me. "Alice? Is everything okay?"

"Yeah, everything's fine." I sat down at the end of the couch, next to his feet. "I just couldn't sleep."

"Yeah?" Jack moved so he faced me more. "What's going on?"

"I don't know." I leaned back on the couch, pulling my knees up to my chest.

"Is it about what happened tonight?" Jack asked, and I didn't immediately answer. "Alice, you've got nothing to be scared of. They would never hurt you, not outside of that club, and we're never going back there."

"No, it's not that," I shook my head. "I'm not scared. I mean, not about that. I know you and Milo would never let anything happen, and they seemed like losers anyway."

"They were," Jack agreed, but he sounded serious. "What are you scared of then?"

"I don't know," I sighed and tried to sort out what I wanted to say. "Maybe scared isn't the right word. I just…. Did you know them? Did you know any of the vampires down there?"

"No, I don't think so. I've seen some around, but I'm not acquainted with any of them. I'm not really into that scene." He propped himself up more, and even in the darkness, I could see the worry and confusion on his face. "What are you trying to find out?"

"I don't know. All the vampires down there were just so... attractive. Olivia's like a goddess, and even Violet with her silly makeup couldn't mask that she was very pretty."

"Oh, come on." He rolled his eyes as he connected the dots. "They barely gave me the time of day. Besides, you were the hot sensation down there."

"That's different." I brushed past it. "And I wasn't complaining about them hitting on you. I was wondering... if you..." I squirmed, finding it difficult just to say it.

"What?" Jack asked. "I think Violet was right. I might've seen her around before, but everything she was saying was just to get you going. We'd never done anything."

"I know." I shivered a little, so maybe my girl boxers weren't such a good idea.

"Take some of the covers." He pushed some at me with his feet, and I scooted closer to him so I could snuggle underneath his blankets. When I felt his leg brush against my thigh, I decided I'd moved close enough.

"This is why I don't wear these pajamas here."

"That's what they made blankets for," Jack laughed.

"What do you use blankets for anyway?" I asked, and he looked at me like I was a total idiot. "No, I mean, you guys love it cold. Why do you need to cover up?"

"Force of habit, I guess," he shrugged. "I don't know. I never really thought about it. I only do it when I go to bed. Why? Does it bother you?"

"Why would it bother me?"

"I don't know! I don't know why anything bothers you!" Jack sighed.

"Oh, whatever. You know why everything bothers me." My chill was fading away, but I pulled the covers up to my neck anyway.

"Okay, fine." He rubbed the bridge of his nose. "What's bothering you about tonight? What are you actually getting at?"

"I'm not..." I decided just to spit it out. "Did you sleep with any of them?"

"That's what you're getting at?"

"Yeah," I blushed at his surprise. He seemed to think it was obviously stupid, and I couldn't see why. "I mean... you're still... you still... I don't know." I buried myself further under the covers, wishing I could disappear completely. "Do vampires even have sex?"

"Yeah," Jack laughed, and he sat up a little. "We do. I have, yes. Both as a human and as a vampire, although probably not as much as you're thinking."

"I don't know how much I'm thinking," I admitted. My mind vacillated somewhere between one and a million, but none of the numbers sounded right. "How much do you think I'm thinking?"

"Do you actually wanna have this conversation?" He looked at me earnestly. "I'm willing to, if you are, but... do you actually wanna talk about this?"

"I don't know anything about your relationship history at all, and I'd like to," I said, peering at him over the top of the blankets.

"You just look so terrified by it."

"Cause I don't know what I'll find out." My eyes met his for a moment before I dropped them.

"It's not bad," he said, but the pit in my stomach only seemed to grow. It didn't help that this topic made him nervous.

"Well... how about a ballpark figure?" I asked.

"Oh," Jack groaned. "I don't know about that."

"Why not?"

"Because it's misleading."

"Misleading?" I raised an eyebrow, and he leaned back on the couch, relenting.

"Fine." He sighed and ran a hand through his hair. "The thing is, I dated this girl from the time I was 14 until I was 20. I mean, she was the only girl I was with for all of high school. After we broke up, I went out with one other girl for like four months, and that's it. I mean, as a mortal guy, I had tons of girls that were friends, but like no action at all. So, two girls as a human. That's it."

"And then?" I asked nervously.

"When I turned... suddenly hot girls wanted me, and even some hot vampires, which you know, when you're new to this, vampires look really hot." He scratched at his head and shifted uneasily.

"You know how we said that in the beginning, you're hungrier than normal? Like Milo thinks he needs to eat every hour when he really doesn't? And all your emotions are right at the top? Well... so..." He trailed off.

"No, I don't wanna talk about this," Jack decided, rubbing his eye and shaking his head. "It's really not that bad. Honest. But I don't want you to think of me like that. Cause I'm not.

"I mean, I never was. Human, I only ever had sex in relationships, and the past fourteen years I've barely done anything. So I don't want to be judged on the first year or two when I was stupid and young. Okay?"

"Its scaring me more that you won't tell me," I said. "Is it like a thousand girls or something?"

"No, no, god, no!" Jack insisted with wide eyes. "It was like... twenty girls. I think it was like fifteen girls and six vampires. I think. I mean. I'm sorry." His cheeks flushed with shame.

"I'm sorry. I didn't... I don't know." He looked away from me and shook his head. "That's not who I am now. That was just me coming to terms with being a vampire, and being cool and sexy in a way I never was before."

"I see." I swallowed. It wasn't that bad, but it wasn't as good as I had hoped. Like under five would've been an acceptable number for me.

"I'm really sorry."

"No, it's okay. You have nothing to be sorry for. You didn't do anything wrong." I wrapped my arms tightly around myself and I couldn't meet his gaze. "So... did you... have you like actually had relationships since you turned?"

"Kinda, once," Jack said, looking more comfortable with this. "A couple years ago. But other than that, for the past like fourteen years I've been celibate. So I think that counts for something."

"Mmm." I refused to confirm or deny that, because I wasn't sure. "Why did you stop?"

"Stop what?"

"You had sex with a lot of girls, and then you became celibate. Why?" I tried to concentrate on the fact that that was a long time ago, and he stopped. He wasn't still some kind of rich playboy that just went out and hooked up with hot girls just because he could.

"It was boring. It wasn't who I was, and it didn't feel right," he shrugged. "What about you? What's your story?"

"I don't have a story," I said, and he laughed. "What? I don't."

"Really?" Jack gave me a stern look. "Cause I'm pretty sure I just picked you up the other night, and you had been making out with some guy."

"Well, that's it. That's all there is to tell."

I grimaced at the thought of it and felt even worse talking about it sober. Regardless of what our actual status was, it felt like cheating, and it was stupid and pointless. I vowed to never drink alcohol again.

"That's the only time you've ever kissed a guy? I mean, other than me... or Peter." He was dubious, and my hesitation made him nervous, but he didn't understand that there really wasn't anything to tell.

"No, I've kissed guys before," I admitted. "But everything is exactly the same. I'd go to some party with Jane, and there'd be some guy there that I would kiss for a little bit. But it'd never be anything more than that. I've kissed a couple guys when I was drinking. The end."

"Really?" He had moved on from skeptical to bewildered.

"Why is that so hard to believe?"

"I don't know." He settled back into the couch again, furrowing his brow. "I guess I must just be impartial."

"What are you talking about?" I turned to face him more, gently pressing my knee into his leg as I did.

"Well..." Jack laughed nervously, but that didn't affect how perfect it sounded, or the way it sent happy shivers down me. "Like tonight, when you walked into that room, everybody turned and stared. You're kind of irresistible."

"That's different," I said. "That's just because of my blood."

No sooner had the words fallen out of my mouth then a painful realization gripped me. My heart ached and the color drained from my face.

"What?" He moved closer, unsure if he should touch me and console me or if that would only make it worse.

"It's my blood." I bit the inside of my cheek as I worked it out in my head. "That's it, isn't it? That's why you're..."

Jack was attracted to me for the same reason Peter was, but on an entirely different level. And unlike Peter, who should feel bonded to me no matter what, Jack's would all but disappear when I turned. My blood would stop smelling so sweet, and all my appeal would disappear.

"This is all because of the way I smell and taste and the way my stupid heart beats!"

"No!" Jack looked offended. "No! That has nothing to do with the way I feel about you!"

"I walked into a room full of gorgeous people, and they all turned to look at me, plain, ordinary me." An awful lump swelled in my throat, making it difficult to talk. "The only thing that makes me irresistible to them, to you, is my blood."

"Alice!" Sitting up, he looked at me directly. "Okay, fine, you want the truth? Yes! The vampire in me does want the blood in you, more than you can ever imagine.

"But if that was it, then I would've just bitten you a long time ago, or just forgotten about you. I've been hungry before. I've tasted things better than you, okay? You might be a fine wine in the vampire realm, but you're not the only one and you're certainly not the finest on the shelf."

"Is that supposed to make me feel better? Because it's really not," I mumbled, and he shook his head.

"No, I'm just saying your blood isn't that amazing," Jack said. "It's not the only thing binding me to you. If it were, then I wouldn't want you to turn so bad, and I cannot wait for you turn. You, not your blood, are amazing."

"You really can't wait for me turn?" I looked at him hopefully, biting my lip.

"Are you kidding?" Jack laughed. "I'm dying to kiss you."

"Humans are capable of kissing just as much as you are." I leaned in towards him, and while he didn't move in closer, he didn't move away either. His breathing had deepened and his eyes met mine, searching for resistance.

He placed his hand on my cheek, resting his thumb on my skin, and leaned in to kiss me. I'm sure it was supposed to be a sweet, short kiss, but whenever he touched me, it ignited something inside me I couldn't control. I threw my arms around his neck and kissed him greedily, and I loved the frantic feel of his tongue against mine.

Wonderful hot tingles spread through me and my stomach fluttered. He sat back on the couch, and I moved onto his lap so I straddled him. His hands searched all over me, smoldering against my skin.

He kissed me so desperately, as if he was terrified to stop. I dug my fingers into his hair, pulling him as close to me as I possibly could.

I stopped kissing him just long enough for me to pull his shirt off. He looked at me questioningly, but I pressed my mouth to his before either of us could think about it. Pushing myself against him, his fingers dug hungrily into my flesh.

My mind became a delirious fog, and I realized we could be closer still. With him, there were more ways than one, and both of them sounded too tantalizing to pass up. The way his lips touched my neck, I knew which one he wanted the most, but I wanted one that would least likely lead to our deaths.

I looped my fingers into the elastic of his boxers, and he moaned with surprise.

- 15 -

"Sorry to interrupt, but I thought I'd let you know I was home." Ezra's deep voice filled the room, making my heart stop. I looked over my shoulder to see him standing in the doorway to the living room.

"Oh, shit," Jack groaned.

We had stopped kissing, and he let me slide off his lap. He wrapped the blanket around us both and kept an arm around me, warmly pressed up against him. I buried my head in his shoulder and tried to hide under the covers.

"Are you hell bent on getting her killed?" Ezra asked wearily.

Jack dropped his eyes to the floor instead of answering, and Ezra flicked on the living room lights. He went over and sat in the chair across from us. Leaning back, he crossed his leg over his knee.

"Well?" Ezra looked at us expectantly.

"What?" Jack asked, and I moved closer to him.

"I'm waiting for you to explain what is going on with you," Ezra rested a hand on his chin, looking at Jack solemnly. "What do you think you're doing with all of this?"

"I-I don't know," Jack stumbled and rubbed the back of his neck. "I wasn't really thinking. We were just having fun."

"That's your answer for this and for taking her to the club?" Ezra asked, and Jack nodded. "I see."

"This wasn't-" Jack gestured to me but then floundered. "It wasn't anything. I mean, it was under control."

"Jack, I hate to be the one to tell you this, but you don't seem to ever be in control of matters that involve Alice," Ezra told him dryly. "Honestly, what do you think would've happened if I hadn't walked in? Do you think you'd be able to stop yourself?" Jack flinched and pulled away from me.

"I screwed up," Jack sighed. "I get it. I always screw up. You don't need to rub it in."

"That's what you think I'm trying to do?" Ezra sounded offended. "I am trying to keep you both alive."

"I keep her safe," Jack said defensively.

"A vampire club? Jack, really?" Ezra raised an eyebrow and shook his head. "Did you forget what happened when you were human? You nearly died. Vampires may try very hard to live a civilized life, but you know what they're capable of."

"Milo just wanted to check it out, and Alice wanted to get out and do something fun," Jack shifted, and by now, he wasn't touching me at all. Several inches of cold distance sat between us. "I'd been there before, and people go there all the time and they're fine."

"It takes so little to take it all away," Ezra said quietly. "She is so fragile."

"Then why can't we just turn her?" Jack asked plaintively. "Then nobody would have to worry about me accidentally killing her."

"You know I can't do that right now" Ezra rubbed his eyes tiredly.

"Why not?" Jack asked.

"Milo is too young. Young vampires are far too dangerous," Ezra sighed. "Vampires require proper guidance to keep them from turning into something horrendous. Morals and restraint are imperative to our survival. We have the power and strength to destroy everything if we don't live in quiet moderation."

"But we're all here!" Jack insisted growing frustrated. "There's three of us here to the two of them. We'd be fine!"

"You say that because this is what you were born into," Ezra said with a mixture of affection and fatigue. "We were always stable and supportive and calm. You don't know what it's like when there are too many vampires and not enough leadership. You've led a very privileged life, and you're taking that for granted."

"It's just two more vampires," Jack said indignantly.

"It just takes one, Jack!" Ezra raised his voice, and I winced. "I've seen what it does, and I don't want that for us."

"But..." I said meekly, peering at him from over the top of the blankets. "Just because it happened somewhere else doesn't mean it'll happen here."

"I'm sure Mae has told you of the unique position you are in." Ezra rested his deep brown eyes on me. "You are one of the few that has a choice in this life. The rest of us were forced into it."

"She did tell me that, yes," I said.

"She also told you of the family she left behind, and how difficult that was." Ezra rested his elbow on the arm of his chair and propped his head up. "But she told you nothing of my family or where I came from. Correct?"

"I think she said you were from England, but that's it." I looked to Jack for help, but he just watched Ezra intently as he spoke. There was something very captivating in the way Ezra talked, even to other vampires.

"I was born just outside of London in 1674," Ezra said. "By the time I was fifteen, both my parents and two of my brothers had already died, leaving me in charge of my seven-year-old sister and the family farm. We managed to do quite well for ourselves, and I was able to support a family. I married at seventeen and went on to have four children of my own."

"You had kids?" I asked. It never occurred to me that he would be married or have kids.

"Two boys and two girls." His lips touched on a smile that quickly faded. "We lived a quiet happy life, but unfortunately, the skills that made my family thrive made me appealing to others. I was strong, hard-working, and diligent.

"A man called upon our house one night asking for dinner and board for the evening in exchange for money. Because of where we lived in the country, it wasn't uncommon for weary travelers to take respite with us. My sister especially enjoyed it. She was at the marrying age and had yet to find a suitor.

"The man introduced himself as Willem, and he appeared wealthy and attractive, so I sent my sister to tend to him, in hopes that he would consider her." He lowered his eyes, thinking heavily on the memory, and then shook his head.

"He stayed in the back room of the house, and he mentioned he was hungry. I sent my sister back with a bowl of soup, and when she

170

didn't return, I went back to check on her." Ezra paused. "Willem stood in front of the window, staring at the black night, while my sister lay motionless on the floor. He drained all the life from her.

"I meant to attack him in some way, but he was much stronger than me and over took me. He commended me on my bravery and strength, and then forced me to drink his blood," Ezra grimaced.

"Before I could really understand what was happening, his blood ripped through me, and he drug me off into the night. Once I had turned and had my power back, I fought him, trying to kill him or at least demanding that he let me go. He refused, saying that he had needed a worker and companion, and I suited his desires perfectly.

"I continued fighting him, but he grew tired of it. He shackled me in the cellar of his castle. He did not feed me for three weeks, and I was a new vampire, so I was mad with hunger." Ezra's face had become an emotionless mask. "Then, he took me to my home, and released me.

"In my desperate thirst, I bit my own wife. My children managed to escape before I got to them, but not before they witnessed me killing their mother.

"When I realized what I had done, I went back to Willem." His expression changed as he shifted in his chair, and he tried to put that memory behind him. "I let him enslave me under the condition that he never let me go. I did not trust the monster I had become, and I didn't know how to destroy myself.

"Over time, Willem would bring in other vampires, turned the same way as I had for the same reasons, in hopes of helping me work. He was always expanding on the castle and traveling, and he liked to live a life of complete leisure. I did absolutely everything for him, even things you wouldn't think a man would dare request." He repressed a shudder.

"These other vampires he brought in, they were always a mess," Ezra went on. "They were rabid monsters, and it was only a matter of time before they would have to be destroyed. Without any guidance, they resorted to their own primal state, relying solely on hunger and instinct. They had to be constantly chained to keep them from hurting themselves and other vampires.

"Only I seemed to have humanity. I stayed with Willem for nearly a hundred years, traveling all across Europe and Asia. Most of other vampires we encountered had some sense of decency and control. Most tended to be cold and cruel, like Willem, but not animals, like the slaves Willem made. As time went on, the other vampires would comment on how wonderful and amazing it was that Willem had managed to create a slave as civil as me.

"That's when it finally occurred to me that I wasn't like them. What had happened with my wife had been a direct result of Willem's manipulation. I could control myself, and I had openly wept for my wife and my children. I was not a monster, although I was capable of being one if I let myself." He exhaled deeply and looked on me for a moment.

"What happened?" I asked when he didn't speak.

"One night, I simply killed Willem, and I left to start a life of my own," Ezra said. "I had made some acquaintances through him that I thought were compassionate, and with them, I managed to learn things about myself and other vampires. They were impressed that I had been able to do what I had done without instruction.

"When you first turn, it is so easy to let emotion and instinct rule your life. It's a constant battle for years that's nearly impossible without another vampire coaching you along."

"I know how hard all of that was for you," Jack said carefully, and then shook his head. "Okay, no. I don't. I can't even imagine all the things you went through. But what happened to you isn't anything like what's happening here. Nobody's going to throw Milo or Alice in the basement and tell them to just figure it out."

"It's not a risk I am willing to take," Ezra said. "I have seen vampires gnaw at their own arms because they haven't fed in days. I've seen them slaughter children. Alice and Milo might never be that extreme, but they could turn out like Willem. He was in complete control of himself, but he was cruel and merciless."

"Don't you think Willem was probably like that before he turned?" Jack asked. "I mean, Mae was all love and maternal instinct before she turned, and she still is. And I was a clumsy idiot, and I still am. Milo and Alice aren't tyrannical or malicious."

"Left unchecked, Milo's jealousy could've gotten out of control. He could've killed her by now. But because you were able to devote all your time to his cause, look," Ezra nodded at us. "You're completely safe to kill her yourself."

"Haha," Jack said dryly.

"You will have all the time in the world," Ezra said. "What are a few more years in comparison with eternity? I'm asking that we err on the side of caution. Wouldn't you rather wait then have something go terribly awry?"

"But there's nothing to be cautious about!" Jack was growing exasperated.

"I'm sorry, but the plane ride has exhausted me, as has this conversation." Ezra stood up, blithely stretching his limbs. "I'm going to turn in for the night, and I suggest you do the same."

When he left, we sat in silence. I thought of everything he had said, and Ezra had a point. But so did Jack. The odds of me or Milo turning into crazed fiends seemed unlikely, but waiting wouldn't really hurt anything either.

Eventually, Jack pulled back on his tee shirt, and I excused myself, heading to his room for a night of sleeping alone.

Of course, it wouldn't be an easy sleep, not after everything the night had held. It was full of endless dreams of Ezra and his lovely wife and small, towheaded children that looked like small versions of him. Then I would see their faces, contorting with fear, as they were splashed with their mother's blood.

Ezra, the most contained person I had ever met, had been so out of control that he had nearly murdered his own children. What hope did that leave for any of us?

Jack took me home just after midnight the next night, citing that I needed to start getting to bed at a reasonable time for school. With less than a week to fix my sleep cycle, it didn't seem possible, but that's not why he really took me home.

After the kiss, and then Ezra's rather unfortunate story, Jack had seemed oddly distant. He still talked to me, but when he put in a movie, he made sure to sit on the far side of the room.

Without Milo constantly straightening up combined with me spending more time at home, the apartment was rather messy. Not enough where Mom would scream at me about it, but enough where I noticed it and decided to do something about it.

I put Fall Out Boy on the stereo and went about picking things up. After that, I took a long shower and crawled into bed. It was still much too early to sleep, at least for me, so I pulled out *A Brief History of Vampyres*, the biography supposedly written by Peter.

After detailing his own experiences with turning, including graphic descriptions of watching other vampires turn, the next chapter was entitled "*Vampyres and the Earth*." I was glad to be done with talk of turning. He wrote one particularly disturbing passage where he recalled seeing a young man's stomach bubble and move as he screamed.

The following chapter opened with a beautiful description of a sunrise and a poem called "Sunrise on the Hills" by Henry Wadsworth Longfellow. In his youth, Peter was apparently obsessed with the sun.

It appeared to be a vampire's one true weakness, and he struggled to understand it. He would spend hours out in the bright afternoon light, trying to discover what exactly it did to him.

"I would bask in the sun, like an afternoon cat, leaving as much of my flesh uncovered as modesty would allow. The rays of light burned heavy on my skin and my muscles started to drain. My energy weakened, my thoughts muddled, but in complete contrast with that, my heart beat grew stronger and faster.

"When I returned to the darkness and proceeded to slumber, once I awoke, all of the effects would be erased. My skin never even changed its hue.

"What precisely did the sun do to me, then? When I asked my fellow vampyres, they speculated very little on the subject. The most informed answer came from my mentor, who said, 'It does a man well to stay in the light, and a vampyre to stay out of it.' The anatomy of a vampyre remains such a mystery that the best we can come up with is merely that the light weakens us.

"But what if I were to stay in the sun always? If I were to exist as a normal man would, sleeping during the night and awaking during the day, what would the outcome be? The sun only seems to dull all our senses, lessening them to the point of mere humans.

"Would that surmise that living a life in the sun could reduce us to mortality? Would we then begin to age and grow old and eventually perish?

"Which leads me to an entirely different thought. Does our immortality, our exotic power, then come from the moon? Are the tales of lycanthrope embellished stories of vampyre?"

For being a document that's meant to answer questions, it faired better at raising them. Peter could find little in the way of scientific reasons for the sun's effect on vampires. He did conduct his own study on whether the sun could return him to a mortal, or at least to aging him some.

He spent a month living during the day and sleeping at night, but all he found was that he was very tired, weak, and inordinately hungry. As a result, he had to eat at least once a day, and it led him to nearly kill three people.

At the end of a month, he decided that was enough and finished his study without any real change to himself.

Lying in my bed, I rolled over and peeked out my curtains at the bluing sky. The sun hadn't risen yet, but it was well on its way, meaning I had failed at following through with Jack's suggested bedtime. I set the book aside and decided that I had better try to get some sleep.

I managed to sleep all day, even through the baking heat of the afternoon. When I finally got up and turned on the TV, the weatherman announced it had peaked over ninety degrees. I was tempted to lie around in my underwear all day long, but Mom was still around, complaining about the heat and her job and life in general.

After she left, I stared at my phone, hoping that someone would hurry and call me and rescue me from the insane heat. There would be no such luck.

As the day moved onto night, I resigned myself to spending the evening parked in front of a fan, sprawled out on the couch watching *Arsenic and Old Lace* on AMC until I died of heatstroke.

- 16 -

"This building needs central air!" Milo threw open the apartment door.

I sat up and looked over the back of the couch at him. His arms overflowed with bags of groceries. His face looked flushed, presumably from the heat.

"What are you doing here?" I asked, surprised by his random appearance.

I got up off the couch and went over to help him with the groceries, until I realized how silly that sounded. Normally, when Milo carried things in, I'd be stuck with the brunt of the load since I was stronger. It was hard to shake the image of him as being my little brother, even though he was clearly so much stronger and better than I was.

"What? You're not happy to see me?" He set the bags on the table and smirked at me.

"No, it's not that. I just…" I stopped and looked over the bags on the table. "What is all this? And what are you doing here?"

"I figured you hadn't eaten a good meal since I moved out, and I thought you'd be bored and dying of heat stroke." Milo dug through the bags and pulled out frozen things, like ice cream and Popsicles, and put them in the freezer. "I know you and Mom don't do any grocery shopping, so you'd waste away without me."

"That's maybe true," I admitted, eyeing him skeptically.

He continued going through the bags to put things away, while I went over to the freezer and pulled an orange Popsicle out. He was actually dead-on about the lack of food and heat stroke.

"Aren't you afraid Mom'll catch you?"

"She's at work," Milo shrugged. "And so is Jack. So it's very quiet at the house and I needed to get out."

"Jack's at work?" I hopped on the counter to watch Milo put the groceries away. "I thought Ezra just came back."

"He did, and he's still at home." With ease, he reached over me to put away cereal on the very top shelf, something that used to require the aid of a chair for him to reach. "Jack went on his own. He's really getting the hang of the business."

"What do you mean? Jack's in charge of stuff all by himself?" I slurped at my Popsicle, trying to keep orange drips of juice from spilling on my legs, but it wasn't working.

"Yeah. Why is that so shocking?" Milo laughed at my apparent surprise.

"It's not." Wiping at the spot of orange on my thigh, I shrugged. "I just didn't realize he was doing that good or whatever. I don't know. I mean, I don't even know what he does really."

"Neither do I. They're keeping me out of the loop for now, but Jack says that once I get more settled in, I'll definitely be able to do it. He says it's actually kind of fun when you get into it, but a lot of the work is already done anyway.

"Ezra has tons and tons of patents on things, and he has to do a lot of legal shuffling around so people don't catch onto the fact that he's the same guy that's been collecting money for the past hundred years or so." Milo said it all matter-of-factly like I would completely follow what that meant.

"So, what? Pretty soon you're gonna be a millionaire?" I bit off the last chunk of Popsicle, even though my gums didn't necessarily appreciate the cold.

"Alice, I hate to break it to you, but I already kind of am." Milo looked rather sheepish as he put away the last of the groceries in the fridge, and then turned to face me.

"Well, they're super rich or whatever, but you just live with them," I said.

"Yeah, but…" He shifted, fearing the worst from my reaction. "I'm like part of the family now. So, Ezra set up credit cards and an expense account for me the other day, and Ezra's working on documents to legally change my name to Milo Townsend.

"Once that's through, I'm going to get a driver's license, but it's going to say that I'm 18, since I can pass for it now and it'll be easier to get things done that way."

"Nah ah," I gaped at him. "You have an expense account?"

"Yeah, I mean, it's just easier that way. So I can buy my own things." He shrugged, then added, "And groceries for you too. I'm spreading it around."

"But…" My face crinkled. "But that's their money. Don't you feel bad about taking it?"

"Not really," Milo admitted. "I didn't really feel bad about taking Mom's money. As soon as I'm able to, and as soon as they'll let me, I'm gonna start working. I'll pull my own share. I'm kind of a kid right now, and they just adopted me."

"They are adopting you, aren't they?" It hit me in a weird way that Milo wasn't really my brother anymore. He was, and he always would be, but at the same time, he wasn't. "Milo *Townsend?*"

"Yeah, it sounds weird, right?" He wrinkled his nose, and I felt a little better knowing it was strange for him too.

"Whose last name is that anyway?" I chewed on the wooden Popsicle stick and tried to seem casual about Milo's news.

"I think its Ezra's. Jack's is really Hobbs, and Mae's is Everly, but I don't really know what Peter's was." He leaned back against the refrigerator, watching me swing my feet and chew on the stick. "They don't really talk much about Peter."

"That's not surprising." The wood splintered so I tossed the stick in the garbage can and looked over at him. "What do they say about him?"

"Mae told me about you guys being bonded and about how Peter nearly killed you before." A shudder ran over him at that. "Why didn't you tell me about that?"

"How could I?" I asked. "You weren't supposed to know they were vampires. It'd be pretty weird to just say, oh yeah, Peter tried to drink all my blood."

"How could you not tell me all this stuff?" Milo looked hurt and offended. "Jack told me you were going to turn last spring, but you changed your mind because of me. And I appreciate that, I really do, but you almost did! And you wouldn't have told me about it? You were trying to make the biggest decision of your life, and you didn't mention anything to me."

"I couldn't tell you anything," I sighed. "They told me not to, and I raised the same argument. How would it be better for me to just disappear instead of telling you something. And they said it would be too hard for you to live a normal life while knowing that they exist."

"But you could've made up something," Milo shook his head. "You could've just told me about the whole triangle thing with Peter and Jack, and said you were thinking about running away with one of them. That was close to the truth."

"I don't know. I didn't think of it, I guess," I sighed. "Look, I'm sorry I didn't tell you anything. But at least I can talk to you about it now, right?"

"On the subject of which," Milo grinned and titled his head. "What's this I hear about you kissing Jack last night?"

"Word travels fast." I avoided his eyes and what they insinuated.

"Come on. There's like four people in that house. You're the only word there," he laughed, shaking his head. "What else would we really talk about?"

Looking down at my feet made me realize how badly the dark purple nail polish was chipping on my toes. In order to reach it better, I pulled my knee to my chest and started scraping at the nail polish with my fingers.

"That's really hygienic." Milo nodded to my foot being on the counter, and I stuck my tongue out at him.

"What do you care? You don't eat here anymore." I smiled, almost sadly. "Hell, you don't even eat anymore. Or get sick. I don't think this is really an issue for you."

"You're avoiding the major issue." He pulled out a kitchen chair and sat down, then tapped the empty spot next to him. "Come on. Have a seat, and tell me all the juicy details."

"There isn't anything juicy to tell!" I groaned and stayed where I was.

"You kissed Jack! There's got to be something to tell!"

"Are you even cool with talking about this?" I looked up at him, studying his face for any jealous aggression that might be brewing underneath.

"Yeah, I'm so over that." He leaned back and rolled his eyes, then shook his head. "Okay, I'm not like completely over him per se, but I'm not crazy jealous anymore. Remember at the club? I didn't freak out then, and he was all over you most of the night."

"He was not all over me," I said, but my cheeks burned crimson. "He protected me a lot, and so he had to touch me. But it wasn't like we were making out or anything."

"No, that was for later." Milo winked at me.

"It wasn't like that!"

"Alice, everyone gets it. You and Jack are seriously into each other. What exactly do you think you're hiding from me? And more importantly, why do you think you need to hide it from me?" Milo asked me directly, and I squirmed a bit.

"I don't know." I kept my arms wrapped around my leg and rested my head against my knee. "I guess I'm just not used to talking about any of this stuff. And I can't really explain it, but I feel weird talking about it because of Peter."

"Peter? He's not even here. What does he have to do with anything?" Milo's brown eyes were filled with confusion.

"Nothing." I shook my head. "Everything. Did Mae explain to you what it meant to be bonded?"

"Yeah. I mean, she did the best she could, but considering I've never even had a boyfriend, it's a little hard for me to get a handle on what you guys feel." Looking the way he did, it would be hard to believe that he'd stay single for much longer.

"It's not like having a boyfriend." I chewed my fingernails and stared down at the faded floor tile, thinking of how to explain it. "In a really abstract way, it's like having a crush, but it's far more physical than that. From what I can tell, from when Jack's really having bloodlust, it's something similar to that."

"What are you talking about?" Milo squinted at me. "You know what Jack feels when he's hungry?"

"Kinda. I can feel what he feels, most of the time. Not exactly, unless it's really intense, but I usually have a sense of what's going on with him. I think he always purposely eats before we're together, just to be safe, but I've felt what he feels when he really wants my blood."

A change inside of Jack was completely visceral when he wanted me that way. Raw and intense, there was something frightening about it, but it was completely exhilarating and always made me want him more.

"Wait, wait, wait!" Milo waved his hands to stop. "You feel what he feels? That's not normal, is it? You never did that before."

"No. I don't know if it's normal." With a wry smile, I added, "But then again, I don't really know what's normal."

185

"So, is it him, or is it you that's behaving unnaturally?" He overlooked my attempt at a joke and kept staring at me severely. That was just like him. He'd discovered something he didn't understand and he had to figure it out. "Is he pushing his emotions on you, or are you picking up on things?"

"Both?" I shrugged helplessly. "From what I gather, nothing about the way Jack and I feel is natural. He's not supposed to be into me, you know? I'm only supposed to want Peter, who doesn't even want me at all."

"Huh." Milo took a deep breath and nodded. "It sounds like a clear case of nature vs. nurture."

He sounded like a doctor giving a diagnosis, and I would've mocked him for it if I hadn't been intrigued. (Something along the lines of "you're gonna have to face it – you're addicted to love" would've fit there nicely).

"What?"

"You understand the concept of nature vs. nurture, right?" He gave me that exasperated look he'd been prone to giving me when he taught me calculus. "It's the basic argument for what compels people to do anything. Is it because of our biology, our animal instincts, or because of the way we were brought up? Do men cheat because of a biological imperative or because they had an absent father?"

"I think those are both too blanket of answers for either of them to really be correct," I said. "Give two men the same biology and the same upbringing, and they could still make two entirely different decisions."

"You're missing the point," Milo waved me off. "Peter and you, that's 100% pure nature. Your biology is what draws you together, but for reasons I don't fully understand, Peter's fighting it.

"At the same time, Jack is falling for you because of who you are and who he is. He nurtured a relationship with you. From a scientific stand point, it's very fascinating."

"I'm glad my quandary of a love life is fascinating. At least it serves a purpose," I muttered dryly.

"I don't really see a quandary." He turned his attention to spinning a bottle top on the table. "You and Jack like each other, and Peter's out of the picture. Problem solved."

"I'm sure that we'd run into Peter in the next millennia."

"What makes you think you'll live a millennia?" Milo replied.

"Immortality, for one thing." I dropped my foot from the counter and leaned back, stretching the kink in my shoulders.

"Immortality isn't really immortality, you know," Milo told me evenly. "It's just very long longevity."

"So you came over to point out that I'm a magnificent specimen in the case for nature vs. nurture, and then tell me that I'm going to die?" I raised my eyebrow at him.

"No, actually." Milo jumped up suddenly, scaring me. He moved quicker than he ever had before, and his movements were losing that clumsy edge they had when he first turned. "I came over to make you supper."

"You can still cook?" That sounded much smarter in my head. Because every single thing about Milo had improved upon from the way he was before, it'd be silly to think his cooking skills magically dissolved.

"Yes! And I'm making your favorite." He went over to the fridge and rummaged through it.

"Hey, can you eat food?" I asked, and again, it sounded smarter in my head.

"Well, yeah, I can eat it. I just can't digest it." Milo turned back to face me, his arms overflowing with food. "Jack dared me to try an orange last week, and it tasted terrible. Like eating acidic salt or something. I don't even know how to explain it to you. But I ate it, and then like five minutes later, I felt terrible and threw up. So that was the end of that."

"Gross." I hopped off the counter and took some of the vegetables away from him so I could wash them up.

"Food isn't appealing anymore. The only thing that ever sounds good is blood. And you know what else? Blood tastes different!" Milo said this really excitedly, like he was shedding light on something for me.

"You mean like from how it tasted when you were human?"

"Yeah, but that's not what I meant. Different kinds of blood have different flavors. It's just really weird cause I'll find myself craving different types. Blood from women tastes different, and Asian blood is different, and then the types, like O or AB positive taste different too," Milo went on, and he was talking the same way he used to talk about ingredients for a new recipe he'd just learned. "There's a whole cornucopia of flavors out there!"

"Good to know," I replied, unsure of what else to say to that.

"I bet your blood tastes really good." Milo stared at me intently, enough to make me nervous, and I moved away a little bit. "It smells sweet and… rich."

"Thanks. And I don't mean to be rude, but you're kind of freaking me out right now."

"Sorry." He shook his head and went back to slicing a tomato. "I just can't *not* smell you, you know?"

"Well, try not to fantasize about eating me at least," I grimaced.

Milo managed to not eat me while he made the rest of my meal. He sat down and watched me eat, but it still felt nice, like we were eating together like we used to. Even though he didn't really look like my brother, and he wasn't really anymore, we were still family.

We were just turning into a whole different kind of family.

- 17 -

Vampires needed oxygen, just not as much as people. Living on minimal oxygen was an important skill vampires could add to their arsenal, if only they could master it. That's pretty much a direct quote from Jack, right there. Maybe not all of it, but the word "arsenal" was definitely in there. That's the explanation he gave for today's exercise.

"Exercise" was another word he used, and I hadn't realized how seriously he took everything with Milo. When he had texted me earlier, he said that I could come over, but he'd be pretty busy with Milo. Ezra had gone somewhere, so Mae could use the company.

Jack picked me up, giving me the briefest of explanations before he and Milo changed into their swim trunks. That only made it harder for me to understand things because Jack shirtless was captivating.

Not to mention how distracting Milo was. Obviously, I wasn't attracted to him in anyway, but I had spent all summer seeing him in swim trunks, and he had looked nothing like he did now. He was all muscle and chiseled abs.

Milo didn't need to breathe as much as he did, but his body didn't realize that yet. The best way to train his lungs would be to put him somewhere he wouldn't be able to breathe. Jack's idea was to submerge him underwater, the same way Peter taught Jack not to breathe.

Apparently, it's terrifying the first couple of times he did it, since his mind didn't understand that it wasn't about to die. So Jack recommended that I stay in the house while he went out with Milo, lest I get freaked out.

I stood at the French doors, staring out at the black lake behind the house. There wasn't a moon in the sky, and a rather eerie cloud cover had swept over, blinding all the stars.

The back deck lights were off, making it easier for me to see the dock and lake, but I couldn't really see much of anything. The water was like a black abyss, and every now again, I would catch something shimmering off it, but Milo and Jack were completely lost in it.

Matilda sat next to me, whimpering with anticipation. Jack left her inside because, like me, she had the habit of getting nervous and freaking out. I knew Milo was perfectly safe. Almost nothing in the world could hurt him, and certainly nothing in that lake. But that's where he had almost died, where his blood still stained the end of the dock, and my heart felt cold and tight in my chest.

"They're going to be fine," Mae reassured me for the seven-hundredth time that night.

She stood behind me, leaning against the doorway into the dining room, with her arms crossed loosely over her chest. In the other room, I heard Nina Simone playing, and I imagined that Mae was curled up on the couch, reading a book. Or at least that's what she was doing when she wasn't busy checking on me.

"I know." I thought I saw something, but it was gone before I could even make it out.

"You're just going to stand there all night then?" Her words came out soft and disappointed.

"I don't know." I wanted to pull myself away, but I couldn't shake the feeling that if I looked away, something would happen. As if the lake somehow had it in for Milo, and it was just waiting to finish the job when I wasn't paying attention.

"You know what? That's not good enough." Before I could protest, Mae looped her arm through mine and pulled me away from the glass. "Come on. That's more than enough for one night."

"Mae." I actually tried to free myself from her. While her grip felt friendly and gentle, it was really a death grip. Any amount of tugging and pulling I did would do little more than bruise me. "I just feel better if I'm watching."

"I know that, love, but it's not accomplishing anything. Honest."

She led me into the living room. It was dimly lit with several candles and a lamp, but my eyes had been so accustomed with darkness that it almost hurt to look around. Everything smelled of lilacs and lilies, courtesy of the candles, and I breathed in.

"What are we going to accomplish in here?" I asked.

"You're going to relax." Mae yanked me down on to the overstuffed couch with her.

Matilda had followed us in and stood in the middle of the room, looking at me questioningly. Apparently, she felt guilty for abandoning her post too.

"I relax all the time. I've done nothing but relax all summer long. Maybe my entire life, even." I pulled my knees up to my chest, and Mae laughed faintly.

"Alice, if you're going to live forever, you've really got to learn how to live!" Mae teased.

Her fingers combed through my hair, and she turned me so my back was to her. I heard the clamor of something, and when I looked out of the corner of my eye, I saw her getting a brush and hair clips off the end table beside her.

Following suit, I patted the couch with my hand, and Matilda hopped up next to me. As Mae played with my hair, I ran my hands through Matilda's thick, white fur.

"What does that even mean?" I asked as Mae pulled and teased at my hair.

"Hmm?" She'd already forgotten what she'd said to me.

"That I have to learn how to live. What's wrong with the way I live?"

"Nothing," Mae replied, but with a heavy sigh, she changes her mind. "Well, you need to worry less."

"Less?" I asked incredulously. "I think if anything, I'm a little over relaxed, given my circumstance."

"But you know you have nothing to worry about. You're always concerning yourself with how things are going to end, when they're not going to end for a very long time. It's much better to live in the here and now."

"Really?" I scratched Matilda's ear and had to suppress a laugh. "Every time Jack and I get caught living in the here and now, we get a lecture. I don't think that's really what you want for me."

"Living in the present doesn't mean giving into your every whim," Mae said sternly.

"I give into very few of my whims," I muttered. "Trust me. I have a lot more whims that you don't even know about."

"Now you're just being vulgar." She made a "tsk" sound.

"Have you heard from Peter?" I asked quietly.

It was hard not to think about him and what his return would imply. My heart always sped up at the mention of him, and while it still made me feel ashamed, I didn't mind as much when Jack wasn't around.

I heard her intake of breath at his name, and the way she braided my hair got tighter and more painful. Maybe she spent too much time trying not think about the future.

"He called Ezra last week," Mae answered tentatively.

"And?" I tried to turn my head to look at her, but she pushed it back away from her.

"Ezra's with him right now." Mae's voice dropped so low, it was almost inaudible, and my heart stopped. Her hands let go of my hair, allowing me to face her. "They're working on some business together. Jack doesn't know."

"How could he not know? Why wouldn't Ezra tell him?" I wanted to shout, and I felt like I was, but my voice came out surprisingly quiet. Just talking about Peter had a way of taking all the oxygen out of the room.

"Jack would probably quit and move out and run away and all that." Mae lowered her eyes. "He can be so melodramatic sometimes."

"That's pretty much what Peter did, isn't it?" I asked.

"Peter had too." She shook her head "You know I don't agree with how he's handled things with you. Especially what he did in the end... That's unforgivable.

"But you've got to understand. Peter and Ezra were together for a hundred years before I was even born. Peter gave Ezra a piece of his humanity back, and without him, I'm not sure Ezra would've stayed sane all those years."

"Ezra told me about his past," I said, and she nodded evenly.

"It's more than that, Alice. They are brothers, probably even closer than you are with Milo." Her expression softened, and she took my hand in hers. "He can't just shut him out. But he can't lose Jack or you either. Family is very important to Ezra."

"I don't want Peter gone either," I said carefully, and I was surprised by how true that was.

My body felt like a livewire that had just been activated. All my veins and cells tingled at the mention of him, and that dull ache I ignored pulsated like a fresh knife wound in my chest. Everything that coursed through me, coursed through me for him, and I knew that.

"You still feel it for him, then?" Mae had gone pale and her eyes had widened with worry.

"I can't stop feeling it," I said wearily. "I want to, sometimes, but I can't. And I don't think I can stop feeling anything for Jack either. But... I still miss Peter, and I'd miss Jack. I don't know how I'm supposed to make sense of that."

"You're not. You're not supposed to feel that way." Mae smiled sadly at me and tucked a stray hair back. "But you already knew that."

"Where is Peter?"

"He's away, Alice," Mae told me firmly. "And that's the way it needs to stay. He's not good for you. At least not right now, not with the way you both feel."

"I didn't want to see him." I shook my head forcefully, maybe too forcefully. "I have no reason to see him. I was just wondering. So I would know."

"Ezra is working on some things," Mae went on, ignoring the fact that I protested a little too much. "Things will be settled soon. It may seem like a long time to you, but that's just your age talking. Things will be better, though."

I settled back in the couch, trying to slow the explosion of nerves inside of me, and Matilda rested her gigantic head on my lap. Mae went back to stroking my hair and trying to convince me that even fairy tales had their share of problems to work through.

I didn't appreciate the way I still felt about Peter. By now, my feelings for him should've faded, especially after what he did to me. They should've been gone. But they weren't.

It didn't help that Jack wasn't around to remind me what truly mattered. He stayed out all night with Milo, practicing in the lake. It was much longer than I was comfortable with, so eventually Mae went to check on them.

Once she confirmed that they were alright, she put in *Breakfast at Tiffany's*, and curled up next to me on the couch. I lay with her, but I couldn't concentrate on the movie. I couldn't concentrate on anything.

Somewhere during the night, I fell asleep. I didn't even realize it until Jack was lifting me up and carrying me out to the car. When I woke up, I put my arms around his neck and snuggled closer to him, relishing the way he smelled and how safe his arms felt.

"I'm glad to see you too," Jack laughed quietly when I moved in close to him. "I didn't mean to wake you."

"No, its okay," I said. When he set me down in the car, I was sad to let him go. "Why are you taking me home?"

"Mae thought it would be better, after what happened last time." He shrugged and walked around to the other side of the car so he could get in.

"How did things go with Milo?" I yawned, and he just grinned at me.

"Good. Real good."

"I really wish I could've seen you more tonight." I let myself slide down in the seat so I was more comfortable. My body felt unnecessarily tired, already readjusting itself for the upcoming school schedule. "I think I needed to."

"Yeah, me too." Jack watched me struggle to stay awake. "Why don't you just sleep? We can talk tomorrow."

Despite my best efforts, I fell asleep again, and I really wondered what my problem was. Thinking about Peter too much had exhausted me, apparently.

When I got home, I didn't even wake up at all. The next thing I knew after being in the car with Jack was waking up in my own bed.

It was reassuring knowing he'd taken me up, but something felt tragic about how little I'd see him. For some reason, I cried myself back to sleep.

This was the last night I could stay out as late as I wanted. Tomorrow would be my last full day before the start of my senior year, and my stomach cringed at the thought of it.

I didn't even want to get out of bed. Part of me knew that my response should be to be party it up until the break of dawn, but I felt too depressed to even get out of bed.

Burying myself deeper in the bed, I ignored text messages from Jane. When broken down, they all said the same basic thing. "Hey girl! Let's get drunk!" That was one of them verbatim, the "hey girl" and everything. I can't imagine when she picked that up, but I hoped she dropped it pretty quickly.

Even Milo had texted me, but I didn't reply to him either. He mostly just informed me that he was bored since Jack was gone, off meeting Ezra somewhere for some stupid business transaction.

I closed my eyes to the night outside my window, and I wondered how Jack wore his hair when he went on this business adventures with Ezra. Did he lay it flat, or gel it into the mess he normally has it? Did he wear a suit and tie? I could only picture him in the corner of some business meeting, playing Pac-Man on his cell phone, with his hair much too cockeyed for what could be considered appropriate.

This was the last night I could stay up all night, and he was gone. That's what had really gotten to me, and part of it was my fault. If I hadn't mocked him about his lack of interest in a career or fiscal responsibility, he might not have felt it necessary to learn the family trade.

"Alice!"

I heard Milo yelling from another room, and I didn't even hear the front door to the apartment open. He was calling my name, and I just pulled the covers over my head. It was really too hot for them, but I just wanted to bury myself and sink into oblivion.

"Alice," Milo said disapprovingly, after I heard the creek of my bedroom door opening. "What are you doing? Trying to give yourself heat stroke?"

"Maybe."

"What's going on with you? I texted you like ten times." He peeled back the blankets when I didn't answer, and I tried to hide how refreshing it felt for my head to be out in the open. "Is this about school starting? It's just school. It's not the end of the world."

"What do you think people will say when it really is the end of the world?" I wondered dryly. "It's the end of the world, but at least it's not school. Or prison. Or shots. Or whatever else isn't the end of the world."

"You're not very good at being contemplative," Milo said. "You always sound like some bad caricature of a philosopher, like those fortune cookies with 'Confucius say' or the Nietzsche guy from *Mystery Men* that's always saying 'when you walk on the ground, the ground walks on you.'"

"This is you cheering me up?"

I turned to look at him, trying to cast him a dubious glare in the light streaming in from the streetlamp outside my window, but he wasn't even looking in my direction. He sat on my bed with his back to me, and he appeared to be filing his nails, or something equally gay.

"Hardly. This is me entertaining myself." He tossed aside the emery board, and finally looked back at me. "Jack's gone and I am bored with a capital 'O.'"

"Why a capital 'O?' It starts with a B. That doesn't even make sense."

"Why does the first letter always have to be capitalized? Vowels are more dramatic."

"It's not grammatically correct to capitalize the second letter. It's just the way the English language is," I said.

"Well, maybe I'll change grammar. I'm a vampire now. I can do anything I want." He flashed a 100 watt smile at me and threw himself down on the bed, sprawling out over my legs. Propping his head up on his elbow, he patted my stomach. "You've gotta get out of this bed. We're gonna do something."

"There's nothing to do," I groaned.

There were plenty of things to do in the Cities on a Saturday night. I just didn't want to do any of them. Lying in bed was the most excitement I could handle.

I hadn't even read any of Peter's book today because it just seemed like too much work. That, and I thought it would be better if I worked at trying to just forget him. I didn't know how or even if that would be possible, but it couldn't hurt to try.

"Oh, Alice," Milo sighed, tilting his head at me. "What am I going to do with you?"

"Nothing. I'm going to stay here. And do nothing."

No sooner had the words left my mouth then my phone started ringing. Before I could even think to reach for it, Milo jumped and grabbed it off the night stand. His reflexes were lightening fast, so at least Jack's training appeared to be working. Not that I fully understood what Milo needed to train for. It wasn't as if he was a soldier, after all.

"It's Jane!" Milo scrolled through my phone and read the text message. "And she has a marvelous idea!"

"I don't even wanna know what it is." I tried pulling the covers back over my head, but Milo grabbed them and stopped me.

"You need to hurry up and get ready." He finished texting her a reply and flipped my phone shut again. "She's going to be here in twenty minutes."

"What the hell for?" I growled.

"We're going out. Clubs." He quickly added, "No vampire ones. We all know how those sit with you."

"We can't get into clubs." I shook my head. "We're too young, and we always get turned away."

"You never went with me before." Milo winked at me. "I'm like a good luck charm."

"I've had nothing but bad luck since you got here." I tried to roll over, but he gently placed a hand on my arm.

"Alice, come on. It'll be fun. I promise. And it's not like you have anything better to do."

"What's in it for me?" I rolled back over to face him, eyeing him up.

"A good time!" Milo grabbed my hand, yanking me out from bed. "You've got to hurry. You can't go to clubs looking all sweaty and hot!"

"Wait, wait, wait!" I protested when he pulled me to my feet. "You're a vampire now. Don't you think Jane will notice?"

"She never sees me or pays attention when she does. Just tell her I had a growth spurt," Milo decided.

"A growth spurt?" I scoffed.

"This is Jane! She doesn't put a lot of thought into anything, except how she looks. We'll be fine."

I let him rush around my room and play dress up with me. Ordinarily, when I got ready, I would at least express an interest picking things out, but I was basically being forced out against my will. If it wasn't comfy pajama type clothes, I didn't really want any of it.

When Milo decided I looked good enough to present in public, I stood in front of the mirror in my bedroom, inspecting myself. He picked out a light weight dress that felt good in the heat, and I smoothed it down.

"Oh, you look good," Milo said. "And I don't know why you care so much if you don't even wanna go out."

"If I'm going out – with you and Jane – I need all the help I can get." At the mention of Jane, I glanced over at the clock. "She's like ten minutes late. Are you sure she's coming?"

"Alice, it's Jane. She's always late."

Besides being vaguely depressed, I was a bit jumpy. I really needed to get out and enjoy myself while I still could and shake this ridiculous sense of foreboding.

"Is this the book?" Milo asked. Peter's book had been sitting on my nightstand, and he flipped through it. "Oh, yeah. It sure is. Huh."

"What?" I turned to face him, wondering what that little "huh" was about it. "What book?"

"This book." He held it up for me to see.

"I know what book you're talking about, but what did you mean by 'this' book? How did you even know about it?" I wanted to walk over and snatch it from his hands, but that felt inappropriate, so I fiddled with the hem of my dress.

"It's Peter's book. Jack told me." He skimmed a page, losing interest in the conversation. When I asked what Jack had told him, he just kept on reading.

"Milo?" I repeated louder, and when he still didn't look up, I went over and grabbed the book from him.

"What'd you do that for?" Milo demanded.

"You were ignoring me." I took a step back from him, finding a peculiar comfort in putting distance between him and the book. I tried to seem nonchalant and tucked my hair behind my ears. "I asked what Jack said about it."

"He said you had a book that Peter wrote about vampires," Milo shrugged.

"That's all?"

My heart had sped up, and I saw a flicker in Milo's eyes as he registered it. I felt protective of the book because it was the only thing I really had of Peter, and I don't know why it was important that I still feel a connection with him.

Thinking about it only made my body scramble, and my best answer was to turn and quickly put the book in my top dresser drawer.

"What was that about?" Milo's voice had tightened. "What's going on?"

"Nothing." I slammed the drawer shut. Taking a deep breath, I gave myself a moment to recover before I turned around to face Milo again. "It's just Peter."

"I wish I had met Peter." His defenses had softened. "I'd love to see what all the fuss is about."

"There's not a fuss. Is there?" I didn't feel like I was making one, or at least I was trying not to.

"Oh, there's a fuss," Milo nodded with raised eyebrows. "That's a big part of what Jack's 'training' is all about." He did air quotes for training, which would've made me smile, if I hadn't been too distracted by the implications of what he was saying.

Jack's use of words yesterday threw me off, but I hadn't really put things together. "Arsenal" and "exercise" and "training." Things that Milo needed to "master," and in my head I had questioned, "Master for what?"

But I hadn't said anything aloud, and now I really wish I had. Because Jack was training Milo to battle Peter, and it made my stomach twist in knots.

"Jack's training you to fight Peter?"

"No, no," he quickly backtracked. "Not to fight Peter. Not like I'm going to seek him out and ask him to duel or anything. He's worried because he doesn't know how Peter will treat me if he comes back.

"And in case Peter tries to do something... you know, to you." He floundered for a minute, showing me a glimpse of the self-conscious boy he had been. "Jack wants to make sure we're both protected. It's not a bad thing."

"Maybe not," I said, but my stomach kept knotting up. "But I don't like it."

"You don't like anything." Milo rolled over and hopped off my bed. "Jane is taking too long. Let's go down to the clubs and tell her to meet us there."

"It's too far to walk."

"How do you think I got here? Magic?" He snapped his fingers, insinuating he'd appeared out of thin air. "No. I took Mae's car."

"You can't drive!" I said. "You've had like one driving lesson and you don't have your driver's license!"

"Easy, girl!" Milo held up his hands. "Jack's been teaching me how to drive, and I'm a different kind of sixteen now. And soon I'll have a license, claiming I'm eighteen. So... get over it."

"But you don't have that license today!"

"Alice! You're supposed to be the fun one!"

"I was never the fun one."

"Well, you're supposed to be irresponsible at least." He gestured to the kitchen. "I mean, when was the last time you did the dishes? You don't go to bed until the sun comes up. You're a rebel without a cause. You can drive a few blocks in a Volkswagen. Live a little!"

"Okay! Fine!" I threw my hands up in the air and gave in. Grabbing my phone, I followed him out of my room and shook my head. "I'll text Jane on the way there. Let's go."

- 18 -

Milo had new sex appeal and wanted to flaunt it. He'd been sexually repressed and awkward his whole life, so he had a few things he needed to work out. The most logical place would be a gay club off Hennepin.

I wasn't thrilled by the prospect of returning downtown to a place a few blocks from the vampire club, but it was a human club, so I figured it would be mostly safe. Plus, I had Milo with me, and he'd act as my bodyguard, if I needed it.

Jane wasn't happy about gay clubs. She went to them sometimes, because they had drinking and dancing and the gays thought she was fabulous. But Jane liked being hit on more than anything else.

Despite her reluctance, she agreed to meet us there. We waited outside the club for her, since she probably couldn't get in without Milo. I didn't have a fake ID, but I doubted that any doorman could withstand Milo. What I've found out from my time with Jack is that when someone's really attractive, they can get away with anything.

We stood in the parking lot off to the side the club. It cost $25 to park but he had an expense account now, so what did Milo care?

Several very attractive young men (and lots of not-so-attractive men) smiled at Milo appreciatively when they walked past on the way to the Saloon. He noticed and blushed.

Jack's obliviousness irritated me. In some way, it should be sweet and romantic that he didn't notice anybody but me, but it wasn't. Because I always noticed everyone else, and I wished he'd tell them all to back off because he's with me.

Jane showed up fifteen minutes late. I sat on the metal guardrail, playing my part as Milo's invisible sidekick. I chewed gum to see how big of a bubble I could blow, and I wouldn't have noticed Jane if it wasn't for the clack of her heels.

"Milo!" Jane exclaimed breathlessly.

I popped the bubble so I could see her. She'd literally stopped in the middle of the road to gape at my brother. She shook her head and blinked, and Milo laughed in embarrassment.

"Jane, maybe you ought to get out of the road," I said as a taxi whizzed around the corner towards her. She didn't move until it honked its horn, and then she flicked it off and sauntered over to us.

"Milo Bonham, as I live and breathe," Jane smiled at him, and I wondered who talks like that? "My, you've grown up."

"Are you channeling a 50's starlet or something?" I asked, in reference to her new way of flirting.

"Hardly." Jane did this horrible flirty laugh, and I rolled my eyes. "I just can't believe it's really you."

"I had a growth spurt," Milo said sheepishly.

He grew four inches in a matter of weeks, his skin changed into porcelain, and he aged from a little boy with baby fat to a Calvin Klein model. But yeah, a growth spurt would sum that all up.

"Yeah, a growth spurt," I chimed in when Jane just kept staring at him.

"Mmm," Jane purred in some kind of agreement. "I just wish somebody had told me."

"He's still sixteen, Jane," I said.

As Milo said, he was a whole different kind of sixteen now, but despite all his fancy new trappings, he's still my little brother. My naive innocent little brother, who didn't need Jane slut eyeing him up like that. It wasn't her fault she felt so attracted to him, but it still creeped me out. A lot.

"And, more importantly, he's gay." I gestured to the club behind us with my thumbs. "Hence, the gay club."

"The good ones always are," Jane complained in a tiny voice, sounding as if she was doing her best Marilyn Monroe impression. She must've fallen asleep to TCM or something last night.

"What good ones are?" I asked and stepped in between them.

"It's just a saying, Alice." She had that tone like I was trying on her nerves.

We walked around the corner to the club, and I looped my arm through Milo's so he couldn't get very far away from me. Jane couldn't stop herself from repeatedly looking over at him, but she did her best to act like she was over it.

Milo grinned at the doormen, and he let us in. We didn't even have to pay a cover charge, and I wondered how many other things in life I was missing out on simply because I was ordinary.

I didn't have much time to ponder, though, because my head was filled with a dance remix of Lady Gaga. I followed closely behind Milo as we left the entry alcove into the first room of the club.

It was all blue lights and strobes and pounding beats. Three square platforms sat in the center of the room where groups of shirtless guys danced. On the other side of the room were a glowing bar and a couple couches, and while I could really use a drink, I doubted I'd be able to drag Milo over there anytime soon.

Within moments of hitting the crowded dance floor, a foxy guy stole Milo from me. Milo tossed me an apologetic smile, but I waved it off. That was the point of the club scene, right?

Since guys weren't hitting on Jane, she settled for really pretty lesbians. They made a sandwich, with Jane as the meat. I was really starting to wonder what the reason for my friendship with her was. At some point, with all my fancy vampire shenanigans, didn't I grow out of her?

But then, when I realized that I stood alone in the middle of a dance floor, that I was afraid that everyone else would leave me. Jane, in her narcissistic desire for a sidekick, never would.

I went over to the bar and tried to order a drink, but I almost got myself kicked out. I couldn't pass for twenty-one, and the bartender thought it'd be good to alert the bouncers that I'd snuck in. I scurried off into the dark recesses of the club so they couldn't find me.

Hiding against the dark corners, I found several couples making out in a way that was only appropriate in pornography. With the lack of lighting, I couldn't really see much of anything, but I put my hands up to my temples to shield myself as best as I could anyway.

Milo danced shirtless on one of the platforms, and he was definitely the most glorious thing here. Everyone vied for his attention, and I hoped that he made the right choices.

We hadn't exactly had the birds and bees talk. Maybe Jack had, in conjunction with a talk about drinking another person's blood. Those topics would probably be coming up pretty quickly, and I could only hope that he was well-informed.

Even over the pulsating music and men moaning disturbingly loud, I heard a noise carry above it. It was sweet yet fragile, like a tinkling bell… on helium.

Someone laughed, and as soon as I heard it, my blood froze. I scanned frantically through the crowd. The strobing lights flashed on a purple head of hair, and then I saw her.

Violet, the Halloween vampire from the club, looked directly at me, cackling her strange laugh. Her lips were done in black, and her eyes were marked with thick black liner and silver glitter. She flicked her tongue at me, trying to pose as something menacingly seductive, but it felt all too villainess.

Something about her reminded me of Harley Quinn, the Joker's would-be-girlfriend, but then I realized what bothered me about that image. She was the girlfriend, the sidekick, the means of distraction while the real trouble moved in.

I rushed forward to grab Jane and Milo, and make an escape, but my path was blocked by a dark haired model of perfection – Lucian. His smile was far more menacing than anything Violet could hope for, but that had to do with how hungry he was. His black eyes were ravenous.

"Care to dance?" Lucian asked, his voice like silk, and my heart hammered in my chest.

"That's a stupid thing to say!" I shouted to be heard over the music, and that did something to keep my voice even. "It's really cheesy and cliché! You should've said something like, 'What's a girl like you doing in a place like this?' or 'Fancy meeting you here.'"

I clenched my fists at my sides, and I wanted to look around for Milo, but I was too afraid to take my eyes off Lucian.

"I know you're talking, but all I can hear is mooing." His smile broadened at that, and I swallowed hard. I wasn't sure if he meant that my blood was like milk, or that I was just a piece of meat, but either way, it wasn't complimentary.

Behind me, I heard Violet's laughter, and she had closed in on me. We were in a room full of people, though. Even if everyone was enamored with them, they wouldn't be able to ignore me kicking and screaming.

And Lucian wouldn't dare bite me, not with all the witnesses. Vampires didn't exactly hide who they were, but they didn't want it broadcast on the nightly news, either.

This was the only thing I had going for me, and if I stood my ground long enough, somebody would notice me.

"You're plotting an escape." Lucian sounded amused. "I'd love to see how that turns out."

"I'm not here alone," I said, and Violet giggled behind me. Lucian glared at her, cutting the sound short.

"Maybe not, but your knight in shining armor isn't here to protect you," Lucian said with unnerving certainty.

"How do you know that?" I asked

"Because he'd already be here if he were!" He reached out to touch me, sliding one of his repulsively long finger nails down my cheek, and I jerked my head back, terrified of what would happen if he drew blood. "Jumpy, are we?"

He wanted to eat me, and I definitely did not want him to. He was much stronger, faster, and probably even smarter than me. The only thing I had was the room full of people and Milo, so I had to utilize them before it was too late.

I bolted out into the dance floor. Someone grabbed at my dress, and I assumed it was Violet, because Lucian seemed too smart to cause a scene like that. The fabric ripped in the back and I felt a breeze through my panties. If I hadn't been running for my life, I would've been mortified.

With one magical leap, I managed to jump on the nearest platform. It was about two feet off the ground, so it wasn't that impressive, except I'm 5'3" running through a crowded gay club with a torn dress and a vampire on my tail.

Milo was on the next cube over, though, and I yelled his name, hoping to catch his attention, but he was making out with the saucy little number dancing with him.

I leapt from one platform to another, and Lucian hissed behind me. Landing roughly on the platform, I started falling into a guy, but then Milo caught me with startling ease and grace.

"What's wrong?" Milo gripped my arm.

"He's here!" I shouted.

"Who?" Milo scanned the floor

Before I could answer, he snarled, and I knew that he'd spotted Lucian and Violet. His eyes narrowed and his pupils dilated, and I could see him transforming into attack mode. There was something incredibly primal and rather terrifying about it.

"Milo!" I yelled when his hand gripping my arm got painful. I broke his concentration, and his eyes snapped back down to me.

"We have to get out of here," Milo said. Underneath his new confidence and strength, I saw genuine fear.

Still holding onto me, he jumped off the platform, and I heard some disappointed boo's from the crowd about his departure. We had made it most of the way to the door when I saw Jane kissing one of the girls in her lesbian sandwich. In all the panic of trying to get out of here, I'd almost forgotten about her.

I thought about leaving her behind for her safety, since vampires were chasing us. But they might have seen her come in with us, so I grabbed her hand. She looked like she wanted to slap it away, but Milo was dragging us, and she saw him shirtless, so she went with it.

Milo yanked us outside. I tripped over my feet, and I wanted to let go of Jane so I could just hang onto to him and concentrate on walking, but Lucian had definitely seen her.

"Why are we rushing? I'm gonna break a damn ankle!" Jane shouted.

"You've got to hurry up!" Milo insisted.

His strides were so long and fast that it was impossible for me to keep up, and I finally fell to the ground. I barely had a chance to scrape my knee and he was pulling me to my feet again, making my arm scream.

214

"Milo! You're gonna dislocate my shoulder!" I winced.

"Your shoulder can be fixed," Milo growled, and his nostrils flared. "Dammit, Alice. You're bleeding."

"It's your fault." My knee was dappled with little drops of blood. My leg hurt to walk on, and I was already slow to begin with. I looked behind us, expecting Lucian to be a few steps back, but there were only other club goers on the sidewalk. "They're not behind us."

"Then they're in front of us." Milo stopped sharply, and I almost fell again. I could see in front of us, and I had no idea what he was talking about.

"What in the hell is going on?" Jane demanded, her voice edged with panic.

"We have to get to the car." Milo picked me up and threw me over his shoulder like a sack of potatoes. I yelped in surprise, but I didn't protest. "Jane, you have to keep up. If you can't, I'm leaving you behind."

"What are you-" Before she could finish, he was moving again, this time even faster than before. He had grabbed her hand and yanked her forward.

Milo jumped over the guardrail into the parking lot, and Jane scrambled much less nimbly behind him. He scanned everywhere, searching for any sign of them, and I could feel his ragged breathing. He wasn't hurrying enough to be short of breath, so it had to be because he struggled with the scent of my blood.

Even if Milo saved me from Lucian, he wouldn't be able to save me from himself.

We had just about reached the car, and I thought we had really made it. Out of nowhere, Lucian appeared, leaning against the drivers' side of the Jetta. He grinned at us, and Milo tightened his grip around me so much it hurt, but I was too scared to complain.

"Who is that?" Jane asked, and if she had it her way, she wouldn't be running from him.

"Just go away!" Milo shouted.

"You know, you've only succeeded in scenting the air," Lucian told him. "It's the same thing they do with sharks. They bait the water with blood to attract them, and it puts them in a frenzy. Did you know that?"

"Please just move," Milo said through gritted teeth.

"How are you feeling about now? A little frantic yourself?" Lucian took a step away from the car, towards us, and Milo tensed up more.

"I'm putting you down, and you just need to get in the car." Milo dug in his pocket for the car keys, and I gripped onto him, unwilling to let him set me down.

"Violet is roaming around somewhere," I said.

"You just have to get in the car," Milo repeated as he handed Jane the car keys. "Jane, just get Alice in the car. That's all you need to do."

"Okay?" Jane replied unsurely.

"Milo!" I yelled, but that only made Lucian laugh.

"Maybe you should listen to her," Lucian said, but Milo lowered me to the ground.

Once I was standing, with my knee threatening to give out, Milo still kept a hand on my shoulder, as if reluctant to let me go. For a moment, he stood there, staring down Lucian, and none of us moved. Then I heard the click of the keyless entry as Jane unlocked the car doors.

That must've been the cue for go, because everybody burst into life. Taking my hand, Jane rushed towards the car, and Milo dove at Lucian. There was the sound of snarling and gnashing teeth, but I tried not to look at them.

I felt hands like talons grabbing at my arms and legs, and I heard Violet's familiar high pitched squeal as she tried to capture me. I just kept running, letting the panic and adrenaline burn through my legs as Jane pulled me to the car.

She yanked open the door and threw me in before jumping in herself. She landed on top of me, but managed to slam the door shut, and Violet slammed into it, screaming in disappointment.

Jane locked the car door. I slid all the way across the seat, pressing my back against the window opposite of the one Violet glared at us through. Jane moved with me, and when Violet smacked her open palms against the window, Jane and I both screamed.

Hysteria was about ready to take over, and if Violet kept beating on the glass with her superhuman strength, it wouldn't be long before she got in.

Milo threw her off the window, and past him, I could see a dent in the car next to us. Lucian wasn't in sight, but bloody scratches were all up and down Milo's torso. He hit the window so we would unlock the doors, and Jane leaned over and did.

Milo opened the car door and Violet lunged at his back. She bit into his neck, using her razor sharp incisors. He pushed her off, and she crumpled to the ground. He hopped in the driver's seat and locked the doors behind him. Blood streamed down his neck, but he didn't even seem aware of it.

"You're bleeding!" Jane gasped.

"Give me the keys." Milo held his hand out.

Violet threw herself on the windshield and pounded the glass with her fists. Her crazy purple eyes stared right through me and she purposely bared her teeth.

"Get us out of here!" Jane screamed as she gave him the keys.

He started the car and peeled out. Violet flew off the windshield, landing somewhere I couldn't see. Milo squealed out of the parking lot with little regard for other traffic, but everybody made room for him as he drove off into the night.

We weren't going in the direction of home, not his house or mine, but by the way he kept glancing in the rearview mirror, there was a reason for it.

We sped down the road, and Jane felt safe enough to move away from where she had me pinned to the door. She looked down at my tattered dress, and without even asking, she tore off the bottom half of my skirt. Balling the fabric up in her hand, she pressed it against the wound on Milo's neck, and he jerked away from her touch.

"I'm trying to stop the bleeding so you don't die." Jane sounded hurt.

"I'm fine," Milo snapped, and his eyes darted back up the rearview mirror.

"Are they following us?" I asked.

"I don't know. I didn't see him, though. But I can't imagine he would just give up." His words rang truer then I would've liked, and I had to swallow hard to keep from throwing up.

"What is going on?" Jane asked. Leaning in between the seats, she still kept the rag pressed against Milo's neck.

"It's hard to explain," I said.

I sunk lower in the seat, keeping myself out of sight from the passing cars, even though I'm sure Lucian already had a good look at the car, and even if he didn't, he could see Milo driving.

Tearing off more of my skirt, I pressed it on my own wounded knee and the scratches Violet had inflicted on my legs, trying to stop the scent of blood from filling up the car. I wanted to crack the window, but letting the night in terrified me.

"They looked like vampires!" Jane said, and my heart skipped a beat. Milo's eyes met mine in the rearview mirror, and neither of us knew how to address that topic. "Did you see the fangs on that girl? And those crazy eyes? She must've been on something."

"Yeah, probably," I agreed hastily.

"What did they want with you guys? They looked like they were obsessed or something." Jane looked back at me, hoping I would give her answers, but I avoided her gaze and shook my head.

"I don't really know." I swallowed hard, because that wasn't exactly a lie.

"You should call the police or something," Jane said. "Or at least go to the hospital. You're covered in…"

She was looking over his chest, and I knew she was getting that sense of confusion and disbelief that I had when I saw Jack's wounds disappear. Blood was still left from where he'd been cut, proving that she wasn't insane, but there were no cuts.

She pulled back the rag from his neck and gasped. Where there should've been a hideous gouge, there was only pink raised flash, like a fresh scar.

"How did you do that? How can you possibly do that?" Jane trembled and all the color had drained from her face.

"Jane, look at me," I said. "You don't wanna know."

"Of course I want to know!" Jane insisted, but she looked as if she might cry.

"Not right now, okay? After everything that's happened. Can we just let it be?" I pleaded with her.

"Are you guys okay? Are you... normal?" Jane asked. I lifted the rag off my knee, revealing my scraped and bloody injury.

"I'm still me. Okay? I haven't changed at all," I tried to soothe her. She nodded and sat back in the seat next to me.

That was apparently enough reassurance for the time being. Or so I thought.

Turning to look at me, tears pooled in her eyes. Her fingers shook as she pushed a strand of hair from her face, and in a quivering voice, she whispered, "They're vampires, aren't they?"

"Some things are better if you don't know them," I said. She bit her lip and nodded, but I didn't know if she took that at as a yes or what.

"I wish Jack were here," Milo said and ran a hand through his dark hair.

"I think we all do," I said.

"I mean, I know I can take care of myself. But protecting you two..." he trailed off. "I don't know. I don't think I'm ready."

Sitting in the backseat of a locked car speeding down the highway, I did feel reasonably safe. But Milo had a point. Jane took my hand in hers and squeezed it tightly. There was a reason she was my best friend.

Despite all her shortcomings, Jane had saved my life tonight, and she let me keep secrets when I needed to most. There had to be something said for her.

"Okay. So. Here's the plan. I'm going to drive around for awhile. When I think it's safe or we're about to run out of gas, we'll go to my house. And Mae will know what to do," Milo decided.

My whole body trembled and the adrenaline wore off painfully. Milo kept his eyes fixed on the road and the rearview mirror, and somehow Jane managed to drift off after awhile. She rested her head against my shoulder, and I stared out the windows, wondering if the car next to us might be filled with bloodthirsty vampires.

When I started getting tired, that's when I felt unsafe. I didn't trust myself to stay awake, and I didn't know what would happen if I fell asleep. I pulled my phone out of my bra, which was the only place I could put it when I wore a dress to clubs.

You need to come home. Now. I think we're in trouble. I text messaged Jack. Then, all I had left to do was wait.

Eventually, Milo stopped to get gas, and Jane woke up from the lack of movement. Before getting out, Milo instructed us to stay in the car and keep the doors locked, no matter what happened.

He went around to the back of the car and opened the trunk, pulling out a tee shirt that had been stowed back there. It was a little big and had a picture of poorly drawn cartoon dinosaurs on it, so I assumed it was Jack's.

After I had seen my little brother take on a vampire, throwing him so hard into the car next to us that it had left a huge body-sized dent, I didn't feel as nervous for him as I had before. He was strong, and smart enough to know that that wasn't enough.

The bright white lights of the gas station made it hard to tell if the sky had lightened, and I'd been half asleep when we pulled in. The streets were deserted, and the gas station was still closed, so Milo paid at the pump.

A semi-truck sat idling in the parking lot, and an SUV with one headlight drove by. A kid wearing a gigantic hoodie even though it was seventy-degrees walked past. Otherwise, we were alone.

I let go of Jane's hand and moved so I could look all the way around the car. It would be impossible for someone to still be following us, even if that someone was a vampire. We'd been speeding all over the metro area, so they couldn't follow by foot, and I'd be able to see a car.

Milo knocked on the window so we would unlock the doors and let him back in, and Jane jumped. Under the harsh light, I saw how pale he looked. His hands shook as he opened the car door, and in the rearview mirror, I noticed his eyes had a frantic quality to them. Perspiration stood on his neck, and he had the air conditioning on in the car so high, I was freezing.

"I think we're in the clear," I told him.

He didn't say anything, but his jaw tensed as he clenched his teeth. I watched the nervous way his eyes flitted about, and the shallow way he breathed. He started the car hard, and the engine brayed in protest.

The vein stood out in his neck as his body tensed up, and he reminded me of a junkie in need of a fix.

"Milo, are you okay?" I asked as he struggled to get a hold of himself.

I don't know how he had even held on this long. Maybe getting out of the car and realizing that everything was alright let his other senses kick back in, and he noticed how hungry he truly was.

"I lost blood, Alice, and the adrenaline did something to me," he said through gritted teeth. "If I hold off much longer, it's going to be dangerous."

"What is he talking about?" Jane asked and met his eyes in the rearview mirror. "Are you okay?" He locked on her eyes, and I saw her breathing change, getting deeper and more sensual.

"No, Milo, let's go back to the house," I said. I gripped the headrest of the passenger seat so tightly, my fingers hurt.

Ignoring me, Milo put the car in drive. Instead of turning out onto the road, he drove behind the gas station, where everything was hidden in darkness. He went somewhere private, and the hair on the back of my neck stood up when he parked the car.

"Milo, come on. There's other things," I begged him, but his mind had been made up. His hunger was too strong to ignore.

"Alice, shut up," Milo told me quietly. His eyes rested briefly on me, and they were all primal thirst, and nothing else. "Close your eyes. Or get out if you need to. This will only take a minute." Then he fixed his eyes on Jane, who stared at him with stupid adoration. "Jane, do you trust me?"

"Yes," she nodded, sounding like a brainwashed zombie.

He turned to face her and placed a hand on her neck, rubbing her veins with his thumb for a second. Abruptly, he yanked her to him. He was half leaning in between the seats, and with extraordinary swiftness, he sunk his teeth into her neck.

She inhaled sharply, and I heard the subtle sound of tearing flesh. Closing my eyes, I pressed my back up against the door as far as it would go. Jane moaned softly, and I wanted to throw up or cry or scream or laugh.

It started feeling like forever, but I'm sure it couldn't have been that long. I stayed in the car because I wanted to be sure that he didn't go too far. I opened my eyes, and somehow, in my reflexive urge to escape, I ended up standing on the backseat. I was all crouched down, with my knees bent and my back against the window with my head pressing against the ceiling.

Jane's eyes had rolled in the back of her head, but I could hear breathy moans, so I knew she was still alive.

Milo's fingers were knotted in her hair, pushing her neck hard against his mouth. He was turned away from me, so I couldn't see his face, but I saw the way his mouth was on her, the way the blood leaked around it.

All I could think of was the time I saw a starving dog eating a dead raccoon on the side of the road. The way the dog held the leg in his mouth was the exact same way Milo held her neck.

"Okay, Milo, that's enough." My words came out small, sounding nothing like myself.

I had been bitten before, but it was an entirely different thing to watch a vampire bite someone else. It was terrifying and nauseating.

When he ate, it became obvious to me for the first time that vampires weren't human. They may have possessed the appearance and some semblance of humanity, but that – my brother – feeding on Jane, that was pure animal.

"Milo! Stop!" I repeated. Jane's eyelids fluttered, and her breath got shallower. She was passing out, and death wouldn't be that much farther behind it. "Milo! You're killing her! Stop!"

When he still didn't stop, I knew I had to take action, but it scared the hell out of me. Tentatively, and almost gently, I slapped him on the shoulder. I figured that like a wolf, Milo would turn to snap at me and take my entire hand off.

He didn't seem to notice though, so I slapped him again, harder this time. And again and again, until finally, he dropped Jane and collapsed back into the front seat.

Jane fell heavily onto the seat, hitting her head against the door, and she moaned softly. Milo had his eyes closed and looked like somebody that was incredibly, wonderfully high.

Absently, he wiped at the blood on his chin with back of his hand, and he mumbled something incoherent. All his features had softened, and he looked younger than he had in years. Resting his head on the driver's seat, he faced my direction, but he was barely conscious.

"Jane?" I leaned over her and lightly slapped her cheek, trying to wake her. The bite on her neck was already pink and raised, beginning the first steps in healing. I slapped her face again, but she just turned her head away from me.

"Jane? Are you okay? Can you hear me? Jane?" Weakly, she slapped at my hand, trying to push it away.

I collapsed back on the seat, pressing my back against the cold window, and that's when I finally cried. A pair of vampires had very nearly killed me. Jane and I had the scratches to prove how close Violet had come to hauling us off into the night.

I survived all that to have my brother consider killing both of us, but he just ended up feeding on her. They both promptly passed out, leaving me the only one awake in a locked car sitting in the dark behind a gas station in the middle of the night.

Meanwhile, we had no idea what happened to the vampires chasing us.

"Alice, Alice," Milo mumbled without opening his eyes. "Don't cry. We're…" He trailed off and reached out for me, but before his hand got anywhere near me, he let it drop.

- 20 -

When my phone vibrated, I was sobbing. Both Milo and Jane were too out to even notice. The car was still running, blasting me with freezing cold air. I had lost some blood, and I was terribly thirsty, so I had a feeling that I was going into shock.

I barely even noticed the phone vibration over my own shaking, but when I did, I answered it quickly.

"Hello?" I said, doing my best not to sound borderline hysterical.

"Alice?" Jack said, sounding rather frantic himself. A lot of background noise was behind him, people talking and what sounded like a radio announcer. "Are you okay? What's going on? What happened? I've been calling. Why didn't you answer the phone?"

"I'm okay." I sniffled. "I didn't hear my phone. Are you coming home?"

"Yeah, yeah, I'm at the airport now," Jack said. That explained all the sounds around him, and I heard Ezra asking him something. "What happened? Is everyone okay? When I couldn't get a hold of you, Ezra tried Mae, and she said Milo was at your house. Is he okay? Did he do something?"

"No, he's okay." I swallowed hard to keep from crying again. "Milo came over, and he said I had to get out of the house, and then Jane texted me-"

"Jane?" Jack scoffed. "I should've known she'd have something to do with this."

"She saved my life tonight, Jack!" I insisted defensively.

In all honesty, I had never felt closer to her than I did now. Looking at her passed out on the seat with faded red marks on her neck, I knew that she actually cared about me. She risked her life for me.

"She did what?" His voice dropped to a panicked growl. "What the hell happened tonight, Alice?"

"We went to a club, just a regular gay club," I said quickly. "And we were dancing and it was fine, but then the vampires from the other club – Violet and Lucian – they were there. They chased us, and Milo fought them, and then we all got in the car and we'd been driving around all night."

"Wait. They chased you?"

"Yeah. I don't know when they stopped, though. Maybe after Milo fought with them." I looked around, suddenly afraid that they were lurking around in the darkness, but the sky was definitely starting to lighten now. "Milo got hurt, though. And lost some blood."

"He didn't bite you, did he?" Jack sounded sick and afraid, and I heard Ezra booming in the background, "What is going on there?" But Jack didn't answer him. He was too worried to stop talking to me, even for a second.

"No, he didn't." Fresh tears sprung in my eyes, and I tried to erase the image of my brother gnawing on Jane like a wild dog. "He bit Jane, though."

"Oh." He exhaled. "Is she… okay?"

"Yeah. They're both fine. They're just passed out in the car." I wiped at my tears with the palms of my hand and wished this didn't bother me so much. I had spent all this time with vampires and I wanted to be one, so it shouldn't bother me.

"You're still in the car?" Jack asked. "It's almost.... It is after five there. You need to wake Milo up and get him home before the sun comes up. He'll be too tired to do anything then."

"They won't wake up!" I cried. Jane stirred a little bit, but she was still out.

"Wake them up. Hit Milo if you have to. You guys need to get home," Jack sighed. "If there are people out there after you, you can't just sit in a car waiting for them to find you. Get Milo up and get home!"

"Okay," I said. Looking at Milo's sleeping face, and the trail of red-tinted drool coming out of his mouth, I figured that was easier said than done.

"The plane is about to start boarding. I'll be home as soon as I can. You just get home, and stay put. Mae can take care of everything until I get there," Jack said firmly. "And take Jane home."

"What about all this stuff?" I asked. "The vampires and... and her being bit."

"She'll be tired when she wakes up but fine. And they're not after her, okay? She's safer without you. So just take her home, and you can call her tomorrow and tell her whatever the hell you want to tell her. Okay?"

"Okay," I said "I'm gonna try and wake up Milo now."

"Alright. Call me or Mae if you need anything. Or even 911. They're better than nothing." He sounded reluctant to get off the phone. "Alice? Just… take care of yourself, okay? Just run. Okay? Always run."

I hung up the phone and went about trying to wake Milo up. I don't think I'd ever seen him so deeply asleep before, not even when he was little. I reached over and shook him, but he swatted at me, like Jane did, but with more force.

"Milo?" I said loudly, and Jane moaned next to me. "Milo?"

"Wha…" Milo moved his head but didn't open his eyes.

"Milo, you've got to get up!" I reached over and slapped his face.

"What?" Milo snapped his head up, glaring at me with startled, bloodshot eyes.

"You have to wake up and take us home. The sun's gonna start coming up." The tears on my cheeks were drying, but the more alert he got, the more he was able to register how distressed I was.

"Are you okay?" he asked me.

"Yes. We just have to go. And we have to take Jane home first," I said.

He looked back at her, watching her breathe for a minute, then turned to me. He was fully awake now, his eyes bright with their usual Milo-ness, and they weren't even bloodshot anymore. He was studying me to see my response to him.

"I freaked you out," Milo said evenly, without letting on how that fact made him feel.

"Can we talk about it later? I just want to go home," I said, and he nodded.

He sped out of the parking lot, and he raced across town to Jane's apartment. She left her car downtown, but we thought it would be better to take her home.

When we got to her place, she was still completely passed out, but this wasn't an unusual way for her to come home. Milo got up and helped her to the lobby, pretending like it was harder carrying around her deadweight than it actually was, and the doorman took her the rest of the way up.

Neither of us said anything the car ride home. I rested my head against the cold glass, noticing how cloud-covered the sky was as the sun started to rise. I thought about telling Milo about my phone call to Jack, but I didn't want to talk about anything that happened.

We walked inside Jack's house, and the instant Mae saw me, her eyes filled with worried tears. She rushed towards me, throwing her arms around me.

"Oh, love, it's okay." She stroked my hair as I sobbed into her shoulder. "Everything's going to be okay. You're safe, love." She turned away from me just enough to address Milo, who followed me sheepishly into the house. "Are you alright?"

"I've been better," he said.

"You'll be okay, too, love." She reached out to touch him gently.

"I need to go take a shower." He pulled away from her touch and walked off.

"Let me have a look at you." Mae held me out at arm's length so she could look me over. She slowly turned me around, taking inventory of all my wounds. "We better get you cleaned up before Jack sees this, or he's going to kill your brother."

"It wasn't Milo's fault," I said through my tears.

"No, I know that, love." She wiped the tears from my face. "You'll feel better when you get cleaned up."

I nodded in agreement, since I was crying too hard to talk. She filled her Jacuzzi tub with lilac bubble bath, and I soaked inside for so long I almost fell asleep.

She stayed in with me for awhile and explained that Ezra had called her and told her everything. He and Jack should be back in a couple hours, but until then, I was perfectly safe and I should take the time to recuperate.

When I got out of the tub, I took a moment to admire the scratches I had sustained. Several nasty claw marks were on my back and my ankles. I had a large purplish bruise forming from when Milo grabbed my arm, but I couldn't fault him for that. My whole body ached, though.

I pulled on clean panties and a plush robe. I dried my hair until it was damp, and I left the warmth of the bathroom for the cold of the rest of the house.

Mae was in the kitchen making me hot soup and tea, which she claimed could cure anything. She eventually confided in me that Milo had made the soup, but he retreated upstairs because he was too embarrassed to see me.

I sat at the kitchen island, dutifully eating the soup and drinking the tea. She watched me with a disturbing level of fascination, but I ignored it. Even though I wasn't hungry, the heat of the food warmed me. The night felt agonizingly long and I looked forward to curling up and falling asleep.

I stood up to do that when Jack burst through the door. His hair was messy and not in a purposeful way. He wore brown drawstring sweats, a tan tee shirt, and a pin-striped blazer, an outfit that I didn't entirely understand.

Just seeing him, the fear and relief in his soft blue eyes and the wonderful warmth that came off him, stopped everything else around me. He reached me within seconds, wrapping his arms around me and lifting me off the ground.

"Thank god you're okay," he murmured into my damp hair.

Almost reluctantly, he set me back on the ground. Holding my face in his hands, he searched my eyes, looking for any signs of trauma, and then looked me over as best as the robe would allow. He saw the cuts on my legs and the scrape on my knee, and his eyes hardened briefly, but he looked softly back at me.

"Are you okay?" he asked, pushing a wet strand of hair from my forehead.

"Yes," I nodded. "I am. I'm just really glad you're home."

"That damn plane couldn't fly fast enough," Jack smiled and ran a hand through his hair.

"I thought he was going to overtake the pilot and fly himself," Ezra added, trying to lighten the mood. When I looked over at him, he smiled at me and I could see the relief in his eyes too. "I'm glad to see you're alright, Alice."

"Thank you."

"I should go check on Milo, though. Where is he?" Ezra looked to Mae for help.

"He's been in his room since they got home." She exchanged a look with Ezra, letting him know that Milo hadn't taken the night so well either.

Jack didn't take his eyes off me. It was as if he expected me to disappear if he did. Out of the corner of my eye, I saw Ezra walk out of the room, and Mae busied herself with cleaning up the dishes so she wasn't staring at us.

"Why are you wearing sweatpants with a blazer?" I asked when it seemed that Jack would go on staring at me forever. I touched the pocket of his blazer, and he laughed.

"Um, we were sleeping when you texted me," he said with a cautious grin. "We had early meetings today, and then I got your text message. We were calling and canceling things and rearranging flights, and I just never changed out of the pajamas. I put on the blazer because it was cold and raining. It's my business suit. Do you like it?"

"Yeah." I rubbed one of his platinum buttons, and there was something dashing about it. "I was wondering what you wore to work."

"This is it. Well, with matching pants." His eyes were lightening, and he was settling into the fact that I really was okay. "You look tired."

"So do you," I said. It was after eight in the morning, and it was too early for either of us to be up.

"Wanna go to bed?" He took my hand in his, preparing to lead me out of the kitchen.

"Jack." Mae stood at the kitchen sink, and she gave him a hard look.

"If you think that I'm letting her out of my sight, then you're crazy," Jack said evenly.

"It's her funeral." She pointed at me while she glared at him, but she wouldn't stop us.

"Thanks for the heads up," he muttered dryly.

Still holding my hand, he led me upstairs. He walked very slowly and kept looking over at me, to make sure I was still there. When we reached his room, he turned on the light and shut the door behind us. Letting go of my hand for the first time, he slipped off his blazer and tossed it aside, then turned to look at me.

"I, um, I don't have any pajamas," I said awkwardly.

All I wore was the soft robe and a pair of cotton panties, because after the bath, that was all that had sounded comfortable against my skin.

"That's okay," he smiled, but it wasn't naughty.

He stepped towards me, and very slowly, he untied the belt of my robe. He looked at me to make sure it was okay, and part of me wanted to stop him. Not because I didn't want him to do it, but because I was about to be exposed completely.

My skin flushed red, and that only made him smile wider. He slipped his hands inside the open robe, resting them gently on my sides just above my hips, and his hands felt unnaturally warm against my trembling skin.

Gingerly, he lifted me up and placed me on his bed. I lay on my back, and the robe fell open, so my body lay open and naked before him. I swallowed hard as he looked me over.

He lowered his head and kissed the soft spot between my breasts, then turned and rested his ear on my chest, above my heart. His skin pressed against mine, and his hands held my sides as he listened to my heartbeat.

It was the way people listened to a pregnant woman's belly to hear the baby. Something was strangely sweet and intimate about that, and I ran my fingers through his hair.

When he lifted his head again, he looked in my eyes, his blue eyes going translucent. He pushed the hair back from my forehead, and his skin burned against me.

"Do you have any idea how beautiful your heart sounds?" Jack asked me quietly, and I shook my head. "You have no idea how beautiful and amazing any part of you is."

He bent down and pressed his lips against mine. He was still fully clothed, but I could feel the heat of his skin smoldering through his shirt. The weight of his body pressed tentatively against mine. Instinctively, my body pushed against his, and I tightened my fingers in his hair.

Jack kissed me, and everything inside me trembled with anticipation. Pleasure surged over me like electricity, and intense warmth spread all through me. My stomach swirled with butterflies, and my heart beat frantically. Every part of me begged for him.

His breathing was low and rough, and his hands eagerly searched my skin. His body moved with me, but stupid cloth separated us. I wanted to rip off his clothes, but I knew that wouldn't be close enough. I wanted to feel his heart pounding with mine, and there was only one way to achieve that.

"Do it," I whispered in his ear, and leaned my head back, revealing my throat.

He pressed his lips softly against my vein, leaving them there as I pushed myself against him. He tried to resist it, but he had an incessant need for me.

The sharp pain lasted only a second, and then ecstasy spread away from my neck. His heart beat heavily, and I felt it thudding in my own chest, above my heart. The double beat felt more amazing than anything I had ever experienced.

I could taste him in my mouth, the tangy, honey taste of his blood, even though I had never really tasted it. I could feel the way his blood coursed through his veins, the way it coursed through mine, like hot, liquid silk.

More than anything, though, I could feel how much he loved me. It was pure and raw, and it felt like it was coming from inside and spreading out all over me. It felt deeper than anything I had ever felt before. I didn't think I was even capable of emotions that intense.

Somewhere, in the back of my mind, I felt embarrassed because I knew that he could feel how much I loved him, and it didn't seem to compare with the way he felt about me.

The intensity of everything started fading, getting hazy around the edges. It all felt spectacular, but I felt more like I was dreaming and less like this was actually happening. I was losing consciousness, and I thought about telling Jack, but it felt far too amazing to stop.

- 21 -

A jolt ripped through me, and I gasped for air. My body suddenly felt cold and alone. Jack stopped biting me, and although he lay directly on top of me, the separation of his blood from mine, his heart from mine, was shocking.

"Oh my god." Jack struggled to catch his breath. His face was buried in my hair, and I felt his body shuddering and heaving. "Are you okay?"

"Yeah," I murmured dazedly. "Are you kidding? That was... amazing."

"I can't believe I just did that..." He shook his head and rolled over onto his back.

"No, Jack, that was..." I didn't even have the words for what it was. Using all my strength, I rolled over and buried my head in his chest. Hesitantly, he wrapped his arms around me and pulled me close to him.

"That was bad. Right now, it feels really, really worth it, but that was definitely bad," he whispered hoarsely. For the first time, his heart beat loudly and quickly. Not as fast or as loud as mine, but something much closer to human.

"No. No. I just hate that it's over. I've never felt like that before."

"Neither have I," he said. "What are we gonna do?"

"I'm going to fall asleep…" I felt weaker than I ever had before in my life. "And you're gonna stay with me. Being this close to you still feels too far away. I don't think I could handle it if you were any farther."

He moved and I felt the blanket on top of me. He had covered me up, and he rolled over so he lay on his side, facing me. I buried my face in his chest, and he wrapped his arms around me. It was like being in a cocoon, and I drifted off to sleep.

The afterglow was more of an aftermath.

I was blissfully unconscious, more so than I had ever been before, and Jack got out of bed before I even stirred. The bed was empty underneath my arm, and when I nuzzled closer to him, all I found was the softness of the pillow.

Heavy exhaustion hung on me, like I slept underneath a wet blanket, but I could faintly hear movement in the room and I just wanted Jack in bed with me.

The light was still on, so I blinked until my eyes started to adjust. I tried to lift my head, but that required far too much strength. Using all my effort, I managed to roll onto my back.

Jack paced, but when he saw me waking up, he stood at the end of the bed and just watched me. His arms were folded over his chest, and his eyes looked moist.

"This is why Peter tried to send you away," he whispered to himself and swallowed hard.

"What?" My voice barely came out, and it took everything I had to muster that. "Jack? What are you doing? Come back to bed…" I patted the empty spot next to me, hoping to entice him back in.

"I can't get back in bed with you!" Jack insisted fiercely. "I shouldn't even be in the same room with you. I obviously can't be around you anymore."

"No, Jack." Fear energized me a bit more, and I struggled to sit up. My mind was covered in a thick fog, and I still felt the way his heart beat with mine. "Jack, just please. Can't we sleep? And we'll talk about this later. But you can't... just... not be around me."

"We need to talk to Ezra. I think I may have just killed you."

"I'm clearly not dead, Jack," I shook my head, not understanding what he meant.

"Maybe there's still time. Maybe we can do something." He wasn't looking at me anymore. His mind was working overtime, trying to think of some way out of this. "You've got to get up. We have to go now."

"But I am so tired!" I whined and fell backwards on the bed. I didn't have the strength to argue anymore. He was saying things that were potentially very serious, but my eyes were already closing.

"Alice!" Jack shouted, and it startled me enough where my eyes opened up again. "You have to get up!"

"No!" I rolled over and buried my face in the pillow. "You have to come back to bed! That's what we'll do. Compromise."

"That's not a compromise at all," he sighed. The bed shifted as he sat down next to me, and hesitantly, he touched my back. "Alice. Come on. You have to do this. We have to talk to him. Maybe there's something he can do. Your neck hasn't completely healed yet."

"I don't care! I am so tired, Jack! I've never been this tired in my entire life!" I was shouting, or at least trying to, but if Jack hadn't had better hearing, he wouldn't have been able to hear me.

"You just lost about two pints of blood, and you only had seven to begin with, so your body's weak right now. Which is also why we need to get up, so I can make sure that you're okay." He shook me, and I tried to pull away from him, not that I got very far. "Alice. Get up."

After that, he was done arguing. Part of his insistence came from how nervous my current state made him, and he wanted Mae and Ezra to check me out to make sure I wasn't about to keel over. He stood up, and gently but firmly, he pulled me out of bed.

"I'm not wearing any clothes," I said in my tired whine. I was still in the robe, but that didn't constitute as clothes. Standing up made me dizzy, but he held me in place until I stopped swaying.

"I'll get you clothes. But you have to stay standing up. You need to try waking up a little bit." He was holding me steady, and cautiously he let me go. When I didn't collapse backwards, he hurried to get me something to wear.

"I don't understand why this can't wait until I've had more sleep. What time is it?" I yawned.

"Um, it's a little after nine in the morning," Jack answered as he rummaged through his closet. He came out a second later, carrying a tee shirt and drawstring sweats. "Here."

"How are you so alert? Milo was like... out after he bit Jane." I shivered at the thought of it and took the clothes from him.

"He's still young. It affects him a lot harder than it does me," he said absently. "Put on the clothes."

"I don't want to."

I tried sitting down, but he grabbed my arm to stop me. I just stood there then, fighting to keep my eyes open. Obviously, since standing and opening my eyes were a chore, I wasn't really up to getting dressed, so Jack took it upon himself. Later on, I'd be incredibly embarrassed, but at the time, I was just grateful that I didn't have to do it myself.

He pushed off the robe and pulled the shirt over my head. I tried to help get my arms through the sleeves of the tee shirt, but I got tangled up. He let me sit down to put on my pants, but I ended up lying down. In the ten seconds it took him to get my pants on and pull me into standing up, I had fallen asleep.

"Alice," Jack said, trying to get me to stand again, but I wasn't having any of it.

He just gave up on it. At least I was dressed. He scooped me into his arms, and my head lolled into his shoulder. The rest of me just hung limply.

There was the sense of motion, and the next thing I knew, we were downstairs, and he was trying to get me to stand up again. The hardwood floors felt too cold and slippery, and I couldn't do it.

"Alice, you're not even trying," he sighed. His arm was around me, but my legs weren't doing anything productive, so my weight was entirely on him. "Alice! Come on."

"Just let me sit down." I decided that would fix everything somehow, if I could just sit down that instant. I was trying to push away from him, so I could just drop to wherever I was at and sit down.

"We're in the dining room. Why don't you wait until I take you to the living room?" Jack said but I just kept pushing on him.

He was much stronger than me, especially considering my extreme state of weakness, but he must've decided that fighting me on this was a moot point. He helped lower me down. Once on the floor, I sat up for about a second and fell backwards. He caught me before I cracked the back of my head, and carefully set me down until I was lying.

"You're just gonna sleep in the middle of the dining room floor?" He crouched over me, and I looked up at him blearily for a minute.

"I guess so. Since you wouldn't let me sleep upstairs like a normal person. Why can't I ever just be a normal person? Like… for once. I just wanna sleep when I'm tired. Why is that such a crime?" My eyelids were too heavy, and as soon as they fell shut, so did my mouth.

"Alice! I just want you awake long enough to talk to Mae." He shook me, and while I was still awake, I was too tired to speak or move. "Alice!"

"You bit her." I heard Mae's voice coming from somewhere behind Jack, and it startled him. It would've me too, if I hadn't mostly passed out already. "You finally did it. Is she okay?"

"That's what I'm trying to find out," he said nervously.

"I'm fine," I mumbled, but I heard Mae's footsteps and felt her next to me, pushing Jack out of the way. Her hands went to my forehead and my neck, and she made a clicking sound with her tongue.

"This happened awhile ago, Jack. Why are you just bringing her down now?" Mae asked.

"I don't know. I fell asleep. I don't know what I was thinking," Jack told her apologetically.

"How is she?" That was Ezra, his deep accent rolling out. I couldn't place where he was at. His voice almost sounded like it was coming from inside my head.

"She pale and cool and her heart's beating fast, but I think she's okay. We could give her a transfusion, but I don't really think she needs it." Mae started lifting me up off the floor, and my eyelids fluttered and I tried to push her off.

"No! Just leave me here. I don't want to move anymore," I said weakly.

"You're on the kitchen floor," she said.

"She's really big into the floor apparently," Jack muttered.

"Just leave her if that's what she wants," Ezra said, and I tried to tell him thank you, but I couldn't.

Mae stood up and moved away from me. Jack asked Ezra what was going to happen now, and I heard the wonderful, deep boom of his voice but I couldn't understand the answer. It was like listening to the adults talk on Charlie Brown.

I was quickly fading out, unable to concentrate enough to hear the most important conversation of my life. The lull of their voices put me to sleep.

Milo yelled, and that's what woke me up. My whole body felt stiff and ached when I opened my eyes. Ezra had his arms around Milo, holding him back, and Mae stood in between Milo and Jack, trying to reason with him.

He kept screaming at Jack, demanding to know what he did to me and why he thought it was alright. Jack wasn't saying anything. He just stood behind Mae, looking remorseful.

"Why would you even think that was okay?" Milo shouted, futilely fighting against Ezra's arms.

"Milo, she's alright," Mae said. Her hand was on his chest, more to calm him down than to hold him back. He couldn't break from Ezra's grip. "She's just weak and this is where she wanted to lay."

"When Peter finds out, she's as good as dead," Milo said, and tears streamed down his cheeks. "You're supposed to care about her so much and you just killed her!" Jack flinched and looked at the floor.

"Stop yelling," I grimaced. Sitting up was difficult, and I saw Jack move to help me, but then he stopped and took a step back. Mae ended up leaving her post in front of Milo and helped me into sitting up. "My head hurts. And so does my neck. And every part of my body."

"That's from sleeping on a hardwood floor." Mae rubbed my back. "Other than being sore, how are you feeling?"

"Tired. And a little a dizzy." I ran a hand through my hair.

Milo stopped fighting against Ezra, but he kept an arm on him. Sniffling, Milo wiped at his face with the back of his arm and tried to pretend like he hadn't been crying.

"Jack, go in the medicine cabinet in the main bathroom and get the vitamins," Mae instructed, pointing down the hallway. "There should be some iron and B12." He nodded without looking at me and went down the hall. "Milo, why don't you get her something to take it with? Something with sugar. We have some Mountain Dew, don't we?"

"I'll check." Milo took a step towards the kitchen, but Ezra held onto his arm.

"Can I trust you?" Ezra looked at him, and Milo nodded sheepishly. "Good." He let go, and Milo hurried over to the fridge to get me a pop.

Jack appeared back with the vitamins and handed them to Mae. As soon as she took them, he took several steps back from us. He stood all the way on the other side of the room, crossing his arms over his chest and staring at the floor.

Milo came back in with a Mountain Dew, glaring at Jack as he handed it to me. I couldn't open the can because I could barely do anything, so Mae did it.

Crouched next to me, she actually held me up with her hand on my back. She handed me a couple pills, and I greedily drank the soda. It tasted better than I remembered it tasting, which I thought was odd.

"Feeling a little better?" Mae pushed the hair behind my ear and watched me closely.

"I guess," I shrugged, but I only felt slightly more alert. "Why did you guys even have vitamins? You don't eat."

"I bought them for you," she said. "We all knew this was a possibility."

"Are you sure she's okay?" Milo stood next to Ezra, looking at me nervously and fidgeting. "She's just so pale."

"She'll be just fine," Mae assured him. "Do you hear her heart?" She paused, and Milo cocked his head, listening for the sound of it. "It's a little fast, but it's strong. That sound means she'll be alright."

"We should get her up off the floor," Ezra said.

Mae took the empty can from me, and Ezra bent down in front of me. I looped my arm around his neck and he lifted me up. Having never been that close to him before, I felt a little awkward, but I couldn't help but notice how wonderfully male he smelled, like sandalwood and spice.

He set me on the couch in the living room, and Mae followed behind us, carrying a blanket. Once he put me down, Ezra crouched at eye level with me and he breathed deeply.

Almost sadly, he looked away and stood up. Mae wrapped the blanket around my shoulders, and left her arms with them, cradling me to her as she sat next to me.

Ezra stood in front of us, resting his hand on his chin, just watching me. Milo and Jack stood off to the side of the room, and I could feel them looking to Ezra expectantly. A decision was in the process of being made right now, one that I didn't understand.

- 22 -

"Guys, I'm okay, really," I said meekly, hoping to ease the tension in the room.

"We know, love," Mae whispered, squeezing me briefly to reassure me, but she kept her eyes locked on Ezra.

"Yes," he nodded, his expression regretful. "You can smell him on her."

"Fuck," Jack said under his breath and turned away, so his back was to us.

Mae let out a sigh and rested her forehead on my shoulder. I understood what Ezra meant as soon as he said it, but I shook my head in disbelief.

"I'm wearing his clothes." I touched at my shirt. "And I don't even know why it matters. So what if I smell like Jack?" I looked over at Jack, but he still had his back to us. "Who cares? Does it even matter?"

"It matters." Mae lifted her head, looking up at Ezra. "But there are things we can do. Aren't there?" He stared at me, to the point where I felt uncomfortable, and ignored her. "Ezra?"

"Mae..." Ezra shook his head.

"What does that mean?" Milo asked, his voice high and shaky. "What do you mean?"

"It means that Peter's not here." Ezra put his hands together, as if he was praying, then gestured widely. When he looked over at Milo, he tried to smile. "He's not here. He can't do anything. And that's what we've got."

"That's all you've got?" Milo bit his lip to hold tears back.

"Milo, it's okay," I said, and somehow my tone was calm and even. Maybe I was too tired to really feel scared or sad yet. "I'm okay. There's nothing to worry about. Not right now."

For whatever reason, that's when Jack had enough. He abruptly stormed out of the room, and I heard his feet pounding as he ran up the stairs. Matilda ran after him, but he apparently slammed the door on her because she started barking and clawing at the door.

"Matilda!" Ezra shouted, and she fell silent.

"Milo, can you go get my phone?" I asked, looking up at him. "I think it's in Mae and Ezra's room somewhere."

"Try the bathroom," Mae suggested.

"Sure thing." Milo looked better being put on a task. If he was doing something, anything, it felt better than just standing there.

Once he had hurried out of the room, I turned my focus onto Ezra. I was a little surprised to find my eyes swimming with tears, but I imagined that being incredibly tired and suffocating in Jack's feelings of guilt probably added to it.

"Tell him not to come back," I told Ezra, and a heavy lump grew in my throat.

It didn't seem right, but part of my sadness came from knowing that I would never see Peter again. The reason I can never see him is because he'd kill me if I did, but it didn't change the way I felt.

My body felt intertwined with Jack's, even more so than before. He wasn't even in the room, but I could feel his terror and shame coursing through my veins. But some part of me still pulled towards Peter and didn't understand how I could survive without him.

"You really want that?" Ezra asked.

"Do I even have a choice?" I swallowed hard. "He's going to kill me and Jack." I looked down at the blanket, fiddling with the corner. "I know you still talk to him. Convince him not to come back." Then I shook my head, realizing how selfish I was being. "No, that's not fair. I should just leave. Peter will never know, and he'll never have any reason to hurt Jack."

"Nobody wants you to leave, love," Mae stroked my hair. "Especially not after last night."

I was about to ask why Jack biting me would make them want me to stay even more, but then I realized she was talking about the fight at the club. Vampires were hunting me, on top of this whole other mess.

"I just don't know what to do." I had to gulp down air to keep from crying, and Ezra shifted uneasily.

"We're going to protect you, Alice," Ezra said. "We just haven't resolved everything yet."

"Have you resolved anything?" I asked pointedly.

"We will," Ezra replied firmly.

"I found your phone." Milo stood at the edge of the room, holding my phone out towards me and looking unsure. When he had left, I was mostly okay, but now I was hunched over, hugging myself tightly, and fighting to keep from sobbing.

I held out my hand, and he brought it over. I was surprised there weren't messages or missed calls from Jane, but it was still fairly early in the morning, and I saw how badly Milo had knocked her out last night.

"I need to get home. I have school tomorrow, and I still have to talk to Jane, and I don't even know what I'm gonna tell her yet."

"It's still very early. You've barely gotten any sleep, and you have plenty of time to worry about all that later. Why don't you stay here and get some rest, and we'll take you home in the morning to get you ready for school?" Mae suggested.

"Why in the morning?" I asked. "Why not tonight?"

"We'd just feel a little safer if you were here tonight." She ran her fingers through my hair.

Jack was probably the least of my worries. My blood was already tainted. He couldn't do anything worse than what he'd already done.

Outside of this house, however, there were Lucian and Violet, and not to mention Peter. Plus, I still felt incredibly weak, and it wouldn't hurt for me to be under observation for a little while.

"Why don't you and Mae take the master room? I can take the couch in the den," Ezra said.

"I couldn't kick you out of your own room," I shook my head.

"I insist." He turned to Milo, who stood awkwardly to the side of us. "Go upstairs and get some sleep. We've all had a long night. Mae will be with your sister, and I'll be right next door. Nothing will happen."

"You're sure you're okay, Alice?" Milo looked at me, and I nodded.

"I'm just gonna get some sleep, and he's right. You really need to do the same."

Reluctantly, he went upstairs to his room. After last night, he had to be exhausted. He'd been in his first fight ever, and it'd been with a pissed off vampire. That had to take a lot out of him.

When I stood up, I almost fell over, and instantly, Ezra's arms were around me, carrying me. I had become accustomed to the feeling of Jack's arms and the way they made me feel safe. It wasn't that I thought Ezra would drop me, but it felt familiar and unusual all at once.

He left me on his bed to sleep on a couch in the den, and I felt guilty. I tried to protest, but he wouldn't hear of it. He kissed Mae before departing, and she smiled wanly at me.

I crawled under the covers, trying to get comfortable in their sea of blankets and pillows, and she climbed in next to me. She was still in her pajamas, as they all had been, because Jack and I had woken them up.

"Are you comfortable?" Mae asked before she turned off the bedside lamp.

"Yeah," I nodded, and she flicked off the light and settled in. "Thanks."

"I'm really glad you're here, even with all of this," she said.

"Can I ask you something?" In the darkness of the room, it felt okay to address something that had been bothering me.

"You can ask me anything, love." She moved in the bed, and although I couldn't see her, I could tell she had turned on her side to face me.

"Milo bit Jane last night, and it was… I don't know." I wanted to say animalistic or predatory, but I didn't want to say that about my brother. "But when Jack bit me, it was entirely different. And I know it was happening to me and I wasn't witnessing it, but I don't think that it looked the way it did when Milo bit Jane."

"And you want to know why it was different?"

"Yeah." I said.

When Milo bit Jane, it really freaked me out. When Jack bit me, it had been perfect and magical, and I wanted to do it again.

"Milo is younger and much more inexperienced with that sorta thing," Mae explained carefully. "He was also starving when he bit her, and Jack wasn't, so Jack was able to have more control." She sighed, as if that wasn't quite what she wanted to say.

"Forgive me for a lack of a better analogy, because I'm not saying anything against your brother when I say this," she went on. "But think of sex and rape. They're both the same physical act, the same way that biting anyone is essentially the same thing. But one is for romance, and one is forced.

"That's still not exactly right, though," she said. "When Jack bit you, he did it for love, and Milo did it for food."

"So… when Jack bites other people, is it like the way it was with Milo?" I asked. For the first time, I understood what he meant when he said that it wasn't the same when he fed on other people as it was with me.

"I wasn't there with Milo, but I would say to a lesser extent, yes. Milo was more aggressive because of his age and hunger," Mae said. "Does that help?"

"I think so."

"Why don't you get some sleep now? I know you're exhausted."

I rolled over, so I lay on my stomach, and she rubbed circles on my back. My mother had done the same thing when I was little and couldn't fall asleep. Not that I really needed that much help.

This fatigue was like nothing I had ever felt before. Even after Peter had bitten me and almost drained me entirely, the blood transfusion Ezra had given me had boosted everything before I felt the extreme effect of it.

I didn't wake up until almost ten o'clock that night, but I was still so tired that I knew I wouldn't have any trouble falling asleep again before school.

Jack was around the house, but he didn't even look at me the entire time that I was there. That hurt like nothing else.

We shared something far more intimate than I had ever imagined anything could be, and he wouldn't talk to me or look at me. He could barely even stand to be in the same room as me.

Milo made me supper, and everyone moved around me as if they were walking on broken glass. Ezra was gone by the time I woke up, and Mae said he had some things he had to look into. I didn't know if he really did, or if he was going to talk to Peter and try to keep him away.

Jane sent me a couple texts, demanding to know had happened last night. I didn't really feel like explaining vampires in text message form, and I definitely did have the strength for that kind of phone conversation. So I ignored her, even though I knew she deserved an explanation.

Eventually, I fell asleep on the couch, and Mae woke me up a little after six in the morning. She dropped me at home, where I could shower and get ready for school. She'd sent me with vitamins and iron, as that would help produce more blood and combat my weakness. I felt frail and out of it, and I wasn't sure how I would make it through the day.

After the August heat, I walked to the bus stop in a rather chilly mist. It still felt incredibly strange going to school by myself. Going back to school was like a return back to real life, but I was going alone. Milo was no longer a part of real life.

On the bus, I pulled out my iPod with the intent of listening to it, but nothing sounded good. I felt so disconnected from everything. I just wanted to sleep, but I didn't want to go back to my apartment. It didn't feel like home anymore, and everything about my life felt wrong.

I stumbled blearily through the first couple hours of school until Jane cornered me in a stairwell. I had put on my headphones to listen to MGMT very loudly to keep me awake, and I didn't hear her calling my name or chasing after me.

I made it up a flight of stairs when her face appeared directly in front of mine. Her makeup was caked on heavier than normal, trying to hide the fact that she looked pale and freaked out. Otherwise, she looked like her usual perfect-Jane-self.

"What the hell is going on?" Jane hissed, ripping the ear buds from my ears.

- 23 -

"What?" I tried to play dumb since people streamed down the stairs around me. I would've tried to get away from Jane, but she had me backed up against the wall.

"You know damn well what I'm talking about." Her face was so close to mine I could smell the Red Bull on her breath and the strawberry gloss on her lips.

"I don't want to talk about it here," I said warily. People slowed down, stopping to watch the scene she was making.

"Maybe you should've thought about that last night when you weren't answering my calls," Jane growled.

"I wasn't thinking about anything." I dropped my eyes to floor so I didn't have to look at the frightened glare she gave me. "I slept a lot yesterday."

"Come on." She grabbed my hand and started yanking me down the steps I had just walked up.

"What are you doing?" I asked, but I didn't even try fighting her.

"We're gonna talk!"

She dragged me to the nearest girls' bathroom and practically threw me inside. I stumbled and fell to the ground, but I blame that on my own infirmity. A freshman washed her hands at the sink, but Jane sneered at her, so she finished quickly and hopped over me on her way to the exit.

As I got to my feet, Jane checked underneath the stalls to make sure we were alone, and then tossed her heavy book bag in front of the door to act as doorjamb.

"What the hell happened, Alice?" She went over and dug her cigarettes out of her bag. I walked over to the counter and leaned on it. "What are they? Who were those people that chased after us? And what the hell did your brother do to me?"

"One question at a time, Jane."

I ran a hand through my hair and tried to ignore that haunting, pale reflection that stared out from the mirror. I turned my back to it and using every bit of my strength, I hopped onto the counter.

The bell rang overhead, announcing that the break had ended and class had begun, but neither of us made any move towards the door.

"Start with whichever one you want," Jane gestured vaguely as she lit her cigarette.

"They're vampires."

When she took a drag from her cigarette, her hand shook. She stared at the yellow bathroom floor tile, and she exhaled smoke out of the corner of her mouth. Her expression didn't look surprised and her skin didn't pale, but I wasn't sure if that was a good thing.

Maybe she just thought I was insane. She took another drag of her cigarette and waved for me to continue with her other hand.

"I don't really know who the other vampires were," I said. "We met them at a club a little while back, and they were obsessed with me because Jack wouldn't share me or something. I don't really know what they want with me." I kept watching her, but she stayed the same, nervously smoking and looking down.

"They happened to be at the club that night. And they chased us. Milo lost blood in the attack, and he was kinda desperate to replace it. So he bit you." I swallowed hard. "I'm sorry. We never meant for you to get involved."

"Milo is a vampire?" Jane said, almost interrupting me. "How long?"

"Over three weeks." It sounded so weird saying it aloud. My brother's been a vampire for almost a month.

"Jack is a vampire?"

"Yeah."

"But you're not?" She looked up at me, her eyes wide and scared.

"No, I'm not."

"Why don't I have bite marks?" Jane pointed to her neck. It was completely bare, the same as mine, even though we'd both just been bitten. "I knew that he bit me, but I didn't have any sign of it."

"Something in their saliva. It makes the wounds heal right away," I shrugged. "It's probably the same thing that makes it so they heal quickly and live forever, but on a much smaller scale."

"That's why your brother looked so foxy. And why I can't get him out of my head." Jane chewed the inside of her cheek and stared off into space. "And why I couldn't get Jack out of my head either. They're vampires."

"I'm sorry," I said softly, unsure of what else to say. "I never thought you would... When Milo invited you out, I thought we would just dance and you'd go home. I never tried to mix you guys. I just..."

"What do they want with you?" She looked at me again, and this time, she was suspicious. "Are you like Jack's blood mule or something?"

"No, it's nothing like that." I shook my head. "He's... We're... There's extenuating circumstances that I'm not gonna get into right now, but we're almost dating. I guess."

"What does that even mean?" Her hand was shaking less when she flicked her ashes. "Are you sleeping together? Does he bite you?"

"No." I let it hang in the air, unwilling to tell her the truth. "We just care about each other."

"So why did Milo turn into a vampire and not you?" She studied me, trying to figure out if I was lying, and I shifted uncomfortably.

"There was an accident," I said. "He was dying, and the only way to save him was to turn him. So they did."

"I'm not gonna turn, am I?" Jane's hand went to her neck, touching where Milo bit her.

"No, it doesn't work like that. You'll be perfectly fine," I said. "Oh. You should take iron and B12 for awhile to help your blood replenish or whatever."

"So... they're really vampires?" Jane eyed me up skeptically.

"You saw them."

"I did," she agreed thoughtfully. "But that girl, she had fangs, like hardcore. I didn't notice any on Milo or Jack."

"Yeah, I don't think those are real." I'd been thinking the same thing. "Hers must be veneers or something. She has to be a real vampire, but I think it's all part of her 'image.' You saw her black lipstick and Halloween make up."

Jane nodded and tossed her cigarette butt on the floor. She stomped it out and pulled another cigarette out from her pack.

Obviously, she'd been thinking of it before I said anything. In the car, after Violet and Lucian attacked us, she'd even used the word "vampires" herself. But it was still a hard thing to come to terms with, even when all the pieces fit.

"So what now?" Jane asked at length.

"What do you mean?"

"I don't know!" She laughed hollowly. "They are vampires! Doesn't it feel like we should do *something*? That we can't just go back to living our life like normal?"

"That's something that I struggle with everyday," I said. "But there isn't much else for us to do."

"I was bit by a damn vampire! And now I'm supposed to go to Chemistry, and flirt with boys, and just pretend like none of it ever happened?" Tears welled in her eyes, and she bit her lip. "I sorta feel like my whole life was a lie. I mean, what else is there that I don't know about?"

"Jane, we hardly know about anything," I said. "There's tons out there. But it doesn't affect us. Or we don't realize it does. This one thing happened to touch home, just for a minute, but it doesn't change anything else."

"It changes everything!" Jane insisted dramatically.

This is exactly why I wasn't supposed to tell people about vampires. It was too hard for a person to take. It completely distorts the perception of reality. When things that are so clearly fiction became fact, it changes everything.

"I don't know what to tell you," I told her simply.

"So you're no help?" Jane smiled wryly and flicked her cigarette into a sink. "I should've expected that from you." She pulled out her ample makeup bag from her backpack by the door and went over to the mirror next to me.

"What is that supposed to mean?" I asked.

"You just take your lot in life, no matter what it is." She took out something to blot the makeup that had smeared around her eyes when she teared up. "You don't know how to fight for anything you want."

"I don't think that's true," I said, but her words stung.

"Really?" Jane's reflection smiled at me as she reapplied eyeliner. "If you really believe that, then how come you're sitting here, still human, going to high school? Cause you've got to be dying to be a vampire." When she finished her makeup, she caught my expression in the mirror and laughed darkly. "That's what I thought."

"It's so much more complicated than that." But my words sounded unconvincing, even to me.

"I'm sure it is." She put on another coat of lip gloss and turned to me. "I'm gonna go to class. And we can just pretend we never even had this little talk, since that's how you want to play this."

"I'm not playing anything!"

"Good job," Jane winked at me.

She sauntered out of the bathroom, swinging her book bag over her back as she left. Her runway walk was already back in full strut, and I gaped after her.

It was as if there was a switch inside her where she could momentarily express real emotions, and then just flick them off when it became inconvenient. She'd been frightened and almost crying, and boom! She fixed her makeup, belittled me, and walked off into the sunset.

I leaned back, resting my head against the mirror, and tried to find fault with what she said. I fought for what I wanted. Repeatedly, I tried to convince Ezra that it was a good idea that I turned now instead of later.

I never really told Jack how I felt, but I still hadn't gotten everything with him straightened out. All I was doing was making the best of a messed up situation. That wasn't the same as just letting life happen to me.

I ended up sleeping a lot in class. During lunch, I'd gone to the nurses' offices and lay down on a cot to get some sleep. After school, walking the block and a half from the bus stop to my apartment left me exhausted. I collapsed on the couch as soon as I got in and passed out.

Milo texted me to make sure I was okay, but I only vaguely remember answering it, and then I was out again. I barely managed to wake up for school the next day, but I took twice the vitamins Mae told me to take.

When they bus dropped me off at school, I ran across the street to the gas station and bought five Red Bulls. I was gonna fight this tired thing if it killed me.

By the end of the day, I actually felt pretty good. Jane avoided me, but it was better that way. She needed to extradite herself from this life before she got hurt.

I made it through the second day of my senior year, though, so I thought that counted for something. It wasn't until I got home and sat on the couch, sipping on my sixth Red Bull of the day, that I realized something disturbing.

Milo texted me twice yesterday, once asking how I was feeling and the second expressing his relief that I was doing okay. He had not invited me over. Jack had not called or texted me.

In fact, since he'd bitten me, Jack hadn't really spoken to me at all. We had shared something immensely intimate, and he was just blowing me off.

He was legitimately freaked out by everything. We were both in serious danger. But we were already in danger. Avoiding me now couldn't take it back or make me any safer in the future. He wasn't protecting me or preventing anything from happening.

Unless...

When he bit me, I felt how much he cared about me, and it was overwhelming. It felt amazing, but conversely, he could feel the way I felt. Maybe it wasn't good enough. Maybe he saw how little I cared for him.

Not that I didn't care for him that much, but I wasn't even capable of feeling the way he did. I cared about him as much as I could, as much as my measly human emotions would allow.

Maybe he'd felt the way I still cared for Peter. Despite everything that should be to the contrary, I had very strong feelings for Peter, and something at the very core of me felt destined to be with him. That came directly from my blood, and maybe Jack tasted that.

Without even knowing it, I may very well have broken his heart and driven him away.

I couldn't live in that kind of panic, so I pulled out my phone. I didn't think I could talk directly to Jack, not yet, so I texted Milo instead.

Hey. How's it going? I messaged Milo.

As time started to slowly tick by, it seemed more and more likely that either Milo was sleeping or he hated me. Finally, after seven o'clock, my phone started to ring, and my heart almost pounded out of my chest.

Pretty good. How are you feeling today? Milo texted.

Good. Better. What's going on tonight? I responded.

We're just working on some things here. You should probably just stay home and get some rest. Milo messaged.

I'm feeling better. I'd like to get out. This was, of course, only half the truth, but I wanted to see Jack.

Not tonight. Just get some sleep. I'll talk to you tomorrow. Milo messaged back, and that was that.

They were shutting me out of their lives. If neither Jack nor Peter wanted me around anymore, it made little sense for me to be around. Milo could still talk to me. Just not at their house.

Peter could just move back home, and they could go on with their lives. Everything could go back to some semblance of normal if they just got rid of me.

I took more vitamins, drank another Red Bull, and paced the apartment.

In retrospect, all that caffeine would seem like a really bad idea. I was tired and weak, and instead of perking me up, it made me fidgety. When I finally decided to try to go to bed, sleep escaped me. Even though I was still suffering anemia induced exhaustion, my nerves and the caffeine made it impossible to sleep.

A cool mist seeped into my room through the open window, so at least I wouldn't have to sleep in muggy ninety degree temperatures. I actually had cool comfort going for me, but I tossed and turned until the covers fell off, and then I was cold.

If only Jack would call me, then somehow we could straighten this all out. I could confess how much I really did care about him, and how little Peter meant to me.

Eventually, my body forced itself to shut down and go to sleep, and I was staring at the phone when my eyes finally closed. The last coherent thought I had before drifting off was that I really and truly loved Jack.

I heard a noise, a banging sound on my window, and my eyes flashed open. The scare from the bang drove away my fatigue, and I sat up, looking around for the source of sound.

Fog had permeated my room, sliding in from the open window. A curtain fluttered in a light breeze, letting in the light from the streetlamp, and it cast onto a figure standing in the corner of my room.

My breath caught in my throat, which was probably only a little better than screaming. I was about to ask who it was, but even in the dim fog of my room, I could see his piercing green eyes fixed on me. He knew that I had seen him, so he stepped out from the shadows.

- 24 -

He was still the most stunning thing I had ever seen. My heart fluttered, and that familiar painful tug pulled inside of me, almost demanding that I get out of bed and go to him. If I hadn't been in shock, I might have. Instead, I just gaped at him.

"Peter," I whispered breathlessly.

"I didn't mean to wake you," Peter said softly, and his voice sounded like velvet.

He moved closer to me, cautiously sitting on the edge of my bed. His thick, chestnut hair fell into his eyes, and he absently pushed it back. His skin was smooth and flawless, and his lips parted slightly, breathing me in.

He wanted to reach out and touch me, but fought it, gripping my blanket and balling his hand up into a fist. There should've been something menacing and frightening about him being in my room, but there wasn't.

"What are you doing here?" I swallowed hard, gauging his reaction, but it was impossible. As always, his expression was impenetrable.

"I wanted to see you. I thought something was wrong." His eyes flashed with something I couldn't read, and I dropped my gaze. My mind was filled with the exotic haze of him, and I wouldn't be able to think at all if I kept looking at him.

"Something wrong? You mean like when you nearly killed me?" I was startled that I'd even been able to say something that biting, but he clouded up whatever part of my senses controlled my inhibitions.

Out of the corner of my eye, I saw him flinch, and that delighted me somehow. He felt remorse about what he'd done to me, as if that were evidence that he actually cared.

"I can never apologize enough for that," he said, and his fist clenched tighter onto my blanket.

"Funny. I haven't even heard you apologize once." I looked up at him, and he turned away from me, his eyes softening with guilt and shame.

"Alice, I never meant to hurt you. I just didn't know how to protect you. Or myself." He exhaled deeply, staring out my window for a moment before continuing. "I'll never forgive myself for what I did. You deserve much better than me, so much better than my life, and that's why I left."

"I didn't want you to leave." I didn't understand why but I was almost pleading with him. Part of me had never stopped yearning for him.

"Really?" Peter turned to me, surprised and relieved.

"I wanted to die when you told me you didn't want me anymore. What does that tell you?" My hands trembled, and my heart pounded so loud I could barely hear myself speak. What was I saying? What was I doing?

"I'll never stop wanting you. I just couldn't hurt you again," he said.

Gently, he placed his hand on top of mine, and electricity jolted through me. It took everything to keep breathing. All my senses went haywire.

"Why are you back?" I whispered.

"I don't think I can stay away from you anymore."

He leaned in towards me, but his lips bypassed mine. Instead they rested softly on my neck, kissing the skin running over my veins. A delirious moan escaped my lips, and a tantalizing heat went through me.

His hand that had been gently touching mine had changed, so it pinned down my wrist, not that I minded. I wouldn't have fought back no matter what he did. I welcomed every touch he gave.

When the sharp prick of his teeth broke the skin, everything was more intense then I remembered. My blood surged through me, hot and silky, making my body quiver with pleasure.

I just started to feel his heart pump with mine, but this sudden darkness stung at me. Just like that, he stopped biting me.

The familiar cold shaking took over me, my body's reaction to the separation. I collapsed back on the bed, but Peter still gripped my wrist. If he squeezed much harder, my bones would snap. He leaned over, spitting onto my floor.

"What did you do?" Peter turned me, breathing heavily. His eyes burned in agony, but his expression was completely bewildered. "Your blood was so bitter. What have you done? Did you let Jack…"

"Peter." I shook my head and tried to reach out for him, but he let go of me and backed away.

"Alice, what have you done?" Peter repeated plaintively, and I had never seen anyone look as tortured as he did then. He ran a hand through his hair, and he looked as if he might be sick.

"Peter. I didn't..." I tried to sit up, but overwhelming dizziness forced me back down.

The exhaustion I felt before came back in tenfold. Even though Peter hadn't drunk very much blood, I could barely handle what I already lost.

I tried to think, to reason with him, but my mind was suffocating. The lack of blood and the haze Peter put on me were too much. I closed my eyes, meaning to clear my head for a minute, but when I opened them, Peter was gone.

I knew I should call Jack or Milo or somebody. I had to warn them that Peter was back, and he knew what was going on. I wanted to move, but it was far too much work.

Nothing seemed to be working, and the best I could manage was reaching out for my phone on the night stand.

Something was shaking me so hard, I thought I would get whiplash. My body flopped back and forth, and hands squeezed my shoulders. I tried pushing them off, but I could barely even raise my arms. A voice screamed my name shrilly, and I realized belatedly that it was my mother.

"Mom!" I shouted, swatting at her wrist the best I could, and the shaking finally stopped.

"Alice? What the hell is going on with you?" Mom looked at me with wild eyes.

She sat on my bed, holding my shoulders, otherwise I would've fallen back onto the bed. Bright sunlight shone in through the curtains, and not only was my mother actually home, she was in my room.

"What are you talking about? What are you doing in here?" I said groggily, and when I tried to push my hair out of my eyes, I poked myself in the eye. I felt like a drunk person when I moved.

"I just got home. It's ten o'clock in the morning, and your alarm clock was going off, as it had been for the last three hours. You didn't hear it? At all?" Mom stared at me, trying to figure out if I was high or drunk or just sick. "When I came in here, I turned off your alarm, and you just laid there. I thought you were dead."

"I'm not dead. I'm just tired." I tried to shake her off, but she wasn't letting go so easily. "I'm fine. Really."

"You slept through an alarm clock and you didn't wake up until I shook the hell out of you. You are not fine!" Her grip on me softened, and she pushed the hair out of my eyes, so she could get a better look and see if they were bloodshot or dilated. "Alice, are you on drugs?"

"No, Mom," I batted her hand away, and she finally let go of me so I could lie back down. "I'm just tired. I think I'm sick. Like I have mono or something."

"Mono? What boys have you been kissing?" Her voice got shriller and higher, and I buried my head in my pillow to block out the sound. "Is it that Jack boy? Did he get you sick? Is he giving you drugs?

"No, Mom, no drugs!" The mention of Jack picked at something in the back of my mind, but I couldn't exactly figure out what it was. "Just go away and let me get some sleep. I'll talk about this later."

"You're just skipping school today?" Mom asked.

"Guess so. I'm sick." I hit at the air above my head, shooing her away.

"If you're not up by this afternoon, I'm taking you to the doctor," Mom relented and stood up. "And I'm having them test you for every drug known to man. Is that clear?"

"Crystal," I muttered into my pillow.

Once she left, I rolled over and tried to clear the fog from my head. I really, really wanted to go back to sleep, but I blamed that on the counteractive effect of the Red Bull. I forced myself to do too much yesterday, and my body completely shut down.

Something about Jack was making my heart panic, but I couldn't put my finger on it. He hadn't talked to me yesterday, and then I had gone to bed, and then...

And then Peter.

I touched at my neck, feeling for bite marks, but there weren't any, not that that really meant anything. Very little of last night remained clear to me. Just Peter's green eyes and the strange fog in my room. But there couldn't be fog in my room. That's not even possible.

And he had spit my blood on my floor. Mom would've freaked out if she saw the floor covered in blood. I rolled over, checking the floor just to be sure, but other than a few pieces of dirty clothing, it was clean.

I lay back down and touched my neck again. What had happened last night? My head still felt fuzzy. Maybe... maybe it had just been a dream.

As tired as I had been lately, it didn't seem likely that I would wake up to any noise. Besides that, Peter moved in almost total silence. I doubted I'd even be able to hear him come in.

It was probably just a bad dream as a result of my own obsessive paranoia, my exhaustion, and too much caffeine all rolled up together.

Just be completely safe, I called Milo anyway. If Peter was in town, it wouldn't hurt to give them a heads up, and if he wasn't, it would give me a piece of mind.

Milo didn't answer when I called but that was reassuring. If Peter had stopped by, they'd all be awake. In fact, they'd call me to make sure I was safe. But Milo not answering meant that he was still sleeping, and everything was okay.

"Hey, Milo, it's just me," I tiredly told his voicemail. "I just had the weirdest dream and I wanted to make sure you all were okay and what not. Just give me a call later, okay? Okay. Bye."

I made sure to set the ringer to loud on my phone, just in case there was trouble, and set it on the nightstand. In the meantime, I was tired as hell. Pulling the blankets over me, I snuggled deeper into the bed and passed out.

I forced myself out of bed at seven o'clock, before my mother went to work, to prove to her that I was still alive and okay. I was feeling better, but not as good as I pretended to be.

Once she left, I took the pills Mae had given me, then downed another Red Bull, and crashed on the couch. While I hadn't the best experience with too much caffeine last night, I figured that a little could probably help take the edge off the fatigue.

Milo came over, disrupting my plans to just fall back to sleep on the couch. He looked amazing, as usual, so it was safe to assume that nobody had attacked him in the night. Leaning on the back of the couch, he looked down at me.

"You look terrible," Milo said, and that was probably true.

I'd pretty much been sleeping the last couple days. The last time I showered was before school yesterday, and I hadn't brushed my hair in just as long. My skin was ashen, even for me, and I hadn't eaten or changed out of my pajamas since the day before. So yeah, I'm pretty sure I looked terrible. I felt terrible.

"Thanks," I replied off-handedly. "So what brings you to my neck of the woods?"

"I came to check on you." He pushed some of my hair out of my face. "You sounded weird on the phone, and Mae thought I should see how you're recovering. Did you go to school today?"

"I overslept," I shrugged.

"Alice, you need to stay on track for graduation."

"Oh, like you are?" I considered sticking out my tongue but decided against it.

His expression only got more disapproving. Too bad. He only wanted what was best for me, and right now, what was best for me was lying down and resting, not worrying about school. Graduation seemed pointless, even if I didn't inherit a fortune from Jack's family like Milo had.

"Have you eaten today?" Milo changed the subject. He glanced over at the kitchen, which was devoid of dirty dishes or any other relics of eating, aside from several empty Red Bull cans. "Hey. You stopped recycling since I moved out."

"You're not here to make the rules anymore."

"So? Doesn't the state of the world seem a little more prudent to you now that you'll be living forever?" Milo walked into the kitchen to sort out the aluminum cans and empty Fruity Pebbles box.

"As of right now, I'll be lucky if I make it to next year, let alone forever," I sighed.

"You're so melodramatic," Milo scoffed.

I couldn't see him, but I heard him puttering around in the kitchen, and my stomach grumbled. I was like Pavlov's dog. The sound of Milo with cookware made me salivate.

"Are you making me something?" I poked my head over the top of the couch again to see what he was up to.

"Yeah. Mae said you need some red meat." He rooted through the freezer, looking for some of the groceries he'd recently bought me. "Why don't you go take a shower and get yourself cleaned up, and I'll make you supper. Sound good?"

"You know, it's so silly," I said as I got up off the couch. "I was staying human so *I* could stay around and take care of *you*."

He laughed, but it was pretty dumb. Milo had always been taking care of me. What exactly had I been sticking around to do for him? Really, I was keeping him company. I should've just gotten him a puppy, and let Jack turn me.

If I had done that, I wouldn't be so damn tired right now, and I wouldn't be on the brink of losing everything.

The bathroom smelled of flowers and cleanliness after my shower, but when I opened the door, all I could smell was delicious. The shower had given me a little burst of energy, so my stomach was even hungrier than it had been before.

Milo had made me steak, and it was so rare, I was a little shocked it wasn't mooing. He already made me a plate, perfectly set up with spinach, and he'd place a single pink rose in a vase in the center of the table.

"This looks fantastic," I said as I took my place at the table. "Where'd you get the flower?"

"I have my ways," he smiled, and I decided to leave it at that. I was too hungry to worry about frivolous mysteries. "You look like you're feeling better."

"I am," I said through a mouthful of food. He sat down across the table from me, watching me wolf down my food, and I couldn't help but feel self-conscious. "It's weird eating when you're not."

"I don't think you'd have much of an appetite if I was eating right now." He tried to make a joke, but a hint of shame was in his eyes. He hadn't forgotten my reaction to watching him bite Jane, and frankly, neither had I.

"Thank you. For this." I changed the subject. "It's really good."

"Anytime." He leaned on the table, propping up his head on his hand. "So. What was your dream about?"

"Peter." I furrowed my brow. "Isn't that strange?"

"Not really. You've been worrying about him since Jack bit you. It's only logical that it would manifest itself in your dreams."

In the back of my mind, I hadn't been entirely certain that Peter biting me had been a dream, but I couldn't see any other explanation for it. Milo made it sound like the only conclusion I could come to. All my thinking and worrying about him had come out that way.

"Yeah, you're right," I nodded, and I devoured the rest of my meal in silence.

"Has Jane said anything to you?" Milo asked when I had nearly finished eating. "Have you even seen her in school?"

"Yes, and yes." I chewed the last part of my steak and swallowed hard, then settled back in my seat. "She knows you guys are vampires. I don't really know how she's taking it. She hasn't really talked to me since."

"Hmm." He looked down at the table, thinking.

"What?"

"Nothing. I just hope she does okay with everything," Milo looked back up at me and smiled. "Knowing her, she'll probably just solve the problem with sex and drinking, and forget that it even happened."

Whenever I'd seen her at school, she acted like her same old self. She was always flirting with a guy, or strutting somewhere and glaring at me. After a couple weekends getting blacked out drunk, she'd probably kill any brain cells that remembered vampires.

"On the subject of how people take things..." I shifted uncomfortably. "How is Jack doing?"

"He's been kind of... stand-offish lately," Milo answered carefully. "I think he's really been beating himself up over what happened."

279

"Regrets are always a fun thing." I looked down at my mostly empty plate.

A lump grew in my throat. I knew he regretted it the second it was over. No matter his reasoning for it, nothing is more painful than knowing the most meaningful thing I ever felt was just another regret to the person I shared it with.

"Alice, you know he just doesn't want you to get hurt."

"Everyone keeps saying they don't want to hurt me. It's just so funny that the only way they can succeed in not hurting me is by hurting me." I stood up and took my plate to the sink.

"Nothing is that cut and dried. At least not when you're dealing with vampires."

"Thanks for making me supper and everything, but I need to get some rest if I have any hope of going to school tomorrow." I leaned against the kitchen sink, purposely not looking at him. I felt like crying, and I wanted to just stop thinking about all this stuff and go back to bed.

"I know you're just trying to politely get rid of me, but you're right anyway." Milo stood up, and he hesitated before he left. "Call me if you need anything. Okay?"

"Will do."

Once he left, I started crying, and I didn't appreciate it. I didn't like how it felt being alone in the apartment all the time, and I wished that I hadn't asked him to leave. I didn't want him to see me cry or know how upset I really was, but I don't know why it mattered if he saw it. Milo saw everything.

My solution was going to bed. The only cure for being sad and tired was rest and time, and sleeping accomplished both of those. I woke up to my alarm the next day, and I blundered through another day at school. Jane glared at me in the halls, the teachers ignored me, and I slept in class when I had the chance.

After school, Milo texted to check on me, but I heard nothing from Jack, and my lack of invitation to their house continued. When I went to bed that night at 8:30, I tried to pretend that my life wasn't so bad.

Unfortunately, I woke up the next morning feeling better. That doesn't sound like a bad thing, but I was kind of hoping that I would just sleep through the rest of my life, and then maybe, I wouldn't notice how much it sucked.

My body finally decided to respond to all the rest and pills I had been popping, and while I wasn't exactly energetic, I felt more like a normal human being.

It was a Saturday, but I woke up at ten in the morning, which felt too early. With my recent almost-burst-of-energy, I decided to put it to good use. Blasting the radio, I went about the house, picking up the mess I had managed to leave even though I had been immobile.

I scrubbed the kitchen floors. I went over the tiles in the bathroom with an old toothbrush to get the mildew. I reorganized my CD collection. I even went into Milo's room and tried to straighten up what was left of his things.

His things had started collecting dust, and there was something incredibly sad about that. It was the nail on the coffin of the life we had. My future was still up for grabs, but his fate was sealed. In most ways, I had come to terms with that, but with Jack currently freezing me out, the isolation of my life felt even more intense.

After the apartment looked cleaner than it ever had before, I had nothing else to do. I occupied myself for the better part of the day, but the sun began to set, and that's when the loneliness started.

I had gotten used to spending my days alone, but the nights didn't seem to get any easier. As of late, I had been able to fill them with sleep, but with that infernal fatigue finally gone, I had nothing to busy myself with on a Saturday night.

I put on some comfy pajamas and put on the Bat For Lashes album. Curling up in bed and reading a good book would be the perfect way to pass the evening, and it would help keep me from noticing how very slowly time passed.

I flopped back in bed and reached over onto my nightstand for Peter's book, but my hand came up empty. The book wasn't there.

- 25 -

I got out of bed and started rooting around for the book. It wasn't on the floor around the nightstand, and since I had cleaned, there weren't dirty clothes for it to hide under. I lay on my belly and squeezed under my bed, which was still pretty full of dust bunnies, but no book.

Milo's ringtone interrupted my search, and the book was forgotten. On my knees, I scrambled to the nightstand and grabbed my phone. A text from Milo wasn't as exciting as one from Jack, but maybe they were ending the embargo.

Jane keeps calling me. She's drunk. Milo texted.

I'm sorry? I replied, unsure of what exactly he hoped I would do about it.

I can't talk to her. I just make it worse. Milo responded, but that still didn't explain what he expected me to do.

Then don't talk to her. I messaged back.

Can you talk to her? She's making weird threats.

Like what? My heart raced and fell at the same time. He wasn't texting me to talk to me. I was supposed to clean up his mess, but strangely, that made me feel special.

Stuff about "exposing" us. I don't know. Can you try reasoning with her? Milo texted.

I'll see what I can do.

I sighed and ran my fingers through my hair, trying to get the dust bunnies from sticking. I climbed up off the floor and sat on my bed.

Texting would be out of the question. Jane was probably drunk and at a party or something, so her typing and reading skills would be sorely lacking. They always kinda were, but when mixed with alcohol, they were illegible.

My best bet would be to call her and try to distract her long enough for her to pass out or hook up with somebody. So it would probably take about five minutes.

"What the hell do you want?" Jane slurred into the phone. I could hear music playing in the background, and laughter and voices mixed with it.

"Nothing. I just wanted to talk." I started shouting too, but I wasn't sure if I needed too. It was loud on her end, not mine.

"Are you with those damn blood suckers? They sent you, didn't they?" Her voice got an edge to it, a fuzzy one thanks to the alcohol, but it was clear that she was suspicious.

"They didn't 'send' me anywhere. I'm at home, sitting in my room. I called to see what you were up to," I said.

"Yeah, right." Jane made some kinda hollow laugh that sounded more like a cackle. "Are you with Milo? You tell your brother that he can't just leave me hanging like this. I'm an attractive girl, you know! I can't wait around forever for him!"

"I don't really know what you're talking about, but I'll be sure to pass along the message," I sighed.

"Why doesn't he want me, Alice?" Jane cried. In the background, I heard a guy yell something about wanting her, but she turned her head away from the phone and shouted, "Shut up, you stupid ass!" When she spoke into the phone again, she sobbed, "I just don't understand what I have to do make him want me!"

"Jane, he's gay. That's a pretty big obstacle," I told her as gently as I could.

"So what are you saying? Like a sex change?" She sniffled and thought about it for a second. "That's expensive, but I think I could do that. Then he'd want me?"

"I think you should just forget about Milo," I said. "It sounds like you're at a party with a lot of other guys, and you can pretty much get any guy you want. There's no reason for you to worry about Milo."

"You think I don't know that?" Jane snapped. "You don't think I don't know how hot I am? I do. But I can't stop thinking about Milo! I can't! You don't know what this is like!"

"I think I do," I muttered to myself.

"I don't know what to do!" Jane cried. "I don't think I can live without him! Really, Alice. I'm trying… and I just can't do it!"

I had never heard her this upset about anything before, not even when she was drunk. Giving her a quick pep talk on the phone wasn't working. This was much deeper than that.

"Jane, where are you at?"

"Why do you care?" she asked.

"Jane, just tell me where you are." I got up off the bed and rummaged through my closet, looking for something that I could just throw on.

"I'm at Dan Kelly's house," she answered reluctantly. "I'll be around if you can make it here." Then she clicked off the phone.

Dan Kelly had dated Jane when we were fourteen, and he only lived a few blocks away from me, so I knew exactly where he lived.

I changed into a pair of jeans and purple top, and I ran a brush through my hair to detangle the dust from it. I tucked my phone into my pocked and darted out of the apartment.

An early morning rain had turned into a dense fog as night rolled in. The street lights cast eerily across the fog, making shadows visible in the air. A distinct chill made me wish I had a grabbed a sweater or a jacket, but if I walked quickly, I could stay warm anyway.

I heard the party before I saw it, but that wasn't really unusual even when there wasn't fog. Jane stood out in front of the house, smoking a cigarette with her cell phone pressed up to her ear. She babbled something about being the hottest thing sliced bread, so I assumed she was talking to Milo.

"Jane," I said, walking across the lawn towards her. She shook her head and waved me away, but I kept going. "Jane, what are you doing?"

"Answer the damn phone!" Jane shrieked into her phone. "I know that you're there!"

"Jane, its voicemail. He can't hear you."

"They sent you." She flicked her phone shut. Mascara and eyeliner made streaks down her cheeks, and her bright red lip gloss had smeared across her face. "Just like I said."

"Nobody sent me. You sounded horrible on the phone. I'm just worried about you." I reached out to touch her, but she shied away from me and shook her head.

"I don't need your damn pity." Her cigarette had burned down to the filter, so she tossed it on the grass and pulled another one out of her bra.

"I'm not giving you any." I crossed my arms on my chest, trying to look defiant in some way.

"So did you come here to gloat then?" She exhaled smoke in my face and tried to glare at me.

"I have nothing to gloat about." I coughed and waved the smoke away. "I just wanted to make sure you were okay."

"You have no idea what this is like." She chewed the inside of her cheek and shook her head. "It's like I can still feel him inside of me, and not in a way I've ever felt before. He's under my skin, and I can't shake him, and he doesn't want anything to do with me."

"I know exactly what that feels like," I corrected her. "Exactly."

"What are you talking about?" Her expression was skeptical, but she started to soften.

"I don't really wanna get into everything right now, but... it's Saturday night, and I have nowhere else to be right now. Nobody has called me in days." I tried to shrug it off, but it stung worse saying it aloud. It had been almost a week since I'd last talked to Jack.

"So why do you look better than I do?" Jane eyed me over.

"Honestly, I don't know. Except that I haven't been drinking." The only thing I had over her was that I had more practice with trying to pretend like vampires didn't freak me out.

"We could go fix that." She gave me a wicked smile and nodded towards the house. "I'm sure there's a drunken guy in there that would just love to feel you up."

"That is probably true, but I don't think that's the answer. Come on." I took step backwards and nodded in the direction of my house. "Let's go back to my place. We can watch bad Lifetime movies all night long. It's far more therapeutic than drunk dialing."

"I think I'd much rather finish off that bottle of vodka, and see what Dan is up to." She looked longingly back at the house, then glanced back at me. "You're more than welcome to join me."

"No, come on, Jane." I wanted to grab her arm and drag her back with me, but I stayed where I was and tried to think of a convincing argument. "Don't you ever have enough of that?"

"You don't have to approve, but this is my life, okay?" Jane said harshly. "I don't know what the hell you do to get you through the night, but this is how I cope. And I'm not gonna change it just cause you don't like it."

"Whatever," I said, but she actually had a point. "You just gotta stop calling Milo, okay? He's not gonna talk to you, and nothing you can say or do will ever change his mind."

"I know," she breathed shakily. "And that's why I need another drink."

"But you won't call him anymore?" I asked her as she turned to walk into the house.

"Scouts' honor." She crossed her finger over her heart as she walked precariously in her heels. "I'll even delete his number from my phone."

Even after she'd gone in the house, I stood out in the fog, debating on what I should do next. I really wanted her to come with me, but mostly for my own selfish reasons. Spending another night alone sounded like torture, and I couldn't even find Peter's book to keep my company.

I thought about calling Milo to let him know mission accomplished and to see if he had taken the book for some reason, but then I decided against it.

The fog made me feel even more alone as I walked home. It blanketed everything around me, making me feel like the only person on a deserted planet. I shuddered at the thought, and I tried not to pretend as if everything wasn't getting to me.

It was pretty amazing that Jane was a crying wreck, but I was holding up still. Maybe it was all the denial. I just kept trying to tell myself that eventually things would have to change. Somebody would have to talk to me. Right?

I had been so lost in thought that I didn't notice the footsteps falling behind me until I heard that familiar helium laugh echoing off the fog, making it sound far away and right next to me at the same time. I froze because I have absolutely no flight or fight reflex, and I was completely unprepared.

It was just me, alone on an especially deserted street, and nobody had any clue where I was, except maybe for one drunk girl. There would be nobody at home to miss me, and it would probably be a few days before Milo would notice if I didn't call him.

I was going to die, and not only would nobody care, nobody would even notice.

- 26 -

Deciding that it was better to die with dignity, I turned to face my attackers. I wouldn't be able to out run them, and since they were probably stalking me, they knew where I was going. For whatever reason, I had gotten under Lucian's skin and he wasn't keen on letting me go.

"I know you're there!" I announced into the fog.

I heard their odd echoing footfalls, and their dark silhouettes materialized. My heart raced, and I knew they could hear it, but I planned to hide all the other evidence that I was terrified.

My stomach flipped but I swallowed hard, and I clenched my fists to keep from shaking. I stuck my chin out defiantly, even though that meant that I would expose my neck more.

It didn't really matter. They would find a way to get to my veins no matter what I did.

They were in front of me. Lucian's black eyes looked at me as if I was a piece of meat or the Holy Grail. His greasy black hair was slicked back, and he smiled widely, revealing his ridiculous fangs.

I glanced over at Violet, and the fog made her purple hair fall flat and dull. Her thick black makeup had smeared, and instead of looking pleased to finally catch me, her smile seemed to falter.

"You spoiled the chase," Lucian said, his voice sounding like venom.

"Well, she's not very much of a catch," Violet pointed out in her gothic Tinker Bell voice. She glared at me, then shifted her gaze to one of pure lust at Lucian.

That's why her smile faltered. After her original appetite for me, she would've been content to forget about me and go on with her life. But Lucian was the one that wouldn't let go, and she was becoming increasingly threatened in his interest in me, which only frightened me more.

Generally, people wouldn't be jealous of a hamburger, so it didn't seem right that Violet would be jealous of me. Unless Lucian's intentions for me were more than strictly food.

"Okay. Let's get this over with," I said as evenly as I could. I wasn't exactly eager to die, but I didn't want a long drawn out death.

"What's the hurry?" Lucian reached out to touch my cheek with the back of his hand, but I flinched and his grotesque long, black nails barely brushed my skin. He smiled at me, and I swallowed back the vomit. "You're still feisty."

"Who cares?" Violet scoffed.

"I've just decided that today is a good day to die, and midnight is rapidly approaching, so we better get this done," I said.

I had unconsciously taken a step back from them. My legs felt like jelly, but they burned to run. My racing pulse suggested that I bolt, but I knew I wouldn't get very far before I felt Lucian's arms around me and his hands on me, and that thought just made my skin crawl. I decided my best bet was pissing off Violet in hopes that she'd just kill me.

"Your makeup looks stupid," I said her. It wasn't really as witty or as painful as I hoped, but panic clogged the helpful parts of my brain.

"You look stupid!" Violet countered, giving me a disgusted glare.

"Ladies!" Lucian held up his hand to silence us.

From his exaggerated fangs to his long black coat, he was every vampire cliché that Jack refused to be. At the club, Violet had even accidentally confessed that his name was really Hector. He had probably been some horrible computer geek that had somehow stumbled onto the vampire underworld. He wanted the gothic romantic vampire lifestyle, even when it ended up just being kinda tacky and making him into a caricature.

"This is stupid!" I shouted, surprised by how strong I sounded. "If you're not gonna kill me, then I'm just gonna go home."

I don't even know how that was really a threat or why it made sense to me, but Violet did her shrill little laugh. I was beginning to wonder if she had surgery on her larynx or something, because she did not sound human at all.

Technically, she wasn't, but every vampire I had met sounded human. That was part of their disguise. But her disguise really sucked.

"I'm not going to kill you," Lucian assured me.

He had something worse planned for me, and he wasn't about to let me go. He placed his hand on my arm, and his touch set something off inside me. It made it real somehow, and I freaked out.

"Get off me!" I screamed and struggled to pull my arm out of his grip. I knew it was futile, but I had to fight it. My skin crawled, and I wanted to throw up. "Don't touch me! Let go! Let go!"

"Alice!" Lucian hissed, and his other hand pressed firmly on my mouth to quiet my screams.

I had never been so scared in my entire life. I was flailing and kicking and hitting and pulling on anything I could. I kept screaming, and I wanted to bite his hand, but the thought of tasting his skin or blood was far too revolting.

He was going to do horrible things to be me, and that certainty was the most terrifying thing I had ever felt. It was even worse than the dismal feeling I had about living without Jack. That was more of slow burning desolation. This was instant and desperate and rabid.

"Let her go!" a velvet voice boomed out in front of me, and I opened my eyes.

He was far enough away where the fog partially masked him, but his fierce emerald eyes were unmistakable. Peter was here, which was simultaneously reassuring and frightening. He would save me from whatever Lucian had planned for me, but then most likely kill me and Jack. It was a win/lose situation.

"What?" Lucian sounded bewildered, and my fight against him lessened. I would've gone completely slack, but he was still touching me with his wretched hands.

Once, I had fallen in the woods, and my hand had somehow ended up in the carcass of an animal full of maggots. I wasn't in any real danger, but that was the most disgusting thing I had ever done and it totally freaked me out. That's exactly how I felt when Lucian touched me. Like I was covered in maggots.

"Let her go!" Peter took a step closer towards us, his eyes burning with rage.

Even though Peter wasn't very large, there was something incredibly intimidating about him. The way his jaw tightened and his fists clenched only hinted at the uncontrolled anger and power he had inside him. Lucian's hands were strong on me, but I could sense his hesitation growing.

"What the hell is with this girl?" Violet asked incredulously.

"She belongs to me," Peter growled. He extended his hand out to me, as if he expected them to hand me over after that statement. Like it was all some misunderstanding, and not an obvious kidnap/murder/rape situation.

"What about the other vampire she was with?" Lucian retightened his grip. He thought he'd found a chink in the armor, but he hadn't.

Peter already knew everything about Jack. He had to have. The dream I had the other night, that wasn't a dream. Peter had found everything out, and he'd been laying in wait over the last few days. But for what?

"He is of no concern to you. Let her go." Peter glared intensely at Lucian. "Now."

"You have to be more careful with your things," Lucian tried to sound light and playful, but Peter had unnerved him.

He let me go, and I bolted a few steps away. I think everyone kinda expected me to run into Peter's arms, and trust me, that was rather tempting, but I didn't. I stood off to the side of them, closer to Peter than Lucian, and shuddered.

Before Lucian could say anything more, Peter pounced at him, reminding me of the way a lion pounces on his prey. Lucian made a surprised scream, and Violet yelped and jumped back from them. I stayed frozen in place, watching as the shadows blurred and disappeared in the fog.

I heard Lucian yelling and Peter growling, and then there was an awful gargling sound and things that sounded like tearing and breaking. Violet chased after them into the darkness, and she screamed at them to stop.

There was a horrific ripping sound, followed by Violet sobbing, and I heard her lighter, high-heeled footfalls vanish into the night.

Trembling, I couldn't figure out what I was supposed to do. Did I wait here for Peter? Did I thank him and try to convince him not to kill me? Or did I run off to my place?

Nothing sounded right, and on top of my rampant panic, there was that incessant longing inside me that pulled me towards Peter.

When he finally emerged from the mist, I was where he had left me. His shirt was stained dark across the front. His skin was completely clean, even though it looked like there would've been some splatter. He must've cleaned himself up, and I wondered if it was for my benefit.

He ran a hand through his dark hair and didn't look at me, but it was better that way. I tended to get lost in his eyes whenever I had the chance. A fading pink scratch ran across his face, amazing me at how quickly they healed. Several tears in his shirt revealed perfect skin underneath.

"What the hell are you doing?" Peter asked quietly, looking down at the sidewalk.

"What are you doing?"

"Alice, I'm being serious," Peter sighed, sounding frustrated.

"So am I!" I managed to be more forceful this time, and he looked over at me, his green eyes mixed with irritation and affection.

"You do realize that giving up and dying isn't the same as being brave?" He looked at me severely.

"What other choice did I have?" I argued, and I tried not to let him haze up my mind. "If I ran, he would catch me! He's too strong for me to fight off!"

"So?" Peter was incredulous. "You fight anyway! You run until he catches you! This is your life, Alice! Why are you always so eager to give it up?"

"I'm not!" I shook my head, realizing how pointless this argument was. "What's it to you, anyway? Aren't you gonna kill me in like ten minutes?"

"What?" He narrowed his eyes in surprise and confusion. "Why would I kill you?"

His genuine shock startled me. Even after he had tasted my bitter blood, it hadn't occurred to him to kill me. He'd known about it for days, and as far as I knew, he hadn't killed Jack yet either. In fact, the only thing he'd done was save my life. This wasn't exactly the picture everyone had painted for me.

"You did already try once." I crossed my arms on my chest, trying not to let on that I was just as bewildered as he was.

"I already told you that would never happen again," he brushed me off.

There was something almost endearingly matter-of-fact about him. Sure, he had tried to kill me, but he said he wasn't going to again, so what was I worried about?

"What about Jack?" I ventured, and my voice gave away how much that made me nervous.

Peter tensed up at the mention of his name and stared off into the night. He bit his lip, thinking of something. There was an agonizingly long span where he didn't even move.

"We need to go home and get things in order," Peter sighed at length.

"What?"

"There's no other way about it." He reached out so I would take his hand, and I did, but hesitantly.

I got the same electric surge I always did, and I hated the warmth of pleasure that flooded over me. His hand, the one gripping mine, could very well be the death of Jack.

I let Peter lead me through the fog towards his Audi, parked down the street by my apartment. I tried really hard not to think about how wonderful it felt when he bit me. Maybe I could have Peter bite me again. That would at least give Jack some time to... I don't know what. That wasn't really a plan.

Once inside the car, I came up with the only idea I could think of. After Peter started the car, I pulled my cell phone out of my pocket. I thought about trying to hide it from him, but he'd figure it out anyway. He didn't say anything until after I'd hit send and we were already soaring down the road.

"Who did you text?" Peter asked, his voice devoid of emotion.

"Jack and Mae."

"What did it say?"

"That I was with you and we were on the way to your house," I said honestly.

He nodded once, and then noncommittally, he said, "That's probably for the best."

I almost asked him if he planned to kill Jack, but decided that I didn't want to know. If he said yes, there wouldn't be any hope for this turning out okay. At least this way, I could sink down in the seat and think that maybe this is all a misunderstanding. Peter obviously didn't have any intention of hurting me. In fact, he'd been kinder to me than he ever had been before.

Then again, maybe that was a rouse. As the old saying goes, he'd catch more flies with honey than vinegar.

- 27 -

When the Audi pulled into the garage, I noticed with some relief that the Lamborghini was gone. Meaning Jack probably wasn't here. I had no idea where he might be, but as long as he wasn't here, that was fine by me.

Peter rested his hand on the small of my back as he ushered me into the house, and I tried to pretend like I didn't notice the tingles it sent through me. My heart beat that funny way again, the one that drove everyone mad, and I hoped that Milo wasn't home.

No one greeted us at the door, which surprised me since I had given Mae a heads up. Matilda barked and scratched at the basement door, which led me to believe that Mae had stepped in. If Jack and Peter were going to start battling it out, Matilda would probably get hurt, so Mae put her in the basement to protect her.

"Hello?" Peter announced, his silken voice resonating through the entryway. He sighed when Mae didn't rush in to greet us, the way she would've any other time. "She did always like Jack better than me. She needs someone to coddle."

"That's why she prefers me," I added dryly, and he smiled slightly.

"Mae?" Peter ventured out into the kitchen.

He kept his hand on my back to keep me going along with him. Not that I would've turned away. Wherever Peter was going, I wanted to be, and not just because my body insisted it. If he was going to stumble across Jack, I had to be there.

"Mae?" Peter repeated, his tone growing irritated.

A scuffling sound came from the living room, and Peter moved his arm so it was in front of me, shielding me from whatever was going on in the other room. His stance had changed, though, like he was ready for an attack, and I tried to think of a way relax to him.

"Mae!" I shouted. I doubted Peter would hurt her, and I needed someone else to break the tension.

"Alice?" Milo tried to hide the nervousness in his voice.

He burst into the kitchen with Mae right behind him, tugging on his arm, and I understood the scuffling sound. Mae tried to keep him in the other room, away from Peter, but Milo had been trying to get to me.

Peter, meanwhile, only deepened his defensive posture, and moved so his body completely blocked mine.

"Is that her blood?" Milo asked, referring to the splatter on Peter's shirt. He sounded horrified and his eyes widened a split second before he bared his teeth and charged at Peter.

Fortunately, Mae's arms locked onto him and slowed him down just enough where I could dodge underneath Peter's arm so Milo could see that I was safe and sound. Peter looped an arm around my waist and pulled me back to him. He was trying to protect me from Milo, who was trying to protect me from Peter.

"Milo, I'm fine," I said, and I let Peter hold me to him.

"What's going on?" Milo growled. He stopped clawing his way towards us, but Mae kept her arm around his chest just to be safe.

"Peter fought another vampire. That's his blood, not mine. I'm fine." I held up my arms and turned my neck, trying to show him that nothing had happened.

"Is that... is that your brother?" Peter's grip relaxed as he narrowed his eyes at Milo, trying to understand that situation. "Your brother's a vampire?"

"Yeah." I moved away from his arm, standing a little bit away from him.

Being so close to Peter had done that thing to me again. My mind got hazy and filled with him, the way a room is filled with a scent. I could smell him, too, hot and tangy, and my mouth began to water. Unnecessary goosebumps broke out on my skin, and I'm sure I was trembling.

Wrapping my arms tightly around myself, I tried to concentrate on the scene around me, like Milo's wild eyes and the heavy sounds of his breath. Mae hadn't spoken since we'd come in, but that was because she seemed to have her hands full keeping Milo contained.

"When did he turn?" Peter looked to me, but I wished that he would ask somebody else. I wanted a chance to clear my head of him.

"About a month ago."

"Why did he turn?" Peter's furrow deepened and his tone got even more confused. "Why haven't you?"

"There was an accident, and Milo was going to die, so Jack turned him," I said. "And I had been waiting to turn until Milo was a bit older."

"Jack's always so eager to turn everything," Peter said more to himself than anyone else. Then he shook his head and looked past Milo at Mae. "You haven't said hello."

"I haven't really had the chance." Mae forced a smile and finally released Milo, but she made no movement towards Peter, no attempt to hug him the way she hugged everyone else. "Peter, maybe you should just go."

"I know that you're not happy to see me, but that's not fair." Peter was genuinely hurt by her reaction, and Mae's eyes filled with soft tears. "I haven't done anything wrong."

"Peter, you know that's not exactly true," Mae said quietly. She kept her gaze on him, but nodded her head slightly to me.

"I'm not trying to justify it, but if…" He bit his lip and shook his head. "Jack overstepped his bounds on every measure of this, yet you're all continually on his side. She was meant for me, not him. And it shouldn't have mattered to any of you if she had died."

"Thanks," I mumbled, and I felt his eyes land apologetically on me.

"Alice, that's not what I meant." He made a move towards me, then dropped his hand.

"We're not on anyone's side," Mae insisted, and she rested a hand on Milo's arm, trying to keep him steady. Hearing Peter so casually talk about my death had him fuming. "Things are far more complicated than sides, and you know that."

"But Jack is wrong!" Peter slammed his hand on the counter, and we all jumped. "What gives him the right?"

"He loves me, Peter," I told him timidly.

He turned, his eyes burning on me, and I felt myself try to shrink away. Milo hissed and Mae stepped forward, blocking Milo from Peter. She knew, just as I did, that Peter had no intention of hurting me again.

"And you think I don't?" he asked.

Peter moved so quickly, I almost didn't see it happen. His face was directly in front of mine, and I was backed up against the wall, but he wasn't touching me at all. Milo freaked out because of his sudden movement, and Mae pushed him into the other room so he could get a reign on his emotions.

"They're fine! He's just talking to her!" Mae kept insisting.

Out of the corner of my eye, I saw her finally wrangle Milo into another room, but all I could really see were Peter's green eyes. He always looked at me is if he was trying to completely look through me and solve a great mystery.

Irrational tears welled in my eyes, and I fought to remember to breathe. He placed a hand on either side of me and lowered his face so it was directly in front of mine. All I could smell and see and feel was him. It was suffocating, and I didn't know how to fight it.

The horrible truth was that I didn't even really want to fight it. My body kept screaming that this was exactly what it needed, that this was how I was meant to feel. Always.

"How am I supposed to know how you feel about me?" I whispered hoarsely. "You were always pushing me away or running away. You've spent hardly a minute with me. All I know about you is that you're repulsed and enraptured by me."

"I'm sorry." For the first time, Peter's voice registered a strong emotion and not just restraint to mask something. He was deeply pained, but he went on, unabashed. "I have not been honest with you. There are a million excuses for the way that I've treated you, but none of them absolve me."

He exhaled deeply, his breath warming my neck. He was hungry in a familiar way, one that I stupidly welcomed. Peter wanted me in the only way he could want me, the way flowers craved sunlight. Our bodies claimed that I was the means to his survival, in more ways than one, and Peter was giving in to it.

"Does it really matter anymore?" Peter continued huskily, and when he lowered his gaze to my throat, his eyelashes fell darkly on his cheeks. "It doesn't really matter how much I love you, does it?" He moved in closer to me, breathing me in, and he sighed reproachfully. "You smell like him."

"I'm sorry," I murmured.

Maybe a little bit of me was sorry, but the rest of me felt oddly proud that I smelled like Jack. As if he had marked me as his, and maybe even my blood belonged to him. Deep down, I had always known it was meant to, and I think that even Peter had, so he always rejected me.

"He's inside you now." Peter brushed my hair back and ran his fingers through it, letting his fingertips graze my cheek and send surges of pleasure over me. His eyes had returned to mine, but they were dull and sad. "I've already lost, haven't I?"

Before I could answer, his lips pressed softly against mine. Emotions swirled through me, and I found myself kissing him back.

When he had kissed me before, it had been harsh and rough, but this time, it was gentle and a little sad. He realized this was going to be the last time that we kissed, and he didn't want to waste a moment of it.

When I heard the low growl coming from across the room, I awoke in the moment, with my arms wrapped around Peter's neck and my fingers buried in his hair. His strong arms had me pressed against the hard contours of his body with little room for breathing.

But as soon as I heard the growl, my heart froze, and I pulled my mouth away from Peter. He almost tossed me to the side, but that was merely for my own protection.

Jack came flying across the room in a blur. He slammed into Peter, and together, they landed on top of the dining room table and crushed it beneath them.

They were gnashing teeth and hitting at each other, and Jack went soaring through the glass windows of the French doors. Peter was on his feet, preparing to follow after him, but Jack was already up, brushing away broken glass.

They stood a few feet from each other, glaring at one another and seething with unbridled rage. I scrambled to my feet, thinking that I had to do something, but Ezra swooped in between them. He stood on the rubble of the table, closer to Peter, but held out his palms to both of them.

"Stop!" Ezra boomed. "This isn't going to settle anything!"

From somewhere down the hall, I heard Milo struggling to get free. Apparently, Mae had locked them both in a room, which was probably the safest bet.

"There's only one way to settle this," Peter replied calmly, his eyes fixed on Jack.

Jack's face had contorted with so much hate, it was almost unrecognizable. His whole body was tensed so tightly, all his veins stuck out against his muscles. His chest heaved, and his lips were pulled back in a snarl.

"Peter." Ezra turned his attention on him, which didn't seem like the wisest decision to me, considering the expression on Jack's face. Ezra took a step closer to Peter and rested his open palm on his chest. "You know what this kind of thing leads to. You don't want this."

"Tell that to him," Peter nodded at Jack, who growled in response.

"Jack!" I said, almost plaintively.

Peter winced, but Ezra tried to keep Peter's focus on him, and it seemed to work. Jack, on the other hand, immediately softened at the sound of my voice, and when his eyes flitted over to me, he looked guilty.

"Come on." Ezra moved his hand onto Peter's back and gestured outside. Jack moved away from the broken window so that Ezra and Peter would be able to get by if they wanted to. "Let's take a minute to clear our heads."

Jack stepped down, even allowing his fists to unclench, and that seemed to convince Peter that he was safe enough to take a break. Ezra led Peter through the rubble, out into the thick fog and mist that had settled onto the night.

Jack watched them until they disappeared outside, but we could still hear the soft, careful tones of Ezra's voice as he tried to reason with Peter.

Once they were gone, Jack hurried silently over to me. I opened my mouth to speak, but he shushed me. Grabbing my hand, he dragged me into Ezra's den at the far end of the hall, and I could hear the bewildered calls from Milo coming from Mae and Ezra's bedroom. Inside the den, Jack closed the door quietly behind him.

Again, I tried to ask him what was going on, but he pulled me into his arms and kissed me so ferociously, it erased everything. I remembered the way it felt when he bit me, his heart pounding with mine, and I could feel all the warmth and love radiating from him and surging through me.

Underneath his kiss, there was a desperation that terrified me, but I tried to concentrate on how amazing it felt to be in his arms again. I wanted to make this moment last forever.

"Alice..." Jack breathed.

He forcefully pushed me away. He didn't want to be away from me, but I clung to him so tightly he had to use strength to get me off him. His placed his hands on my cheeks, his skin smoldering hot against mine, and his blue eyes pleaded with me.

"What?" My voice cracked.

"I'm so sorry about all of this." He smiled sweetly at me. "Alice, please don't cry. Okay? We don't have much time. Once Peter realizes we're gone together..."

"We can just run!" I said and tried to keep the tears from spilling down my cheeks.

"No, he'll never let you go. And neither can I." His face filled with agonized apologies. "But I know that I might not come back from this."

"No, Jack, this is stupid," I said through the lump in my throat.

A pain so deep grew inside me, I thought it might kill me. It felt as if the ground had been ripped out from underneath me, and I was free falling into nothingness.

"Alice, you're worth fighting for," Jack smiled sadly. "You're even worth dying for."

"No!" I tried to fight him, so I could break away from him and stop this suicide mission he had himself set on. "This is stupid! This is the stupidest thing you've ever said to me! You're such a fucking idiot, Jack!"

I hit him as hard as I could, desperate to escape from the strength of his arms, but they were unrelenting. He let me struggle in his arms until I tired myself, and he pressed me against him. I could feel the slow, heavy thud of his heartbeat, and it made me sob.

"Alice, listen to me." Jack had buried his face in my hair, and his words came out muffled. "He's not going to stop until he has you, not anymore. He's finally realized he loves you and…. And I saw you kissing him-"

"No, Jack, I'm sorry!" I sobbed. "It'll never happen again. I promise! I'll never-"

"Alice, no. It's not you. This isn't to punish you, okay?" His fingers were knotted in my hair, and I could still feel the heavy beat of his heart against mine. "I just know I couldn't live with that. And you can't fight it. It's in your blood."

"Jack…" I tried to think of an argument to counter that, but there wasn't one.

He was right. I had been fighting the way I felt about Peter for almost as long as I'd known him, yet somehow we had ended up in an embrace when Jack walked in.

Jack moved so he looked me in the face, but he kept his hands strong on my arms, in case I would decide to bolt and spoil his ridiculous plan.

I knew what he was saying almost made sense. He wanted to fight Peter for me, and there wasn't any other way to reason with him. I could follow that logic right up until the point that one of them would die.

That's the only conclusion that Jack could come to. One of them had to die, and I knew there had to be something else.

"Alice, I just need to make sure you're okay," he said thickly.

"I'll never be okay without you," I cried, and he winced at that, but recovered quickly.

"That's not what I meant. I have to go back out there, and if something happens-"

"We can run away. Don't go back out there. Then you'll always know I'm safe!" I interrupted him, but his mind was already made up.

"If something happens, I don't think he'll hurt you, but I need to know that you'll be safe," he said, and I saw tears forming in his eyes, which only made me cry harder. "I need to know that no matter what, you have a long happy life!"

"You're not listening, Jack. I will never be happy without you!"

"Please, Alice, for me." He was begging me now. "I want you to turn." He must've heard something because he glanced back at the door nervously, and when he looked back at me, he was even more insistent.

"What? No! You expect me to live forever without you? No!" I shook my head fiercely, revolted by the idea.

"Alice…" He leaned his forehead against mine and breathed in deeply. "I love you so much. Please. Just do this one thing for me."

"If you love me, I don't know how you can even ask me that," I said.

Without warning, he bit into his wrist and tore open the skin. The room was filled with the intoxicating scent of his blood, and suddenly, his heart beat became palpable.

I had never felt thirst before, not like that, but something about his blood triggered this very animal hunger inside of me. Since he'd bitten me, his blood had become everything to me. He knew as soon as he opened his veins, I wouldn't deny him.

Pressing his wrist to my mouth, his blood tasted nothing like I had remembered blood tasting. It was sweeter than honey, and flowed like wine down my throat, burning with thrilling warmth. Before it even hit my stomach, an intense pleasure exploded inside me, making my vision blur into white and everything about me felt alive for the first time.

I felt his love flow through me, pure and unadulterated. Even when he had been biting me, I hadn't felt it like this. Drinking his blood was drinking him, and while so much about him was loving me, everything about him was love.

He only tasted of kindness and innocence and boundless happiness. The worst things he had ever done he had done because I had driven him to it. I was the worst thing that had ever happened to him, and yet he loved me more perfectly and more eternally than anything he had ever loved before.

When he pulled his arm from me, I stumbled backwards. I would've fallen if he hadn't caught me, and fresh tears burned hot down my face. The room spun, and I felt disoriented and dizzy.

The after effects of drinking his blood made me feel like I was incredibly intoxicated, complete with nausea and confusion, and I knew it was only a matter of time before I passed out.

His arms felt strong and safe around me as he laid me down on the couch. There was something different in his expression, in his face, and I realized belatedly I had weakened him. Going into the biggest fight of his life, Jack had the horrible disadvantage of being weaker than ever before.

"Oh, no, Jack! You're so weak! I've killed you!"

"No, Alice, I'm fine." He brushed the hair back from my face, and I rested my hand on his. He was lying to me. If he walked out of the door and fought with Peter, he would die, and we both knew it.

"Jack... I love you!" I told him fiercely. He was going to leave no matter what I said, so I decided to use my time the best I could. "You were always the one I loved. It was always you."

"I know," Jack forced a smile, and even though I was fighting it, my eyes shut. His lips press warmly against my eyelids, and I felt a tear splash on my cheek.

I wanted to say more, and I really tried, but nothing came out. Epic blackness settled over me, but just before everything went completely blank, I heard the sound of hell breaking loose just outside the door.

- 28 -

The days I spent turning were unquantifiable. In his book, Peter had once described the change as feeling "as if my gut had been cut open and filled with eels," and that description is the most accurate I have ever heard.

Of course, that says nothing for the incredible agony my body went through as organs moved about and died. Everything inside me shifted and reconstructed itself to fit an entirely different way of being.

The turning was nothing short of a delirious blur. I was never asleep, but I was never truly awake. Everything felt vaguely like a nightmare, and it was nearly impossible to tell reality apart from everything else.

The pain and the hunger turned my mind to mush, and I had dreams of beetles and snakes eating my flesh. Nothing I saw when I closed my eyes was very pleasant.

The first truly coherent thing I can remember is waking from a dream where I had been on fire. Somehow, in my sleep, that had translated to me singing "Ring of Fire" by Johnny Cash.

When I started to wake, I realized that my voice wasn't the only sound in my ears. There was another one sounding amazingly perfect compared with the dry, crackled sound of my voice.

I opened my eyes, which screamed painfully at the dim light in the room, and I could barely see anything. Eventually, my vision would be better than that of an eagle, but then, I was nearly blind.

Faintly, I made out a silhouette. The details were still invisible, but the cockeyed hair was unmistakable. Even in my confused pain, delight went through me.

"Jack," I whispered in a voice that sounded like dry firewood. "You're really here?"

"Shhh." Jack brushed the hair back from my forehead, and it hurt like hell, but I relished the touch because it was his. "Get some rest."

"But…" I tried to sputter some kind of an argument, but my throat was burning from singing and speaking.

"I'm right here, and I'll be right here until you really wake up. So you just rest until then, and we can talk about everything."

Nothing had ever sounded as wonderful as the sound of his voice, and I wanted to keep him talking. Unfortunately, I was drowning in pain and exhaustion, and I succumbed to them both. But every time I awoke with any momentary clarity, he was by my side.

Eventually the thirst took over me, and I could hear the sound of his heart beat. Instead of finding that reassuring, it just made me even thirstier.

There was a point in the beginning where I was hungry and thirsty, for both blood and actual food, but my body was at a transition where it couldn't digest either. I had to wait until I was completely through the change and thoroughly weakened by the process until I could eat.

A vampire's thirst is unlike anything known to man. It's more than an unquenchable thirst. It's more than starving hunger. It's more than a passionate lust. It's all of those things combined and multiplied, and it's none of them.

Everything inside me focused on getting one thing, and it blotted anything else out. My body felt wrong and diseased until I finally drank blood.

Jack gave me a bag of blood to drink from, and Mae and Ezra chaperoned on the sides of the room. I gulped it down greedily, but it felt nothing like when I drank Jack's blood. Well, not nothing. It tasted wonderful, and it made me feel amazing and warm, but it was nothing as intense or amazing as Jack.

Like before, and like when Milo drank, the blood intoxicated me. I passed out almost immediately after downing the bag of blood, but I slept better than I had in days. It felt like the first time I had really gotten any rest, and for once, it was dreamless. Sometime later, I'd wake up from all this.

I opened my eyes to see the world as a vampire for the very first time.

Read an excerpt from the first book in Amanda Hocking's new paranormal romance the Trylle Trilogy:

Switched – available now

- 1 -

Drool spilled out across my desk, and I opened my eyes just in time to hear Mr. Meade slam down a textbook. I'd only been at this high school a month, but I'd figured out that was his way of waking me up from my naps during his History lecture. I always tried to stay awake, but his monotone voice lulled me into sleeping submission every time.

"Miss Everly?" Mr. Meade snapped. "Miss Everly?"

"Hmm?" I murmured.

I lifted my head and discreetly wiped away the drool. I glanced around to see if anyone had noticed. Most of the class seemed oblivious, except for Finn Holmes. He'd been here a week, so he was the only kid in school newer than me. Whenever I looked at him, he always seemed to be staring at me in a completely unabashed way, as if it was perfectly natural to gawk at me.

There was something oddly still and quiet about him, and I had yet to hear him speak, even though I had him in four of my classes. He wore his hair smoothed back, and his eyes were a matching shade of black. His looks were rather striking, but he weirded me out too much for me to find him attractive.

"Sorry to disturb your sleep." Mr. Meade cleared his throat so I would look up at him.

"It's okay," I said.

"Miss Everly, why don't you go down to the principal's office?" Mr. Meade suggested, and I groaned. "Since you seem to be making a habit of sleeping in my class, maybe he can come up with some ideas to help you stay awake."

"I am awake," I insisted.

"Miss Everly, now." Mr. Meade pointed to the door, as if I had forgotten how to leave and that's what was holding me back.

I fixed my gaze on him, and despite how stern his gray eyes looked, I could tell he'd cave easily. Over and over in my head, I kept repeating *I do not need to go the Principal's office. You don't want to send me down there. Let me stay in class.* Within seconds, his face went lax and his eyes took on a glassy quality.

"You can stay in class and finish the lecture," Mr. Meade said groggily. He shook his head, clearing his eyes. "But next time, you're going straight to the office, Miss Everly." He looked confused for a moment, and then launched right back into his history lecture.

I wasn't sure what it was that I could do exactly – I tried not to think about it enough to name it. About a year or so ago, I'd discovered that if I thought about something and looked at somebody hard enough, I could get them to do what I wanted.

As awesome as that sounded, I avoided doing it as much as possible. Partially because I felt like I was crazy for really believing I could do it, even though it worked every time. But mostly, I didn't like it. It made me feel dirty and manipulative.

Mr. Meade went on talking, and I followed along studiously, my guilt making me try harder. I hadn't wanted to do that to him, but I couldn't go to the principal's office. I had just been expelled from my last school, forcing my brother and aunt to uproot their lives again so we could move closer to my new school.

When class finally ended, I shoved my books in my bookbag and left quickly. I didn't like hanging around too long after I did the mind control trick. Mr. Meade could change his mind and send me to the office, so I hurried down to my locker.

Bright colored fliers decorated battered lockers, telling everyone to join the Debate team, try out for the school play, and not to miss the fall semi-formal this Friday. I wondered what a "semi-formal" consisted of at a public school, but I hadn't bothered to ask anyone.

I got to my locker and started switching out my books. Without even looking, I knew Finn was behind me. I glanced back over my shoulder to see him, getting a drink from the drinking fountain, but almost as soon as I looked at him, he lifted his head and looked at me. Like he could sense me too.

This guy was just looking at me, nothing more, but it freaked me out somehow. I'd put up with his stares for a week, trying to avoid confrontation, but I couldn't take it anymore. *He* was the one acting inappropriately, not me, and I couldn't get in trouble for just talking to him. Right?

"Hey," I said to him, slamming my locker shut. I readjusted the straps on my bookbag and walked across the hall to where he stood. "Why are you staring at me?"

"Because you're standing in front of me," Finn replied simply. He looked at me, his eyes framed by dark lashes, without any hint of embarrassment or even denial. It was definitely unnerving.

"You're *always* staring at me," I persisted. "It's weird. You're weird."

"I wasn't trying to fit in."

"Why do you look at me all the time?" I rephrased my original question, since he kept avoiding it.

"Does it bother you?"

"Answer the question." I stood up straighter, trying to make my presence more imposing so he wouldn't realize how much he was rattling me.

"Everyone always looks at you," Finn said coolly. "You're very attractive."

That sounded like a compliment, but his voice was emotionless when he said it. I couldn't tell if he was making fun of a vanity I didn't even have, or he was simply stating facts. Was he flattering me or mocking me? Or maybe something else entirely?

"Nobody stares at me as much as you do," I said as evenly as I could.

"If it bothers you, I'll try and stop," Finn offered.

That was tricky. In order to ask him to stop, I had to admit that he got to me, and I didn't want to admit that anything got to me. If I lied and said it was fine, then he would just keep on doing it.

"I didn't ask you to stop. I asked you why," I amended.

"I told you why."

"No, you didn't," I shook my head. "You just said that everyone looks at me. You never explained why *you* looked at me."

Almost imperceptibly, the corner of his mouth moved up, revealing just the hint of a smirk. It wasn't just that I amused him; he was pleased with me. Like he had challenged me somehow and I passed.

My stomach did a stupid flip thing I had never felt before, and I swallowed hard, hoping to fight it back.

"I look at you because I can't look away," Finn answered finally.

I was struck completely mute, trying to think of some kind of clever response, but my mind refused to work. My jaw slacked, and I imagined that I looked like an awestruck school girl, and I hurried to collect myself.

"That's kind of creepy," I said at last, but my words came out weak instead of accusatory.

"I'll work on being less creepy then," Finn promised.

I had called him out on being creepy, and it didn't faze him at all. He didn't stammer an apology or flush with shame. He just kept looking at me evenly. Most likely, he was a damn sociopath, and for whatever reason, I found that endearing.

I couldn't come up with a witty retort, but the bell rang, saving me from the rest of that awkward conversation. Finn just nodded, thus ending our exchange, and turned down the hall to go to his next class. Thankfully, it was one of the few he didn't have with me.

True to his word, Finn wasn't creepy the rest of the day. Every time I saw him, he was doing something inoffensive that didn't involve looking at me. I still got that feeling that he watched me when I had my back to him, but as it turned out, I couldn't seem to do much about feelings.

When the final bell rang at three o'clock, I tried to be the first one out. My older brother Matt picked me up from school, at least until he found a job, and I didn't want to keep him waiting. Besides that, I didn't want to deal with anymore contact with Finn Holmes.

I walked quickly over to the parking lot at the edge of the school lawn. Scanning quickly for Matt's Prius, I absently started to chew my thumbnail. I had this weird feeling, almost like a shiver running down my back. I turned around, half-expecting to see Finn staring at me, but there was nothing.

I tried to shake it off, but my heart raced faster. This felt like something more sinister than a boy from school. I was still staring off, trying to figure out what had me freaked out, when a loud honk startled me, making me jump. Matt sat a few cars down, looking at me over the top of his sunglasses.

"Sorry," I opened the car door and hopped in, but he looked at me for a moment. "What?"

"You looked nervous. Did something happen?" Matt asked, and I sighed. He took his whole big brother thing way too seriously.

"No, nothing happened. School sucks," I brushed him off. "Let's go home."

"Seatbelt," Matt commanded, and I did as I was told.

Matt had always been quiet and reserved, thinking everything over carefully before making a decision. He was a stark contrast to me in every way, except that we were both relatively short. I was small with a decidedly pretty, feminine face. My brown hair was an untamed mess of curls that I kept up in loose buns.

He kept his sandy blond hair trim and neat, and his eyes were the same shade of blue as our mother's. Matt wasn't overtly muscular, but he worked out a lot. He had a sense of duty, like he had to make sure he was strong enough to defend us against anything.

"How is school going?" Matt asked.

"Great. Fantastic. Amazing."

"Are you even going to graduate this year?" Matt had long since stopped judging my school record. A large part of him didn't even care if I graduated high school.

"Who knows?" I shrugged.

Everywhere I went, kids never seemed to like me. Even before I said or did anything. I felt like I had something wrong with me, and everyone knew it. I tried getting along with the other kids, but I'd only take getting pushed for so long before I pushed back. Principals and deans were quick to expel me, but I think they sensed the same things the kids did.

I just didn't belong.

"Just to warn you, Maggie's taking it seriously," Matt said. "She's set on you graduating this year, from this school."

"Delightful," I sighed. Matt could care less about my schooling, but my aunt Maggie was a different story. And since she was my legal guardian, her opinion mattered more. "What's her plan?"

"Maggie's thinking bedtimes," Matt informed me with a smirk. As if sending me to bed early would somehow prevent me from getting in a fight.

"I'm almost eighteen!" I groaned. "What is she thinking?"

"You've got four more months until you're eighteen," Matt corrected me sharply, and his hand tightened on the steering wheel. He suffered from serious delusions that I was going to run away as soon as

I turned eighteen, and nothing I could say would convince him otherwise.

"Yeah, whatever," I waved it off. "Did you tell her she's insane?"

"I figured she'd hear it enough from you," Matt grinned at me.

"So did you find a job?" I asked tentatively, and he shook his head.

He'd just finished an internship over the summer, working with a great architecture firm. He'd said it didn't bother him, moving to a town without much call for a promising young architect, but I couldn't help but feel guilty about it.

"This is a pretty town," I said, looking out the window.

We approached our new house, buried on an average suburban street amongst a slew of maples and elms. It actually seemed like a boring, small town, but I'd promised I'd make the best of it. I really wanted to. I don't think I could handle disappointing Matt anymore.

"So you're really gonna try here?" Matt asked, looking over at me. We had pulled up in the driveway next to the butter colored Victorian that Maggie had bought last month.

"I already am," I insisted with a smile. "I've been talking to this Finn kid." Sure, I'd talked to him only once, and I wouldn't even remotely count him as a friend, but I had to tell Matt something.

"Look at you. Making your very first friend." Matt shut off the car and looked at me with veiled amusement.

"Yeah, well, how many friends do you have?" I countered, and he just shook his head and got out of the car, so I quickly followed him. "That's what I thought."

"I've had friends before. Gone to parties. Kissed a girl. The whole nine yards," Matt said as he went through the side door into the house.

"So you say." I kicked off my shoes as soon as we walked in the kitchen, which was still in various stages of unpacking. After as many times as we'd moved, everyone had gotten tired of the whole process, so we tended to live mostly out of boxes. "I've only seen one of these alleged girls."

"Yeah, cause when I brought her home, you set her dress on fire! While she was wearing it!" Matt pulled off his sunglasses and looked at me severely.

"Oh come on! That was an accident and you know it!"

"So you say." Matt opened the fridge.

"Anything good in there?" I asked and hopped onto the kitchen island. "I'm famished."

"Probably nothing you'd like." Matt started sifting through the contents of the fridge, but he was right.

I was a notoriously picky eater. While I had never purposely sought out the life of a vegan, I seemed to hate most things that either had meat in them or man-made synthetics. It was odd and incredibly irritating for the people who tried to feed me.

Maggie appeared in the doorway to the kitchen, flecks of paint stuck in her blond curls. Layers of multi-colored paint covered her ratty overalls, proof of all the rooms she had redecorated over the years. She had her hands on her hips, so Matt shut the fridge door to talk to her.

"I thought I told you to tell me when you got home," Maggie looked at him.

"We're home?" Matt offered.

"I can see that." Maggie rolled her eyes, and then turned her attention to me. "How was school?"

"Good," I said. "I'm trying harder."

"We've heard that before." Maggie gave me a weary look.

I hated it when she gave me that look. I hated knowing that I made her feel that way, that I had disappointed her that much. She did so much for me, and the only thing she asked of me was that I at least *try* at school. I had to make it work this time.

"Well, yeah... but..." I looked to Matt for help. "I mean, I actually promised Matt this time. And I'm making a friend."

"She's talking to some guy named Finn," Matt corroborated my story.

"Like a *guy* guy?" Maggie smiled too broadly for my liking.

The idea of Finn being a romantic prospect hadn't crossed Matt's mind before, and he suddenly tensed up, looking over at me with a new scrutiny. Fortunately for him, that idea hadn't crossed my mind either.

"No, nothing like that," I shook my head. "He's just a guy, I guess. I don't know. He seems nice enough."

"Nice?" Maggie gushed. "That's a start! And much better than that anarchist with the tattoo on his face."

"We weren't friends," I corrected her. "I just stole his motorcycle. While he happened to be on it."

Nobody had ever really believed that story, but it was true, and it was how I figured out how I could get people to do things just by thinking it. I had just been thinking that I really wanted his bike, and then I was looking at him and he was listening to me, even though I hadn't said anything. Then I was driving his motorcycle.

"So this really is gonna be a new start for us?" Maggie couldn't hold back her excitement any longer. Her blue eyes had started to well with happy tears. "Wendy, this is just so wonderful! We can really make a home here!"

I wasn't nearly as excited about it as she was, but I couldn't help but hope she was right. It would be nice to feel like I was home somewhere.

Other titles by Amanda Hocking:

My Blood Approves series

My Blood Approves

Fate

Flutter

Wisdom

Letters to Elise: A Peter Townsend Novella (Christmas 2010)

Trylle Trilogy

Switched

Torn (coming September 2010)

Ascend (coming January 2011)

Connect with Amanda Hocking Online:

Twitter: http://twitter.com/amanda_hocking

My blog: http://amandahocking.blogspot.com/

Facebook Fan Page: http://www.facebook.com/amandahockingfans

Made in the USA
Lexington, KY
08 May 2014